My Home Somewhere Else

T0312646

Sandorf Passage books are available to the
trade through Independent Publishers Group:
ipgbook.com | (800) 888-4741.

Library of Congress Control Number: 2024936002

ISBN: 978-9-53351-477-2

Also available as an ebook;
ISBN: 978-9-53351-526-7

The citations in Chapters 14, 18, and 25 are taken from: Coldplay, Yellow,
text and music by G. Berryman, J. Buckland, W. Champion, C. Martin
© 2000 Universal Music Publishing MGB Ltd.; Igo Gruden, Sinku, in Pesmi,
Ljubljana, Slovenski knjižni zavod, 1949; Ivo Andrić, "A Letter from 1920"
(Pismo iz 1920), in The Damned Yard and Other Stories,
(tr. C. Hawkesworth), London & Boston, Forest Books, 1992.

This book is published with financial support by the Republic of Croatia's
Ministry of Culture and Media.

The European Commission support for the production of this publication
does not constitute an endorsement of the contents which reflects the views
only of the authors, and the Commission cannot be held responsible for any
use which may be made of the information contained therein.

Co-funded by
the European Union

Federica Marzi

My Home Somewhere Else

TRANSLATED FROM ITALIAN BY JIM HICKS

SAN-
DORF
PAS-
SAGE

SOUTH PORTLAND | MAINE

In memory of my grandparents,
Gemma and Mario

The characters and family stories associated with them as told in this work are exclusively the expression of the author's imagination. Any reference to actual people or historical events is entirely coincidental.

The Istro-Venetian speech of Norina and other characters from her family circle largely follows the dialect of Buie d'Istria, as well as particular inflections, intonations, and lexical characteristics of the Triestino dialect.

Translator's Note

FEDERICA MARZI WAS born to write *My Home Somewhere Else*;
after all, this first novel does borrow from her own family's
history of forced migration. As I write this—as hundreds of
thousands of Gazans are fleeing Rafah, or just yesterday, Su-
danese trying to escape the fighting in Khartoum, or, not long
before, a million Rohingyan refugees expelled from Myanmar,
plus, for years now, the Mediterranean and US-Mexico border
migration claiming untold numbers of lives—readers may also
feel, with equal justification, that Marzi's story has been ripped
from the headlines. Thinking historically, moreover, an argument could also be made that this tale is the story of humanity
itself: both of its nomadic past, and of—given the already visible effects of climate crisis—its inevitable future.

My Home Somewhere Else is situated in and around Marzi's
hometown of Trieste, in the far northeastern corner of Italy,
on the border with Slovenia, and close to Croatia. It recounts
the lives of two Triestine women, and, by extension, of two

generations of refugees. The story of the elder protagonist, Norina, is rooted in the post-World War II era, when thousands of Italians left their homes on the Istrian peninsula behind after the borders were redrawn between Italy and Yugoslavia. The family of the younger protagonist, Amila, became refugees during the 1992–95 war in Bosnia-Herzegovina. The novel's chronology is thus necessarily complex, with frequent flashbacks from its narrative present, as the backstories of both protagonists slowly get pieced together. On the level of plot, however, the novel's real story begins one summer, when Amila decides to stay in Trieste rather than go back to Sarajevo with her parents and sister, as she has each summer until then. Amila finds employment, helping out with errands, cleaning, and odd jobs for Norina, and, despite their differences, the two women get on quite well. When Norina's great-nephew, Simon, the son of her sister's daughter, travels to Trieste from his home in Australia, the two women find something else that will unite, yet also divide, them.

This brief summary, which I hope does not give too much away, will indicate much of what is at stake in this novel; it intends to suggest as well the purpose that historical fiction can and should have in our culture as a whole. If our goal is to make sense of the global and epic phenomenon of migration, without a doubt the work of demographers, sociologists, and historians will be essential. Yet numbers, charts, and macrohistories that map migratory waves and flows will never tell the whole story; indeed, when it comes to the actual experience of individuals, families, and peoples, what is not told in such accounts may be, in some sense, the real story. That story—the actual, personal history, with all of its tensions, with its legacy lasting across generations—is a microstory, one that must register and represent every nuance, every complex emotion, every impossible yet inevitable choice; if the reality of migration is ever to be anything more than maps and numbers, that story needs to be told, heard, and understood. Such truths, paradoxically, may be found most fully in fiction.

To make this point, however, and leave it as an abstraction would be unjust; it would also misrepresent much of the important work that Marzi's novel undertakes. *My Home Somewhere Else* is not just any microstory, it is a novel with two female protagonists, and that matters. Focusing on maps and numbers is not the only way to miss the reality of migration; it also matters whose stories get heard. In *Crimes of War: What the Public Should Know*, Roy Gutman and David Rieff offer an astounding and memorable statistical comparison. In World War I they tell us, ninety percent of the casualties were soldiers, and only ten percent civilians; in the World War II, with its death camps included, the numbers became roughly equal. By the last decade of the twentieth century, however, these percentages were fully reversed, with ninety percent of the casualties civilian and only ten percent military. Refugee populations, for obvious reasons, have always been primarily women and children; only in our time, however, has the story of war become a tale of what wars do to the lives of civilians. By centering her novel on two female protagonists, and on the relationship between them, Federica Marzi is surely doing the work of feminism. Yet she is also, it must be noted, reflecting our contemporary reality.

In presenting the English translation of this novel, there is one additional subject that can't be overlooked: what you are about to read is not simply a novel in translation, it is also a novel about translation. These days, within scholarly circles, it has become cliché to note the etymology of this word—from the Latin "translatio," or "carried across." Obviously, in a novel about refugees, this etymology is actual—neither history nor metaphor. Just as clear is how, given the lives it describes, any overemphasis on this root meaning in Romance languages risks neglecting the reality that not everything does get carried across, and that the crossings are inevitably multidirectional.

One of the real beauties of this book, in point of fact, is its demonstration of the complex nature of migration and the history of migration within language itself. Right away in the novel, Amila references the presence of at least three languages. Moreover, Norina's most salient characteristic is her insistence on speaking dialect, rather than Italian, despite her half century of life in the Italian city of Trieste. Readers of the original text, whether or not they are familiar with Triestino or Buiese, will understand Norina's dialogue, but they will also be aware of how it keeps her at a certain distance, and how it demonstrates a certain force of character. Frankly, as a translator, the care, nuance, and indeed elegance in Marzi's inclusion of this and other multilingual realities were what first sold me on the book; its multilingualism has also been the greatest challenge in bringing this text into English. For the lines in dialect, as you will see, my first solution was simply to render the words of Norina (and other speakers of languages other than Italian) in italics. A prosthetic device, perhaps, but better than nothing, and surely better than inventing any accented English and passing it off as equivalent to Buiese. As in any translation, other solutions,

FEDERICA MARZI

for this and other challenges, were necessary as well; whether they work is not for me to judge.

I should add as well that, if there is merit in this translation, much of it is owed to the meticulous editing and insights of the other two members of our translator team—veramente una bella squadra. My wife, Anna Botta, first read every line of this work and saved me from countless errors, many silly and others serious. Then, in an act of great generosity combined with indispensable insider knowledge, the author herself, Federica Marzi, did the same. Buzz Poole, our editor at Sandorf Passage, then did another fine-toothed combing. The end result is surely a better work, but I'm also pretty hardheaded, so no doubt a few problems remain, wherever I wasn't wise enough to listen or talented enough to respond adequately.

With that, I'll leave you to your reading, adding only one brief final comment. As I noted, I can't imagine how the reality of migration and its legacy on the lives of immigrants and their descendants could ever be fully understood if we don't know, and we don't learn from, the lives of those who share the experiences of Marzi's protagonists. As you will see, however, in the novel it is first the protagonists themselves who must learn about their own lives. In doing so, they are changed by what they learn. It is my hope, and I believe that of Federica Marzi as well, that, by following their stories, you too may be changed, as Amila and Norina are.

—JIM HICKS

Part One

CHAPTER ONE

The Language from Before

MARCH 2005, IZOLA/ISOLA (SLOVENIA)

AMILA CLOSED HER eyes, blinded by the light. She understood she'd arrived, but didn't yet know where.

For a while, she wavered in doubt. It must've been just past one of those long, narrow hairpins. As she was driving, the turns had already taken her by surprise, forcing her to brake at the last minute, inches away from the guardrail. It had happened while going downhill, the road going in and out of the dark, through woods and then fields. Then the lights intensified, punctuating the siren's reflection on the windshield. Amila knew they'd reached an urban center.

"We're in Isola," a voice announced, in Slovenian. The man was behind her, in front of the gurney. He brushed against her shoulder, which was immobilized; the pain was centered there. "Don't worry," he added. "Everything's fine, okay?"

The ambulance pulled up to the emergency room entrance with its siren turned off. Amila explained that she absolutely had to go back home. That they were waiting for her. She didn't have a moment to waste.

A young man prepared an injection. "We give you something for pain. Just relax, okay?" he said, in an odd Italian, without saying anything more.

A woman took her arm and bared it, forcefully. In Italian— this time perfect—she commanded Amila to keep still.

Amila tried to insist, though a bit more politely. As her father always told her, politeness has to come first. "Please," she asked, and she even tried in her other language, the one everybody there ought to understand. "*Molim vas.*" But no one paid any attention to her. They told her only that they'd arrived. Just a few kilometers from the Italian border, which she hadn't managed to cross.

In the emergency room, a doctor with small, dark eyes adjusted a lamp above Amila, blinding her. He put on latex gloves and informed her that what he had to do would hurt a bit. He spoke her own language.

"I'm from Osijek. My family and I immigrated to Slovenia years ago," he explained, smiling, as if he had to excuse himself or justify the fact that they shared a common language. Even though his accent was a bit different, and his grammar wasn't perfect.

But then Amila, too, couldn't always find every word in that language from before. The language of her family resided in an advanced stage of prehistory. She could speak it, but not write it. She spoke without hesitation, but at times it didn't sound right, like a sum that didn't add up.

When she went back to her former country, they always took her for a tourist—Macedonian, or Russian, or Bulgarian. Even if no one ever saw any tourists like that there. Only when she was under pressure did the words from before sprout from her mouth, like a gaudy flower. No way of telling from what reservoir of memory they came, or where that layer might be buried. A nurse came up to her cot without saying anything. That one must have her language all sorted out. Amila felt something metallic move over her stomach and chest. Her sweatshirt was cut in two.

She saw the doctor again after the X-rays. Through the crowded hallway, he came up to her wheelchair. He extended his hand and asked how she was feeling.

"Everything hurts." Her shoulder was the least of it.

"That's normal. You just need to stay calm. And don't strain anything. The operation was a complete success."

"But when will I be able to go home?"

"In a couple of days. And then you'll be able to start therapy to help with the pain. Where will you be?"

At first Amila didn't understand. "In Trieste," she replied. Where she lived. That was her city.

"But you're from Zvornik, right?'

"Yes. I was born there."

The doctor pursed his lips. Between them, there was a moment of silence, the usual embarrassed, guilty silence shared by people who knew. He must know more than most. Her first name and family name, written on her chart, were all he needed to decide where to situate her within the complex of Balkan geography. But Amila, too, hadn't needed much—where he came from, his language, and, most of all, looking him in the face— in order to know what had happened to him and why he was in Slovenia. He was one too.

"And your family?" the doctor inquired.

"My parents are in Bosnia."

"For a vacation?"

"Maybe you could say that. Our old apartment got flooded and they had to rush back there."

"I see. Nonetheless, you'll need someone to take care of you. When will they be coming back?"

"Soon."

"Good," the doctor said. "I have to go now, but I'll be back again later."

In the room, the wall facing her was flooded with light. Surrounded by a metal frame, the view from the window showed an expanse of rough sea. A merchant ship was barely moving forward. A small, dark shape slid along the line between sea and sky. At any moment it might disappear.

Amila wore a gown that tied in the back. The material was coarse and synthetic, making her skin itch. She found a tiny fragment of glass between her pinkie and ring finger, which made her feel like she had glass in her everywhere. She began to remember. She heard again the sound of metal crumpling, and the thump of the windshield. She squeezed her eyes shut.

The accident had occurred at some undefined place in the Istrian countryside. The fading light had softened the edges of things, making them seem tenuous, almost unreal. Amila had crossed the border at Dragogna, a flat stretch of street-lit cement between Croatia and Slovenia where she had shown her passport and visitor's permit. The customs official, a blonde woman, had waved her on. After that, nothing. Nothing but black between the brief pause at the border and the crash—the black that, in fits and starts, filled her memory.

She hadn't heard anything more about the car, even if that wasn't the real problem. The old, wine-colored Fiat Panda wasn't hers; it belonged to Norina, and she hadn't gotten permission to use it. Especially not to leave, cross two borders, and drive toward some place nobody was supposed to know about.

People probably assumed Amila was Norina's caregiver, but it wasn't like that. She wasn't an in-home nurse, and Norina had never even wanted one. At most, Norina spoke about needing some company, having some odd jobs, occasional errands to do. She said she needed to have someone stay in the house whenever she went for walks in the woods or took the dog out for a pee.

It had been during one of those moments, when Norina wasn't there, that Amila jumped into the Panda and took off. She'd only meant to borrow it, intending to return it that same evening, but then she hadn't come back.

By now she ought to have responded to Norina's phone calls, finding some way to explain to her what had happened, to assure her that she hadn't stolen the car. The main thing to avoid was having her think something like that, since she would only get upset and then do who knows what. The voicemail on her phone was already full. Amila nervously drummed her fingers on her phone. Her nails were the same, chewed down to the nubs.

"*Sant'Iddio*, look at those hands!" Mamma Selma often scolded her. But when they spoke this time, Selma didn't scold her. First, with her most worried tone, she asked how Amila was doing. And then second, third, and fourth, how she was doing.

She gave Papà Željko the phone, and, fifth, he asked her what car she'd been in during the accident, since they had the Nissan Micra. And, sixth, where had she been.

But phone calls between Bosnia and Slovenia swallow euros by the second, so they'd have to discuss points five and six in person. Precisely what Amila was afraid of. She was in a real fix now. Plus there, at the hospital, in this land where she didn't know anyone, between the country where she was born and the country where she lived, she didn't even have medical insurance. The nurse on the morning shift had told her, "*Privat, privat,*" shaking her long, red ponytail, making Amila understand that she would have to pay the medical expenses on her own.

And Norina's Panda was also in terrible shape, she understood at last. The car would be an additional expense. So, between doctors and mechanics, her family's savings were going to be sucked dry—their whole life savings, everything Papà Željko and Mamma Selma had earned working abroad. And the two of them definitely hadn't had things easy, not with their lives.

On one occasion, invoking her God in Italian, Mamma Selma had exclaimed, "*Sant'Iddio*, are you telling me you want to spend the rest of your days in a hardware store in Trieste?" That happened not long after the Dayton Accords that put an end to the war.

"So what do you want me to tell you?"

Zvornik had become part of the Serb Republic of Bosnia. The apartment close to the Drina, where Amila spent part of her childhood, had been occupied by the family of a cop.

"In Sarajevo, they're looking for good teachers for our children. And you? You just said you want to keep working in a store!" They were all together, in the living room of their house on Via Pascoli in Trieste.

Željko had seemed undecided; he was thinking. "We lived happily in Yugoslavia. It's not the same country now."

"In Sarajevo we'll live in peace."

"But in a postwar country." Željko had straightened his glasses. "And then, there are the girls," he added, without even glancing at them. Amila and Majda were sitting at the same table, their eyes lowered, mute as eleven- and nine-year-old fishes. "They have the right to a better life. We have to choose."

"Exactly. Either one side or the other." In the living room, crammed into a corner, were the boxes from the Refugee Center, still taped up, waiting to find out their final destination.

"Not necessarily," Željko countered, starting a tug-of-war that could go on forever. "Let's take a sabbatical year. School is our way of life, so we ought to allow ourselves the benefits."

"Željko Hadžigrahić, I'm warning you. Don't joke about our tragedy!"

"What tragedy? Our girls will be really happy here, and you know it. They'll study, they'll get a European degree, they'll be able to work. When they grow up, they'll make their own decisions about where to live. And we have the sea here too."

"The sea? You don't even know how to swim!"

Amila had to force herself not to laugh.

"The sea is for everyone. Even for people who can only look at it."

"I'm telling you—it'll be a life without roots."

"It won't be like that."

"What am I supposed to say to someone who tells me 'it won't be like that'?"

"'It'll turn out fine,' for example. You could say that."

Mamma Selma had raised her eyes to her heavens—the high, wide, and discolored ceiling of their Hapsburg-era apartment building.

"All we need to do is behave ourselves, and we won't have any problems."

"Behave yourself" was one of Papà Željko's favorite admonitions. It was something he always said, even when the rest of the world was doing exactly the opposite. And Mamma Selma thought the same. It's how Amila's parents were made.

And so there was no doubt that at least Papà Željko would help her. With his calm, patient words and his somewhat shaky Italian, he would figure out a way. He would pay the health-care costs without saying a word. And he would speak with Norina to apologize for what had happened and, above all, pay her back. Everything can be fixed—that, too, was one of his sayings.

About the other things, though, there wouldn't be any words exchanged—not in their family language, and not in the language Amila used for everything else.

How could she have revealed to her father, or to Norina, that she had been in a stone house, in the middle of the Istrian countryside, a place she had found after following waves of red dirt, olive trees, and vineyards? To have told them about how she'd been sitting at a table—rough wood, she remembered it was rough—in a kitchen heated by a woodstove, across from a man who, in Norina's house, they called Franco?

FEDERICA MARZI

So far as the people in that house knew, he had disappeared. One moment in the slow fade of their family story.

But Amila had been in his home, she'd asked him questions. She'd left before evening fell. At the border, the blonde customs official had waved her on. Then there had been the road, full of twists and hairpin curves. Then the straight line. Amila had accelerated. Distracted for a moment, she'd looked at her hands and the chewed-up fingernails she hid from Mamma Selma, and—*sant'Iddio!*—she lost track of the dotted white line. A semi was heading toward her in the opposite lane. Amila had heard the howl of the horn. Then nothing.

Franco's face surfaced for an instant after the accident. The doctor from Osijek was examining her; he'd been saying something to her. "Try to move your arm. Now I'll touch here." Her breastbone. "Does it hurt?"

It caused her sharp pain, bad enough to scream. And then, as she squeezed her eyes shut, she saw the face of Franco, that man who had challenged her with his mocking grin, sipping his homemade grappa and wiping his moist lips with the back of his hand.

CHAPTER TWO

The World Turned Upside Down
MARCH 2005, IZOLA/ISOLA (SLOVENIA)

NORINA WAS SITTING on the icy stone of a small bench in front of the hospital, a giant, green-and-blue-striped building corroded by the salt air. Her tongue felt like dried cod, ready to be pounded and then left to soak.

From this elevation the sky seemed within reach. She no longer could see the interchanges and exit ramps that had delivered her there. Behind a long, yellowish wall of glass on the second floor, a patient in pajamas and another in a T-shirt moved by, as if in an aquarium. A cloud covered the sun, and Norina pulled her coat tighter, rubbing her hands together. The cold was stinging. She stood up.

She looked up again and saw that the two patients from before had been watching her. Amila, too, was somewhere up there, having vanished with the Panda while she had been in the woods, without a word of explanation.

Bless it, girl, what sort of trouble have you gotten into?

The reason why Amila had done what she'd done remained a mystery. Sure, she had left a note saying that she'd come back before nightfall. But instead, she'd disappeared for an entire day and then called Norina, swearing that she hadn't stolen the car, begging her not to jump to any conclusions.

So then, what was she supposed to think? Norina wondered.

She had also received a call from the highway patrol. At first she had lost her composure, blushing, but then she managed to stand her ground against the masculine voice on the other end of the line. She was asked to confirm her statement. Norina had answered with a firm voice—as if she were reciting a Hail Mary—that she did confirm it. She no longer said Hail Marys, and that's why her confirmation went so well this time. But also because she'd never been able to stand those macho *milissia* guys.

As soon as she turned the corner, she saw the building's oval windows and the sky- and dark-blue porch roofs, shaped like waves. In the view below, Isola could now be seen, a small patch of earth with a church steeple. Norina stopped for a moment and looked at the sea—a calm, sparkling expanse interrupted by two merchant ships. This Istria was all new, buffed to a shine. It was no longer hers, even if it had been, once upon a time.

But the times were gone when she and Mariano would go once a year to visit Buie, the city where she had been born, in order to take care of the family gravesites. On those occasions, Norina would wear something elegant. She would pack some green-and-red foil packages of coffee, for gifts, and put ice in the cooler, to fill with fresh sirloin on the trip home. She packed her large second billfold with big, coarse dinar notes—purple, light blue, maroon—which she would count, wetting her fingertips. There had to be enough to pay for a full tank of gas; otherwise, they'd need to change more money. She would check the expiration date of her *propusnica*, the pass that allowed her to cross the border.

Norina used to go to see her former home. The house with the *rosèr*, a tall shrub of roses that had grown from a handful of soil wedged between the stones. On the exterior, everything seemed the same; more than anything else, it was the country that had changed. She saw unfamiliar people walking around, some new breed that had come *de via*, from outside. Their pronounced cheekbones set them apart, although those also made them look a lot like her father, or Mariano. A few houses had been abandoned, even in the main square, next to the towering Venetian steeple.

Norina always took photos so as not to draw attention from the new tenants. She knew them; she knew they would have invited her in, with all sorts of ceremony, for second-rate coffee and oversweet pastries that would ruin her appetite. She preferred not to go back inside her old house, which now belonged to others.

When they'd finished their tour, Norina and Mariano would have lunch at the restaurant. They'd eat for the whole afternoon, as if they owned the place. They would pay in lire; it never cost much, yet something would always be difficult to digest. They had become two Sunday tourists from Trieste who get fooled by tasty gnocchi, sauces, and set Italian phrases.

When her photos were developed, Norina would put them away, in a drawer of the end table in the living room, and she wouldn't think about them again until the following year. Above the end table were displayed the few trophies life had given her: a photo of her with bangs and a veil, and Mariano, stiff and serious; a more recent snapshot with Luli, at the lookout on Monte San Primo; her mother and father, Ederina and Pietro, back together again—two photo IDs made into a single image with Photoshop. It was all she still had of them.

In the small drawer there was also a pile of publicity brochures for hot springs and tourist resorts across the border, in Slovenia and Croatia, the territory that Norina still called Zone B. She had refused to recognize the two new republics, for which a war had been fought, one that had caused world leaders to intervene. Their names didn't come naturally to her. But she wasn't planning on going back. To tell the truth, she never really went anywhere.

At the hospital, Norina slipped cautiously through the transparent sliding doors. She brushed past an elderly couple, avoiding the stare from the nurse at reception. The empty, spacious atrium had a series of dirty windows that looked out toward Trieste and the sea. Within the city you could recognize, in miniature, the Vittoria Lighthouse and the Temple of Monte Grisa. Norina had forgotten about that view, even though it had once belonged to her. Now, in contrast, seen from there, the world seemed upside down.

A sign in Italian said, "Common Elevator." She turned on her heels, not understanding if she could use that elevator or not. To her right was the gynecology ward. A gurney with flaking paint had been left in front of the door. To her left the hall

FEDERICA MARZI

led to the ophthalmology ward and a waiting room. The wooden furniture with rounded corners and the small, cabin-sized windows made her feel like she was on an ocean liner. The sort of ship she'd never taken, but once had seen, as it departed.

She went back to the "common elevator," which she concluded must be for visitors, since there was no other way to get upstairs. She traced with her index finger the embossed lettering and the translations of the various names of the wards. *Dejavnost travmatologije.* There it is, the trauma ward; that's what Amila had told her on the phone. Second floor.

Once she got up there, she took a deep breath. The signs with room numbers were lined up, sticking out from the walls. An ocher-colored light flooded the hallway. Norina moved forward cautiously until she got to 9A. The door was open. It was hot, and an antiseptic odor mixed with the smell of food, even though the lunch hour had been over for some time.

A blue shirt was protruding from under the sheet, with Amila's dark hair falling around it. You could detect some padding up around her chest. From the needle stuck into her bare arm twisted small rubber tubes that led to an iv bag. Behind her eyelids, her eyes quivered. Norina coughed, as if she were clearing her throat, but Amila didn't move. She had a purple-and-blue bruise on her cheek. It must've really been painful.

"*There, there, kiddo, c'mon now,*" Norina murmured, in dialect. She stroked the arm that had the iv, but quickly withdrew her hand.

The second bed was empty. Norina sat down on it, completely exhausted. Seen like this, Amila seemed like a defenseless child. What sort of wrong could she have done, even if, for who knows what earthly reason, she'd taken the Panda without asking, and even if now, after the accident, the police were holding the car?

When Amila came to their place for the first time, Norina and Mariano had been waiting for her in the living room, dressed up for the occasion, the way they did when they traveled to Buie. Mariano stayed seated, on a beach lounge chair.

"It's for my hip," he explained.

He was wearing a heavy jacket that made him hot. He shielded himself from the light filtering in past the blinds, which had been broken for months. His unshaven face and uncombed hair definitely weren't making a good impression.

It had been Anika, their neighbor and their only friend, who convinced them to look for some help, at least on a trial basis. At first Norina had said *yes, no, maybe.* She didn't want any outsiders in her home, but she couldn't manage to do everything by herself anymore. Anika suggested to her that she could try with female students, the friends of her niece, that they could be trusted. And that's how they ended up with Amila.

Anika had made clear right away that Amila was Bosnian, to apologize, or as if that would be the deciding factor, and Norina would have to think about it first before accepting. But those weren't the sort of things that would worry her.

When she showed up at their place, Amila was wearing the usual sort of tight, faded jeans, with sequins on the pockets, cut short over the ankles. On her feet were pink canvas sneakers. Her legs crossed, she sat rocking her foot, as if she were in a hurry.

More than anything, Norina regretted that such a girl had ended up in Italy because of the war Norina had seen on television. She had no idea how someone like her could have come from a country where the houses were destroyed, where repulsive men in camouflage were surrounded by microphones, where green and yellow explosions from shells ripped through foggy nights, and where old women like her wiped their noses with the back of their hand.

None of that fit, though, with the sight of Amila in front of her in her living room, sitting on their red couch. Not with this female student from the university who spoke Italian, not dialect, without an accent. No, better. With a slight Triestino accent.

"But our dialect, you speak that too, right?" Norina had asked her, as if that were an official pass needed for entry to her life.

"Yes, of course."

"Good."

But then Amila didn't actually say anything in dialect, and Norina felt as if she were facing a particularly demanding professor.

"So what do you do with yourself, study?"

"Yes. Communicational sciences." Amila had the habit of using difficult words. "I want to be a journalist."

"Ah." To Norina, that seemed like an excellent plan.

Amila would arrive with a bag full of books and a beach towel. Luli would go up to meet her, happily wagging her tail. She would take off her earbuds, in order to answer questions, and follow the list of things to do, either nodding or shaking her head. Norina stayed seated, leaning forward in her chair, her hands folded. Even she was in the mood to chat a bit, though she never spoke with anyone.

Once Amila had been putting things away in the fridge. She was amusing herself, crumpling up the old aluminum foil and shooting it into the wastebasket. She had played basketball in a fairly important league. Norina, plucking up the courage, asked her if she had ever been in a camp.

"Norina, I'm sorry, but 'camp' in what sense?"

"A refugee camp."

"Ah, that sense. Yes, when I was very young. The Jesolo Reception Center."

Amila used words that had no color or odor—studied choices. She responded politely, saying, "Yes, of course." But then she would slip out the door and escape upstairs, where Mariano was, and Norina would be once again left alone. Bless that girl.

So, Norina would stop talking and start getting herself ready.

In the woods, where she went whenever she could, she didn't care anymore about asking anyone questions, or about worrying what was the matter with others, especially if they seemed depressed. Breathing in the tall pines and holm oaks, her head quit cooking and her legs remembered where to go.

That place, to tell the truth, was the only place Norina would ever go.

CHAPTER THREE

Rough Sea

MARCH 2005, IZOLA/ISOLA (SLOVENIA)

WHEN SHE OPENED her eyes, Amila could make out a blurry figure on the bed beside her, wearing a camel-hair coat. She heard Norina stand up and say hello, in her raspy voice. Closer up, her hair looked freshly done; her scarf was loose around her neck. Two deep wrinkles circled her mouth. Her large, dark eyes were fixed on Amila, worrying.

Amila had grown used to Norina wearing the heavy lilac sweater when she went to the woods, or the gray cardigan—it hung down to her knees and was worn through at the elbows—whenever she stayed at home. Dressed up like this, Amila could barely recognize her.

"*How're you?*"

"More or less intact."

She looked for the remote control, so she could raise up the head of the bed. Norina helped her support herself with pillows, carefully, because of the tubes.

"*The doctors, what d'they tell you?*"

Amila did her best to explain; she needed to translate every-thing from the language in which it had happened. She summed up: fractured clavicle, titanium plate to realign it. And the brace. Norina listened calmly and quietly, her eyebrows furrowed. Her eyelids were trembling, and her right eye twitched a bit. Amila suspected that her slightly crossed eyes allowed Norina to both stare and shift her gaze at the same time. She would watch you, concentrated or disconcerted—which at times seemed the same thing—but then she would suddenly be far away, looking off somewhere else.

To her, Norina often seemed a tragic figure, standing before a choppy sea, with her curved legs spread wide and her feet plant-ed on the shoreline, as if a big wave were about to crash. When the wave arrived, she would stagger. And then she'd raise her voice in protest, with her gritty, rough words, spoken in dialect, because she never spoke Italian except with the dog. It was her way of protecting herself, staying on her feet despite everything.

"Did the highway patrol call you?"

At the hospital after the operation, two Slovenian police of-ficers had shown up. They were looking for the owner of the automobile and wanted to know why Amila had been behind the wheel. They'd carefully examined her passport and residency permit, just as they did at checkpoints or the border. Customs officials always held her papers in their hands, their expression blank, silently thumbing through the pages. They checked and rechecked what was already written on them but still never seemed entirely sufficient. These were moments of pure panic.

"And what did they tell you?"

"*Dunno. To go to Capodistria. The car was up there.*"

"Capodistria? And did they ask you about me?"

"*Yes.*"

Amila swallowed. Maybe Norina wasn't fully aware of her status as a foreigner. Even if they had spent a whole summer together, they'd never thoroughly discussed all that business. They'd come to an agreement without worrying about certain details. Amila and her passport that wasn't Italian. Norina and her foreign worker. And between them a car had been taken without permission, not stolen, but that fact didn't change anything now, now that it was damaged and in the possession of the highway patrol.

"And what did you tell them?"

"*Nothing.*"

"Norina..."

"*Don't always interrupt!*" A blush of red surged over Norina's cheeks. The big wave was getting nearer, but this time Norina stayed firm on her feet. She had told the police that Amila was a friend who drove her Panda from time to time. Not a word more.

"Thank you," said Amila, easing herself back on the pillows. "Thank you."

Norina didn't appear touched by Amila's gratitude. Instead, she seemed to be looking around, warily. Lowering her voice, she asked, "*But do they know, or not? That you work for us with no permit?*"

"No, I don't think so..."

"*What does that mean, 'I don't think so'?*"

Amila clutched the hem of the bedsheet. She couldn't remember if or what she'd told them about it. When those two men showed up, she was confused, still in shock.

"Holy Mary, Mother of God!"

"I don't really think the highway patrol cares what I do on Saturdays at your place."

"No? So what're they doing all day long? Twiddling their thumbs?"

There it is—the big wave crashing at last. *"Me, I don't want any problems with police, got it?"*

"But no, no, you'll see . . ."

"But what?"

Amila pursed her lips tightly. "Okay. I'm really sorry. But I swear, I really needed to take the car. It was an emergency."

Norina shrugged her shoulders. *"But why? Bless it, girl, could we at least know where you were going?"*

Amila shook her head. "I can't tell you."

Norina let out a loud sigh. Her arms fell back to her sides.

Amila could have invented an excuse, but she wasn't able to lie, and so she told Norina the truth. That she couldn't tell her the truth.

"But that's crazy."

For a short while they both stayed silent, without looking up. Then Norina took the Nokia out of her purse. She pushed the keys with her index finger, stiffened by arthritis. *"Anika's waiting for me in the parking lot."*

"Ah . . ."

"I have t'go." She turned around.

"Norina?"

"What is it?"

"If you're worried about the money, you shouldn't. Tomorrow my father will be here, and—"

"Okay," Norina interrupted, adjusting the strap of her purse.

"Norina, try to understand. I'm an immigrant. Me too—I don't want any problems with the police . . ." A slip of paper with her ID photo, stapled through her forehead, gave her permission to reside in Italy. Nothing was more important.

Norina simply said, "*No*," in a low voice. It was an affirmative no, but a no nonetheless.

"And Mariano, how is he doing?"

"*Just the same*," she replied, on her way out.

Amila didn't know how to explain it to her, but what Norina thought she saw now—a foreign girl who came to work for her without a permit, the wrecked Panda held by the highway patrol—was just the tip of the iceberg. In reality, in that house, for months everything had been falling into place so that all this would happen, without Norina ever realizing anything was going on. Amila would have liked to keep her from leaving, but Norina pushed out of the room, pained and bent, as if forced to step out into the middle of a storm.

Outside, however, the sea was flat and lined with light from the setting sun. The sky seemed to lower like a curtain, and on the walls of the room a purple shadow lengthened.

A heavyset nurse arrived, his face covered in freckles. He was carrying a metal tray with medications. He checked Amila's IV and turned its valve. She asked him if he could get her phone, which was charging. The nurse obliged and added that the physiotherapist would be coming by to teach her some exercises. He swallowed his words, so that his tone seemed to scold—as if, by not understanding half of what he said, Amila was just being lazy.

He left without saying anything more.

What could she do now?

For Amila it was impossible to see in advance how Norina would react to the news about her Panda or to the questions of the highway patrol. It was important, though, that she not get confused, that she didn't lose control of the situation, and above all that she didn't let some inopportune detail slip out. Neither of the two women should have problems because of what had happened. Which meant someone needed to help her stay calm and say the right things, without a moment's hesitation.

Amila decided to try to get in touch with this someone. The number—with its two extra international digits—was still at the top of her favorites list. She quickly wrote a message to the one person who could help: Norina's nephew, Simon.

I'm in the hospital.
There's a problem—I had an accident with your aunt's car. Nothing serious, I'm more or less fine, I'll explain. But she is really worried.
Please call her as soon as possible and tell her to stay calm. I'll take care of everything. Ciao.

The way things were now had all been started by him. Arriving from Australia, with all his questions, inventing some person who perhaps never even existed. He had started playing with the past—the one thing you should never mess with. So it was Simon's job, not Amila's, to confront Norina with questions about their family—and, if possible, to put those questions to rest. He was her nephew; she wasn't.

But in Melbourne, where Simon lived, it was the middle of the night, and Amila's phone stayed silent. Everything, in fact, stayed silent.

CHAPTER FOUR

Back Then, We Were a United Country

JUNE 2004, TRIESTE/TRST (ITALY)

FOR AMILA NONE of this was easy. With Mamma Selma and Papà Željko, she already had plenty of problems to sort out. One was named Italy. The other was now officially Bosnia and Herzegovina, divided into two separate entities: the Federation of Bosnia and Herzegovina, and Republika Srpska.

She lived with her family in Trieste for most of the year, but in July and August she would go—whether she wanted to or not—to Sarajevo, one clause in an ironclad family contract. After the report cards came out, and after the end-of-year exams, anyone who, like her, was the child of two countries had their duties to perform.

For eight hours, if everything went well, or for ten or eleven if things went the way they always did, they would be glued to their seats in the Nissan Micra with Trieste plates. Željko and Selma sat in front, Amila and Majda in back, in the middle of a pile of bags and boxes. They would stop to stretch their legs and fill up the gas tank at the last station in Croatia. They'd each get a small bottle of water and a bag of Dutch snack food. On the highway they made good time. On the side of the road, just before the border, the first ruined houses appeared. At Slavonski Brod, after crossing the Sava River and waiting in line, the real journey began. No more highway, just patchy asphalt roads, slow trucks, cars with German plates passing them in no-passing zones, and towns that in some cases weren't even towns anymore, their names written on signs in Cyrillic, and stretches of road immersed in darkness. Only when they got to Doboj, with its brightly lit buildings and the Bosna River, did Amila begin to breathe more easily.

In Sarajevo, it was better. For her it was not much more or less than a city surrounded by green hills. That's how she saw it when she first went there, after the war. And their vacations were not much more or less than a pilgrimage, moving at the same slow pace of the city's rebuilding.

With Mamma Selma and Majda, she went to see the iron inlay that supported the new arches of the National Library. Amila stared at the building's crenellated exterior. From a certain perspective, near the entrance, it looked a lot like the Miramare Castle outside Trieste. It had the same Liberty or Art Nouveau style, except more orientalized. She always looked at it on purpose from that point of view, even if it annoyed Mamma Selma, since for her it would only be okay if a Bosnian monument or landscape could be moved to Italy, not the reverse.

Mamma Selma got back into a good mood by wandering with her daughters around Baščaršija, the old city, where they'd just be tourists, but not simply visiting famous sites from the war. They were an odd sort of tourist, though, in the midst of the others who might really be sightseeing. For once, they did get to eat out, but Mamma Selma would only grimace, chewing slowly and declaring with pride that her own *pita* and *somun* were a thousand times better.

Each year they stayed in Marijin Dvor, near the mosque and not far from the Catholic Church of St. Joseph and the Orthodox Church of the Holy Transfiguration. Mamma Selma always said that there was no other city in the world that united so many holy sites, a paradox that Amila found irritating. And besides, as far as she was concerned, there was another place like that, with the sea and the Greek church a stone's throw away, but no mosque. Ponterosso, in Trieste.

Every year Mamma Selma would inspect the neighborhood buildings one by one. She'd look at the holes in cornices and facades left from the shelling, hoping that some would have disappeared. Some did, in fact, disappear.

"Look, they fixed it up!" she'd exclaim, satisfied, as if she were waiting for the day in which everything would be back in place. Or else she'd say, "Look, what beautiful curtains, what lovely geraniums," observing something nicer that contrasted with the pockmarked buildings.

Amila, too, noted some of those punctures, wondering what sort of shell would be capable of penetrating that deeply through cement. Holes so deep she couldn't see where they ended. Falling plaster, one hole in a concentric spiral, with a smaller one inside it, and a burst of small holes surrounding the biggest. What could have caused actions with that measure of precision from the surrounding hills? What thoughts had possessed the hearts and minds of the shooters?

For her the hills around Sarajevo had continued to be an unimaginable place. She could only imagine what was happening below, because she'd seen it, on the TV news that had marked her refugee childhood in Jesolo like a religion. Everything else was like those holes. Empty and dark.

The second part of the family contract signed them up for sharing a rented apartment with Papà Željko's brother's family, which luckily at least included Olga, Amila's cousin. They were the same age. If they hadn't had their richer aunt and uncle, who had emigrated to Vienna and helped the poorer family members who lived in Italy, they never would have been able to afford an apartment with two bathrooms and six beds (even if there were actually seven of them).

For Amila that was the best part of their vacation—whenever she sat together with Olga on the bench in the apartment block's square courtyard, under an enormous, unpruned plane tree that hung over their heads like a weeping willow.

Riddled with bullets or not, falling plaster or worse, that was their refuge. Olga brought an ashtray, and she left it on the bench right until the moment they both had to leave for their homes abroad. She left her packet of Gauloises in plain view, evidence of imported luxury goods. The conspicuous display of her better life was a reflex with her. Fit compensation for having a life somewhere else, for being an expatriate. She would put out one cigarette and light another immediately, then straighten her hair. She'd offer the pack to Amila, who would accept but take only one, just to do something transgressive—and to be able to say she knew how to smoke. They would look up from their apartment block at the narrow skies of July and August, and then Amila's words, vacuum-packed all winter long, would liquefy at last. Her speech had a different weight there, and words flowed easily. There were some things she could only discuss with Olga.

It was from Olga—who was always a step or two ahead, and not only because she lived in Vienna—that Amila had learned everything necessary about the use of contraceptives. Speaking quietly and giggling, together they would translate all the illustrated instructions, written in German and Italian. They didn't always know the full vocabulary in Bosnian, so they got by with the Latin they'd learned in school, which worked perfectly for that sort of thing. Olga explained to her the importance of foreplay and what to do, for him and for her, since otherwise it would be difficult to reach orgasm. Which could be either clitoral or vaginal. And if you were lucky, also multiple.

"What're they like for you?" Olga once asked her, exhaling a big puff of smoke. Amila was left speechless, with all that smoke hitting her right in the face.

Olga always had a boyfriend, and always a new one, never someone steady. She'd say that Austrians had no sense of humor, and with *dijasporci* like them it was even worse, because those boys could make her laugh, but they had no idea how to sort out their uprooted lives. They were unreliable. So clearly none of it was easy for Olga either.

And then nothing. Amila told her about the brief story she'd had with Lazar, her friend for ages, even if those ages were only a part of everything else—life in Trieste, in Via Pascoli, from fifth grade on. They'd both left their childhoods at home somewhere else. Feeling grown-up now, Lazar had kissed her. His mouth had the taste of tobacco and mint. Parked in a dark stretch along the coast, he'd squeezed her breast too tightly. A police car passed by, but luckily didn't come close. They quickly started up the engine again, zipping up hurriedly and driving back to town in silence.

Olga responded only by exclaiming, "Oh," without asking anything more about him. For instance, if he was a Croat or Serb. Olga was awesome.

"But was he good?" Olga was, however, a bit obsessed about some subjects.

"Meh," Amila admitted.

And as it turned out, that "meh" also meant Lazar would stay just a friend. Amila was still waiting for her first love. And she was certain that the reason the business of love was taking so long was because she'd never spent even one summer in Trieste. In Vienna, where Olga was, summer wasn't such a big deal, because they didn't have the sea. Amila, on the other hand, spent the best time of year out of town, in her other country, where she'd never even had a decent opportunity. Back there, surrounded by green hills, stuck in a city under construction, within the small sisterly spell of Marijin Dvor, she knew that there would be no future for her.

And so, for once in her life, Amila dug in her heels. It happened in June, when the summer session of exams was beginning and the city was already focused on its beaches. Without any great to-do, she broke the family contract. This summer, for once, she wouldn't be going to Bosnia.

To succeed in putting her plan into action, she needed to have a good excuse. If she had simply said she would have to study or write for a small local paper, it wouldn't have worked. She had needed to find something more believable. And that, as far as her parents were concerned, could only be work. A summer job that would pay her university fees. Papà Željko's salary wasn't enough anymore, and Mamma Selma shouldn't have to go back to cleaning houses. And Majda, too, would be enrolling in college now. How could they manage?

Norina had appeared at just the right moment. Amila would do simple chores around the house in order to help out an elderly couple—who would be paying her well. And who, above all, lived really close to Canovella, the city's best beach. For her it all seemed made-to-order.

Then, in the Via Pascoli apartment, when she'd explained what her plans were for the period up to September, all hell broke loose.

"So now we can't even go to Sarajevo," Mamma Selma blurted out. She'd been taking a blue dress with white polka dots off its hanger, weighing which of three suitcases, lined up like coffins, she should put it in. Their lives would be divided up once more into baggage; whenever it was necessary to put or get something packed in there, everything suddenly seemed to shrink in size.

"And of course it has to be this year that you're not coming!" Mamma Selma was sitting on the bed, getting wrinkles in her best dress. "The very year we also have to go to Zvornik!"

Exactly. Amila had absolutely no intention of leaving with them. First of all, not for Sarajevo, for the by-now annual vacation with the relatives from Vienna. And, second of all, definitely not to go to Zvornik, this year's latest development.

What would there be for her to do in Zvornik, in an apartment next to the Drina, in the house they'd managed to repossess after making an official request to the Office of the Interior Ministry of the Serb Republic of Bosnia, following an eviction order? An apartment that so far only Papà Željko had gone to visit, shortly after the war, showing up there with all the nerve and stubbornness of a schoolteacher, while it was still occupied by the family of a police officer. Now that the official decision had been reached, the apartment, which they had owned, was once more in their possession, even if it was in terrible condition.

And so, in addition to their Sarajevan apartment in Marijin Dvor for the summer, as well as the other in Via Pascoli in Trieste for the whole year, now they also had another place in Ruska Zgrada, the Russian Building, in Zvornik. And they'd need to decide what to do with it, for who knows what period of the year or of their lives. Keep it, give it away. Who knows?

For Amila, however, its uncertain fate mattered. They'd gotten it back, yes; it needed to be renovated, okay. It had been their home. But that wasn't okay at all. She lived in Trieste, and that was where she wanted to spend her summer vacation. She wanted to go to the seaside. "Every blessed day," as Mamma Selma would have put it.

Amila was sitting on the parquet with her legs crossed, next to the suitcases and leaning on the armoire. She had decided not to move until she'd won. Majda had shown up in the doorway and was winking at her.

"Well, if it's just for this summer…" Papà Željko had started thinking out loud. "Why don't we let her take that summer job?" he continued, calmly. "Girls need so many things."

"She shouldn't stay here all by herself. Do I have to ruin my vacation too?" Mamma Selma was hugging her fancy polka-dot dress tightly.

"C'mon. At her age you weren't staying at home with mamma and papà either. In case you don't remember, you were already going out with me."

"What does that have to do with anything? Back then, we were a united country. It was peacetime."

"We can't drag her along just because we no longer have that country."

"It's our duty to go back."

"C'mon, Mamma." He always called her that when he wanted to persuade her. "For this once, three of us will be plenty."

"And so now even families get divided?"

"What are you saying? Did you ever see a family split up because one of the daughters decided to help out?"

Eventually Mamma Selma gave in, but she still wasn't convinced; in fact, she kept sulking until it was time to go.

Still, Amila didn't allow herself to be intimidated. Home or no home, country or no country, whatever it turned out to be, or might be, wouldn't have changed her mind. She lived in Italy, and summer was part of a normal life. She didn't intend to waste it.

CHAPTER FIVE

Kitty

MARCH 2005, KOPER/CAPODISTRIA (SLOVENIA)

AT THE POLICE station, Norina presented her ID card and confirmed that she was the owner of the impounded Fiat Panda. The thought that all this could have been a side issue—Amila, her illegal employment, taking the car for inexplicable reasons—didn't trouble in the slightest the distracted police officer sitting in front of her. He took her statement, typing on the keyboard with a single index finger and asking for information about the car and everything else from Anika, who spoke Slovenian. He gave Norina the keys and sent her to a storage lot where she could retrieve the vehicle. Under the desk, she noticed his white socks, peeping out from a pair of dark beach sandals.

When she came out of the single-story building, Norina stopped in front of a big tomcat with thick red fur, calmly squatting atop a short electrical post. He couldn't even be bothered to look at her, even when she came close to him and coaxed him, calling out, "*Kitty, kitty, kitty.*" The most he did was perk up his ears, with his fur raised, making visible a wave of irritation.

It was a relief to get out of there, to get back in the car and leave behind those silent hills, with their rows of vineyards and gray-colored soil. For a brief moment a glimpse of Capodistria could be seen, the sea appearing where the barren, ash-gray mountains petered out, and behind that, the storage tanks and multicolored cranes of the port. And then the twists, turns, and roundabouts returned. Anika drove quickly, using the accelerator unevenly. Norina hung to the strap above the passenger car door. She'd left the window open a bit to let in the brisk air. It helped calm her nerves.

"*Didn't they use to call this Albaro Vescovà?*" Norina asked, commenting on the yellow road sign that pointed in the opposite direction.

Anika answered no, saying that she'd always only heard it called Scoffie in Italian.

The radio was tuned to a Slovenian station. Radio Koper, Norina heard them say, as she closed her eyes and thought again of the red, thick-furred cat she'd met outside the police station. Back in Buie she'd had a cat like that: Luli, the same name as her black mutt with bristly fur. And her cat, too, had been big, red, and wild. No stranger would dare go near him.

One day, Norina had been coaxing him to come out from under the bed. It was one of the last things they'd told her to do before they had to leave. *Kitty, kitty, kitty.* She needed to convince him to come out, before her father showed up with a broom or who knows what else. If that happened, there'd be trouble, for Luli and for Norina—their animals couldn't come to Trieste. Luli stared at her with his yellow eyes wide open. He was watching her, like a cat, sure, but a cat who was scared to death, a cat who no longer trusted her, as if he knew what was about to happen.

When she slipped under the bed and managed to grab him by the paws, Luli tried to wiggle away, scrambling backward. Norina set him down carefully by the outside door, next to the bare *rosèr*, which needed pruning. Luli shook it all off, coldly, without giving her another glance. Norina clapped her hands, once, two times, *G'on! G'on!* He'd manage to survive. After all, he was a cat, not a dog. A dog would've died of a broken heart, or they would've thrown it into a ditch, to save it from suffering.

Norina thought about petting her old cat one last time but hadn't dared. He wasn't one you could betray with false flattery. Instead, she kept it simple, telling him once more, "*C'mon, go!*" but Luli wouldn't move. His ears were pulled back, and he looked straight ahead, as if nothing were wrong. That was the day Norina left Buie behind, the city where she was born.

At the vehicle storage lot, Norina handed Anika the carbon copy of the statement she had given the police. A big, heavyset man took them over to the Panda. He must've been the boss; he gave off a sour smell, like burned sauce at the bottom of a pot. The Panda had crashed into the guardrail, and as a result the passenger-side door was crushed and the windshield was gone. That Amila was still in one piece, that she'd gotten out of it with just a broken shoulder and bruised cheek, seemed a miracle.

Norina thought again about the cat in Capodistria that had made her remember her Luli. All that commotion, and then the long drive, and now the car in this condition. *And that chump of a cat* couldn't even be bothered to acknowledge her presence. It was too much.

"Me, I just don't get it. Any of it," she protested, worn down by it all.

Anika continued an intense conversation with the man who ran the garage. Norina watched them, bewildered. It didn't reassure her at all knowing that the Panda was in the hands of such a rude guy. She couldn't say why, but she again thought of a red cat—first running under the bed, then grabbed by the scruff of his neck and lifted up like a rag. She imagined it hanging from his fat fingers, which now were squeezing a half-smoked cigarette butt.

But she really shouldn't, Norina thought, she shouldn't let such stupid ideas into her head. No. This man definitely wouldn't have a cat. Only a wife, judging from the ring on his finger.

Anika, meanwhile, was trying to get Norina to focus, because they had only three possibilities. They could call a tow truck to take the car back to Italy. She did have international auto insurance, didn't she? Norina shook her head. Well, then they needed to see if the car would start, and if it was worth getting the Panda repaired. They would have to come back to get it some other time. Norina held up her hand, making it clear she didn't want that.

So then, it was the salvage yard. That area was full of them. Everyone in Slovenia was changing their cars. But if the engine was still good, the salvage yard would send the Panda to Albania or Montenegro; she would still lose out, and others would cash in.

Norina put her hand on her forehead, forcing herself to find a solution, but her thoughts had gone cloudy. Questioningly, she looked at Anika, who cleared her throat and pushed back her thin, gray hair. She, too, seemed to have reached her limit, which was saying a lot. That meant the situation was serious. The man began to get impatient. Anika made a decision, saying they should first see if the motor would still start. Norina muttered something, *yes and no*, but Anika stood firm and signaled to the mechanic. He called two young men and then got in the driver's seat. He turned the wheel, yelling instructions through the open window. The mechanic closed the garage door with a remote control, and Norina and Anika were left outside.

Norina started to sob, but with no tears. To tell the truth, Norina didn't know how to cry.

Anika put an arm over her shoulders and convinced her to take a short walk. They were near a highway off-ramp, and there weren't any cafés, bars, or supermarkets nearby. Nothing but a field full of broken automobiles, surrounded by other cars hurtling in all directions.

They got back to the garage just as the men were coming out. The engine had started up, and the car could be repaired. At the kiosk that functioned as an office, Anika asked for an estimate. It would cost about a thousand euros. And yes, you could pay in euros. Better, in fact.

The man, who, according to Norina, grabbed big red cats by the scruff of their necks, looked at her, puffing out smoke, his legs spread wide and his thighs about to burst from his jeans.

In Slovenia, Anika assured her, auto repairs cost less and were done better than in Italy. Norina listened in silence, biting her lips.

"*And who will pay?*"

"*You, for now.*"

"*What're you all thinking? Who am I, Berlusconi's banker?*"

And who would get the car once it was repaired? Definitely not Norina.

Anika shrugged. Then she said, "*C'mon, Norina, lighten up.*" There'd be some way to do it. Norina sighed. Her legs felt weak and her brain fried.

Anika was trying to reassure her, saying they'd manage to sort things out. But Anika saw everything in her own way. The glass was always half-full, in her eyes. For her, everything was easy. She had a neat little house, a garden where everything she planted would grow, and a husband, son, and niece who ate lunch together every day. And she still found the time to stop by and see Norina and Mariano, who would otherwise be on their own.

Ultimately, Norina had to understand. Anika repeated, endlessly patient, that there was no other solution. Norina bowed her head, defeated.

"*Prav.*" Anika spoke to the man in Slovenian; he answered with a nod of his head, contented. For the first time, he let slip a polite smile.

Part Two

CHAPTER SIX

News from a Very New World

JUNE 2004, BRISTIE/BRIŠČE (ITALY)

ONE MORNING, THE call of a cuckoo woke up Norina. She downed a quick cup of barley coffee, laced up her leather boots—the pair good for both summer and winter—grabbed her walking stick, and went off to look for it.

The woods thrummed with chirps and trills, but he could be heard above it all—a male with his rhythmic call, pining away for his mate. She found him perched on the branch of a maritime pine. A small, hawklike bird with an orange beak and feet and plumage like a pigeon. *You merlo!* That birdbrain had somehow managed to get an old lady out of bed, and after all these years, she was still running after him. The cuckoo reminded her so much of her childhood.

Norina had heard on television that its eggs get put into other birds' nests. The parents leave the nest, and when the cuckoo egg hatches, the insolent chick gets rid of the others, to become the boss of the nest. But sooner or later it, too, leaves the nest behind. It does so by instinct, or out of some biological imperative or necessity. That story disturbed Norina: it spoke about life itself, and, when it came down to it, her life in particular.

"You're really a merlo, aren't you?" she said, with barely a whisper.

Luli had gone on ahead, toward the oak grove. Up there, you had to leave the dirt road and cut straight through the coarse, thick grass until you came out on the county road. Norina walked along the roadway, but seemed less sure now, because her boots were on hard asphalt, not dirt, and the boots slowed her down. A car hurtled right by her without slowing. Luli pulled hard on her leash. It had been a terrible idea to come this way.

"C'mon, girl." There was only a short stretch of road before the city limits sign.

Bristie.

The village where Norina lived was only a handful of houses, with a sign on the road at each end: one written in two languages that marked the beginning, and, not far from that, one with a red slash through it, marking the end. Again in two languages. A narrow downhill road connected them to the town of Santa Croce and the sea.

Brišče, its Slovenian name, could hardly be read. The word had been covered with a black cloud of spray paint, as happened a lot, as if years hadn't passed and it was still necessary to draw or erase lines and divide up their land. In that neck of the woods, they still told the same old stories, getting attention with a load of graffiti painted over the walls of houses. In Italian, "Fascists in foibas, now and forever" and "Poor, lost Istria"; in dialect, "Rotten Slavs"; and in Croatian, "Trieste is ours." Norina thought she could guess who'd done it. She would see them around, young men loafing about in the village square. They were louts who parroted everything they heard at home but knew nothing about history. Nothing. If they'd only gone through what she had, they'd be looking for a better job, and they wouldn't be wasting their time dirtying other people's walls. *Manigoldi*. Scoundrels.

Norina turned down the dirt road that led back home. In Anika's garden, the hortensia had dazzling shades of pink, blue, and pale purple. She came to her own gate and collected her mail, lost in thought. The ivy was growing up again around the roses. It was a strange sort of ivy, one she'd never seen elsewhere, with thin stalks and spreading roots that could never be weeded out entirely. A bad sign, she thought.

"*Mariano? You here, or d'you go out dancing?*" she called from the doorway.

Ever since he'd gotten that ulcer on the sole of his foot, Mariano had been lost in a world of his own. Now this problem, on top of the news from that last orthopedist, who figured out that Mariano's hip was worn out and they'd have to replace it. They were on a waiting list, and only God knew when the hospital would call them. In the meantime, Mariano was walking slower and slower, more and more dependent on his walker.

But at least Amila had accepted the job. Norina would be able to go out more often, and not just to shop for groceries in Prosecco or take Luli around the corner to pee. Already years ago, a '*sichiatrist*, who didn't seem to take depression in women all that seriously, had recommended that Norina should try taking walks. Getting out of the house and exercising might help get rid of her negative thinking and bring back her appreciation for the good things in life. At least for the small things.

Except, though, things lately had become so tiny that you could fall right down into them. All day long she and Mariano talked about practical issues, so they at least had something to say to each other, as the days stretched out. *You wore it, you did it, you took it.* Mariano would do something, and Norina would undo it. He'd put something in its place, and she'd move it someplace else. This was their way of coming together: bumping into each other and, in the end, tolerating each other. Nothing all that bad, but also not all that good.

Norina would neglect housework out of apathy; nobody shined up her house. It just didn't matter to her. The only things she cared about happened in the woods. Things that came out of the ground. Everything else could fall apart, on its own.

Mariano stayed upstairs, in the study, where he had set up a single bed. He'd wear a shirt and tie, as if he still had to go to the office, and he spent his time doing math problems on his computer. According to him, in a few years global warming would put Trieste's Piazza Unità d'Italia underwater.

"*Mariano?*" Norina tried to call him again. "*Everything okay, or is the flood coming?*"

"*Yes, yes. Everything's okay.*"

"*Good.*"

But at least thoughts of catastrophes filled up his days— between internet research, studying the layout of the piazza, and compiling the data. All that would take a lifetime, and for Mariano there wasn't that much life left. He'd have to hurry, if he wanted to discover a way to save the city from the sea.

Norina tossed onto the kitchen table the packet of envelopes and brochures that she'd gotten from the mailbox. It didn't take long before she noticed it. The envelope, which she wasn't expecting, was white like all the rest, but its edges were striped in red and blue. She picked it up, her hand trembling. The koala-bear stamp and the postmark in English were unmistakable. Inside would be news from very far away. News from a very new world.

Norina couldn't remember how long it had been since Nevia had last written to her. It must've been quite a while ago, but that didn't matter all that much, because for years Nevia had always told her the same things: about her daughters and their husbands, about what her nieces were doing, and about her only nephew. Her handwriting was tiny, and her crooked words densely filled the sheets of onionskin paper.

They talked on the phone from time to time, on official holidays, even if Norina wasn't one to waste time. The calls were expensive, and she wasn't good at chitchat. Plus she never knew whether to laugh or cry. Nevia always spoke as she did back in the day, but those days were gone. She also had acquired a strong accent from down south, from Southern Italy, like that Carmine Giarrusso she'd married, though he'd died a few years back. And, what's more, she pronounced her "o's" and "u's" like something that could barely pass through a funnel. Or, as they said in Buiese, *dal cul strento de una galina,* through the tight butt of a hen. And then, well, Norina just didn't know. Nevia kept saying "fantastic" this and "fantastic" that, in her other strange new accent: English. No, that woman wasn't her sister anymore.

Nevia sent a card for her birthday, and others at Christmas and Easter. Norina never did. And, frankly, Norina wasn't overjoyed with those colorful cards, with their musical jingles that sounded like TV commercials when you opened them. They always arrived right on time, at most a day ahead. Norina always wondered how Nevia managed it. Of course, it wasn't news that her sister knew how to organize things to her advantage, even from the other side of the planet. She'd always been calculating, despite her cute little face and how naive and timid it might seem. Norina remembered very well how she looked as a girl, with her thin lips and eyebrows, with her luck in having that small, French, aristocratic nose, and her gleaming, wavy hair, embellished with a single pearl barrette. Her mother had given the barrette to Nevia, the younger daughter, rather than to Norina, who had thick, straight hair.

Luli came in the room and lay down between her legs. Norina sighed and decided at last. She opened the envelope.

"My dear, dear Norina."

In total, there were three pages. The usual onionskin paper.

"I'm writing from Moonee Ponds. I just finished making a batch of walnut bread, and it made me think of you. Probably because it didn't come out all that well, and I wanted to ask you for advice. I don't remember anymore if you need to add poppy seeds or not. I forget so many things lately, it's really distressing. How are you all doing?"

Nevia talked about how down there it had stopped raining, and the temperatures had gone down some. She would still have to stay home inside for another month. And then she'd be going to the public hospital for therapy. "Asthma is a dirty beast."

Next she began with the usual rundown of her daughters and grandchildren: Ann, according to Nevia, had too much money, which meant that she was never happy; Louise seemed a bit down in the dumps, after filing the papers for her divorce; but Maria Vittoria, Nevia said, "Well, it's fantastic." She ran the business with Salvatore. Those two worked like demons, exporting doors and windows—"to Malaysia!" And then news about Adele, Teresa, and Laura. They had long hair and were wearing tight jeans. And Christine was already in college.

"And about Simon. He's fantastic." He'd just completed a law degree. "He'll be a lawyer. Our little boy a lawyer, Norina, can you imagine that?"

"And here's some real news."

As a present, Nevia wanted to give her grandson a vacation. "He'll be coming to Europe, and he'll make a quick stop in Trieste. I told him that's fine, so long as he brings me back photos."

"And so, my dear sister, that's also why I'm writing." Norina closed her eyes, so she wouldn't read any farther. "To ask you for a huge favor—big as a house." Too late. She'd read it, and she was struggling to breathe.

The favor, big as a house, that she was asking was for Norina to let Simon stay with her, for two weeks at the end of August. After that, he'd be going on to Greece, for some windsurfing thing he'd arranged. Simon was a wonderful kid, Nevia assured her; he wouldn't be any trouble at all. He could always find a hotel, of course, but he'd certainly be more happy staying with family. Simon was the only one of all the kids who ever asked about Trieste, maybe because he had also studied history. Honestly, he'd studied so much that he really needed to have some fun before starting his career.

"We're as old as the hills. Let's sort out things between us, okay?" No. That was the one thing Nevia shouldn't have said.

"Please write back to me. You can write directly with the computer. Regular mail is slow. Write to simon.monforte@melbourne.com.au. Mariano can help you. If you write back in a letter, I'll already be at the hospital. So write me an email—it's the modern thing, and quicker.

A big, big hug.

Nevia."

So, in her old age, that's what Nevia had become. After a life spent in Australia. A woman who baked walnut bread in the summer, which for Norina was the winter, mixing up bread pudding and bread, poppy seeds and currants.

Annoyed, Norina threw the letter on the table. Her sister's chatter filling her head was like nettles, irritating. Luli jumped up, alarmed, and she put her nose in Norina's lap. Norina petted her in return.

Simon—her blond Australian great-nephew with glasses, the future lawyer who liked to windsurf—was hoping to visit at the end of August. Norina had seen him at most once or twice, in photos that ended up in the drawer of her side table. The long-hoped-for male child, which Nevia never had, because her womb had generated only women. First Ann, and then the twins, Maria Vittoria and Louise. And even they had a gaggle of girls: Adele, Teresa, Laura, Christine. The girls with jeans, long hair, and all the rest. Except that the anxiety-ridden Ann had become the mother of Simon, the son that neither Nevia nor Norina ever had. Simon, the most Istrian of all the grandchildren—the only one who didn't have even a single drop of Calabrian blood.

Norina had been left without sons or daughters, because she and Mariano weren't able to have children. And now, in her later years, a flight was about to arrive with a nephew unknown to her. The boy she'd never had. Some youthfulness, in the midst of these seniors, herself and Mariano. Maybe, for once in this blessed house, someone who would talk to her. Someone whom she could talk to.

Norina shook her head resolutely: no, definitely not. Because first and foremost, Simon belonged to Nevia. And she didn't want anything from her sister. Between the two of them, things could never be sorted out.

Even so, a decision would have to be made, and, this time, it had to be the right one.

And so she stood up suddenly, ignoring the tremor in her legs. She put on her apron. She blew vigorously into her rubber gloves. She walked toward the kitchen sink, still full of dishes from last night, as if she were starting to put some order in her disordered house, which often seemed to reflect the disorder in her head. Or vice versa. Because August would be here soon, and, in some corner of her heart, something was still stubbornly fluttering, despite all the years, the entire life, which had passed. She'd never be able to stand up to that.

Norina wanted to see that unknown nephew, to have him there. But their house would need to be put in order, from top to bottom, even if she'd never been able to do that with her life. All the more reason—it was high time to start.

CHAPTER SEVEN

Rubble

AUGUST 2004, BRISTIE/BRIŠČE (ITALY)

WHEN NORINA NOTICED the paintings, it was only a few days before Simon's arrival. Lengthwise on a mustard-colored background, the two pictures each depicted a child—a boy and a girl—with big, sad eyes. She was wearing jeans, standing pigeon-toed, and holding on tightly to a teddy bear. His eyes were even larger and rounder than hers; he seemed lost in thought, with some gadget in his hands and a runny nose.

Norina had forgotten about those two. Maybe that's why they now seemed so ugly next to the newly repaired window, with its freshly laundered drapes. Or maybe it was because, for once, she was sitting in a different place on the couch, far away from the TV.

She didn't know when they'd been put there, although during the sixties those sorts of paintings were often bought as part of the decor, and you'd see them in a lot of houses, not just hers. The two children had gone undetected, as if for months or years they'd been the ones observing her, spying on her, not the other way around. And that wasn't good at all.

She'd been working together with Amila throughout the whole summer. They'd flipped over the mattresses, cleaned out the armoires, filled black, oversized garbage bags, and probed into corners and crevices with brushes and rags. Yet somehow those two were still there, above suspicion and unconcerned with the occupants of the house, overlooked despite "the biggest housecleaning of the new millennium," as Amila laughingly referred to it.

Norina wondered to herself how long it had been since she had stopped making decisions about things—where they should be put, when they should be thrown away. And why? Was it lack of time, or maybe because she had too much time?

The days, months, and years had fallen over her, without commotion, crumbling to pieces imperceptibly but unstoppably, and that made it all the more shocking. All this had happened while Mariano, hunched over his chair on the second floor, stubbornly continued to calculate the extent of an immense, imminent catastrophe.

Norina blew her nose (it couldn't possibly be a cold), then stuffed her handkerchief back in her pocket.

Who would have the job of moving those paintings? What would be done with them after she and Mariano were dead? No one would be coming from Australia, not for her funeral, and not to take on the problem of the house and all these old things. Nevia would have written a letter, yes, and it would have arrived on time, but it wouldn't have changed anything. Because it was just paper. It wasn't flesh and bone.

And so, Mariano's only grandson, Robby—whom they never saw, not even on major holidays (and a good-for-nothing,

FEDERICA MARZI

according to Norina)—would hustle over, snapping up the inheritance before the Australians could get there. Robby, so massive that you'd expect him to be a carbon copy of Mariano, would go through the place. He'd hire a couple of Serbs or Albanians to tear everything down, including the paintings, and throw them away, along with the rubble, in their cement-coated buckets.

Norina couldn't do anything about it. That's exactly how it would have to happen.

But Simon was about to arrive, so there might be some hope. Maybe, someday, that house far from the city and from floods, up in the high plains, would belong to him.

What sort of impression would all this make on the future lawyer when he arrived? Simon came from a world where everything was fantastic. What would he say about her paintings, her furniture, these old walls? How would they look to him? Would he be curious? Respectful? She couldn't say why she felt this way, but to her Simon seemed special, and not just because they shared the same blood. More because Nevia had always had all the luck.

But now, nonetheless, that luck might have turned—for once, luck might be on Norina's side, opening up windows and doors that had been left closed for years.

"*Dìo benedetto, you're going to give me a stroke!*"

Amila had come in without knocking.

"Oh, sorry. I wanted to know if everything was set. If I can go."

Amila had her beach bag over her shoulder. *Black as a babàu*, a bogey. And fresh as a rose, even if her sleeveless shirt was sweaty and her hair was falling in her face. She'd been going to the beach all summer. It was never too hot for that one.

"*Wait a second.*"

"I told Mariano to rest for a bit. With heat like this . . ."

"*Good girl. Let him sleep.*"

"You ought to lie down too. We're finished here. And be sure to drink some water."

When Amila was there, Norina felt secure, sheltered from storms, floods, ruin, and destruction, even if Amila herself was a raging river. With her you could never get a word in. She talked too quickly. Norina couldn't even follow.

"No, actually, just wait there. I'll bring you a glass."

You see. Norina never even got to say what she thought.

"Luli is in the entryway." Amila handed her a glass dripping with water.

"*Listen.*" Norina downed the water in a couple of gulps. "*Can you help me take down those paintings?*"

Amila looked at her in dismay. "What paintings?"

"*Those two monsters.*" Norina pointed, her finger trembling.

"Why?"

"*Do they look nice to you?*"

"No, but . . ."

"*Exactly.*"

"And where should we put them?"

"*In the basement.*"

"There's not enough room there for a mouse!"

"*We'll pack it in there somehow. It's not that much trouble, is it?*"

"Yes, okay, okay. I get it."

Norina started to smile. She stood up and took Amila by the arm. She moved forward carefully, as if two enemies were lying in wait for her. Amila was a head taller than her—only beanpoles in that house. Everyone except her. For some things, though, tall people were useful.

Amila first took one painting off its nail, then the other, and she set them on the ground.

"*But is that even possible?*" Norina cried out, dejected. Not only were they ugly, but those two paintings had also left two rectangular stains on the wall.

Amila put her fists on her hips in irritation. "Okay then. We cleaned up during the entire end of the millennium. But we're not going to start over now and clean during the next one too, are we?" That's just the sort of tangent her comments always took. "To make those stains go away we'd have to repaint the whole living room. You decide if it's worth it." Then she added, more gently, "C'mon. Just relax, for once."

Amila was right. There wasn't enough time to take care of that too. The paintings had won, but Norina felt anything but relaxed.

"*Okay. Hang them back up, and that's that.*"

If Norina had been able to say what she felt, she might have responded, Okay, put them back up—some things just can't be resisted. Things have a force of their own. Things have inertia on their side. And that gives them permanence, even when time caves in on you.

Amila took off on her scooter.

Norina felt useless and transient in that big house, where the two children were once again staring at her with their big eyes and deep sadness. Yes, Norina could feel all of it, the force of things that go the way they go, and are the way they are, and it wasn't a good feeling. She felt she was sinking into her sofa, just sitting in her usual place, with the remote control in her hand, but she had no desire to press the "on" button. So she put it away and gave up.

She wouldn't be able to make Simon see her as someone else, with taste she didn't have and didn't want to have, with organization that had never been her strength, and with courage she'd never possessed. Or that she had once, yes, but in speaking her mind. She could try as hard as she wanted. That was true before, and it still was. But maybe it would have been fine for Simon, without all that effort. He was so young. And she was old, falling apart. What would he expect?

With the years, with their slow, inexorable pace, she had sunk into a state of torpor, a condition she was no longer able to resist.

When had it begun? When had she stopped caring about anything that happened around her? When had everything become the same to her, no matter whether they were on one side or the other, if they hung there for a few hours or for a thousand years, on a wall with faded color?

It had been years since Norina last thought about that distant day in May. Back in those days she had been the same age as Amila, and her future seemed written in stone. She'd been a happy girl, but then, after the war and the Germans, Yugoslavia had come.

She closed her eyes, and the memory of that day came so strongly that it stopped her in her tracks and forced her back into her old bedroom.

Norina lingered over one detail after another. The chest of drawers made of walnut with gold handles and a marble top. The pink floral design along the edges of the drawers. She saw herself again framed by a standing mirror, the rebellious curls in her chestnut hair. Wait, she told herself. Stay still, still. Don't go away.

In the middle of her room in Buie, in front of the big bed, there was another mirror, framed in bronze spirals. Now she could see it from the back as well, with the names, Norina and Nevia Benci—Buie—1955, written there by her, in chalk. Her handwriting looked crooked and uneven, as if she'd been a dunce at school. But it wasn't true; she'd never been a *mussa*, a donkey. It was simply that school, too, had gone as it had gone. Like everything in her life had gone—all those things that she hadn't been able to resist, that she'd never been able to accept, but that, in the end, she had to get used to.

CHAPTER EIGHT

Amor, Amor, Amor

MAY-OCTOBER 1954, BUIE/BUJE (FREE TERRITORY OF
TRIESTE—ZONE B, MILITARY ADMINISTRATION OF THE
YUGOSLAV PEOPLE'S ARMY)

IN THE LONG mirror with a bronze spiral frame, all of Nevia's slender, though not-so-tall, figure could be seen. Back when she was twenty, she didn't mix up anything, she didn't talk with a strange accent that made you want to laugh or cry, and she didn't write letters. She was simply Nevia, that's all, and she was getting dressed for Mass.

She was admiring, with satisfaction, the dress that she had sewn by hand, working until late in the night. It was cut to fit her slight, shapely frame. She'd chosen jersey, with elbow-length sleeves, cinched by a belt around the waist. The skirt cut midway across her knees. If the hem had been a bit higher, her father would definitely not have let her out of the house. If it had been a bit lower, she wouldn't have gone.

Only one thing was missing. Nevia pinned a big white bow to her hair. Despite its childish appearance—nothing but a simple bow—that inventive headdress challenged and provoked; you could tell it wanted to be much more than it was. Nevia's hair was the shade of honey, and it fell softly over the nape of her neck. With the sunny weather it lightened, though you couldn't figure out why, since Nevia spent her days stuck in the house with Mamma, mending the mountain of sheets and uniforms that Dalia sent them. During the evenings she worked as well; she would start sewing again, hurriedly, for herself or for the customers who would come knocking cautiously at the door, before it got dark and no one would dare venture out through the narrow, twisting lanes of Buie.

Norina was sitting behind Nevia's back with her legs crossed, on the bed where they slept together. She, too, was in front of a mirror, a smaller one. She was taking out, one by one, her own locks of smoothly falling hair and wrapping them around the hot curling iron, tapping it with her wrist and burning her calloused fingers.

Once Norina's hair was done, the red of her lips got touched up, and her raven-black curls fell in disobedient waves. The usual wave in front was gone. Her forehead wrinkled slightly, an expression of angry satisfaction, giving her a commanding, decisive look. A face like that belonged to a young woman who was tired of living in a state of suspension, in a land they still hadn't decided which country should have, Italy or Yugoslavia. At her age, she was right to expect everything from life. She was fed up with waiting. Fed up with delays. She wanted to have what belonged to her.

A little later, the two Benci sisters answered their father's summons.

Nevia gave one last touch to Norina's dress, with its sky-blue and fuchsia flowers, adding two more stitches to secure its nicely

FEDERICA MARZI

cut neckline. She fastened a lock of Norina's hair with the pearl barrette. Nevia didn't need it that day, so Norina could keep it for the hours of the Mass.

These days Nevia was wearing her hands out, working with fabrics that no longer came with a lavender fragrance, like the material the monks at Dalia's monastery used to send; this stuff had a yellowish color and a slightly rancid smell, because it came from an old people's home. That's how this new era smelled. How unlike this odor was the tailoring that came from Nevia's expert hands, sought after by everyone in Buie and all the way to the coast. Norina's dress was another marvel, and it smelled of violets. Norina imagined the rows of pews in the Duomo, and how she would attract looks of admiration from everyone. She was proud of her sister's hands.

Her feet, though, were an entirely different subject. But you couldn't do anything more about the shoes. Norina and Nevia had the exact same kind: sandals, crossed by thick white canvas laces. Baba Antonia—she wasn't really their grandmother, or even an aunt, just one of their mother's cousins—had bought the sandals for them in Trieste, on a day when the border was open. She'd suffered a beating because of that trip, in the square where the bus stops.

The shoes weren't exactly what the girls had asked for. The wedge heels were only two inches high; Baba Antonia hadn't managed to find anything higher. She'd wanted them to wear high heels to spite their father and all those people who tried to stop her from trafficking goods between Zone A and Zone B. But in the end, she'd had more important problems to worry about.

"*It's a shame, a shame, a shame,*" Nevia complained, sticking her wrist through the strap of her handbag.

"*C'mon, c'mon, get a move on,*" said Norina, chasing her away and pushing her from the room.

Their laughter echoed through the stairwell.

As soon as he saw them, their father straightened his beret and ran his fingers over his gray, bristly mustache. With a quick glance he measured the hemline of the skirts and, reassured, clapped his hands to get them going, as if he were moving cows along in a field, though his gestures seemed less enthusiastic than usual. As it happened, the People's Committee had taken away some of his cows. Since then, he hadn't been the same.

Their mother checked more closely, inspecting first one daughter then the other with her small blue eyes, two pearls from the sea on a gaunt face. Her hands examined necklines, sleeves, and hems. She judged whether the bows and curls were good enough. She sighed, but let it go. She folded her hands and gave a nod. Perhaps she was hoping that Nevia's bow and Norina's curls might give fate a gentle nudge. It was time for one of the two to find a husband, before the decision was made about where the border would fall.

Norina was the daughter who came first and the one who gave the family most concern. She detested learning to sew, that one. Their mother had taught the trade to both her daughters, but Norina would have tears in her eyes, as if she'd been to a funeral. Her buttonholes would pucker, and then when she redid them, she'd ruin everything. She'd become impatient, and her stitching would go sideways; her hands were unsteady, when instead the blade of the scissors needed to cut through quickly and neatly.

If she had been a man, Norina would have gladly gone with her father into the fields, after his shift at the old Arrigoni factory. As a woman, she went into the fields anyway, but it wasn't the same. Either she would weed in a frenzy around the lettuce or hoe through the big clumps of clay, to make herself look like a man. She'd dig furrows for potatoes without stopping to catch her breath, and, with her bare knees on the cool earth, she would bed out rows and rows of seedlings: savoy cabbage, peppers, tomatoes, eggplant.

It never crossed her mind to go to the factory with her father, to process sardines, even if the "New Socialist Woman" did work side by side with men. And she would never have gone to clean rooms in some hotel in Umago. She felt good in the fields, and on days when her father was in a bad mood, hurling curses at the heavens, she would stay home and slave away at some other form of heavy labor. Those jobs were left to her, since she didn't sew or work at the factory, and hotels were out of the question. To tell the truth, though, she didn't mind at all. It suited her to have things that way, so long as her work was for her, and not given to "the people."

On that Sunday in May, however, it wasn't the white, flowered dresses of the Benci girls that attracted the stares of villagers clambering through the backstreets of Buie. And, before Mass, when people were chatting in hushed tones so no one would hear, it wasn't about the two of them. In the Duomo, people were distracted and only pretended to listen to Don Mario reading from the Gospels. "To me has been given all power in heaven and on earth." The priest, too, was in a rush, and his sermon wasn't appreciated. No one paid the girls any attention, not even beneath the bell tower, where groups of the faithful assembled after the call to "go in peace."

Even at the old cemetery of San Martino, at the end of the street where the youth of Buie gathered, the dresses of the Benci sisters were left nearly unobserved. There the news of the day, which had the whole town upset, was joked about and made fun of.

WE MUST EXPOSE
THE DEADBEATS AND SABOTEURS
OF THE PEOPLE'S COMMITTEE

The graffiti had appeared during the night, on a wall at the bottom of Via Lama, the way into town, where everyone would see it in the morning. Perhaps a warning to straighten things out before it was too late? A while ago, they'd again started having volunteer labor rallies, and a lot of people hadn't been showing up to lend a hand. Who were those people?

Norina and Nevia walked past the commemorative gravestones recalling the magnificence of the Crevato and Festi families. Welcoming them there was the happy, hypnotic call of a cuckoo, hidden on some nearby branch. They stopped to sit on a low wall where some other girls, in the shade of a lush fir tree, were seated, across from the small church and large stone cross, planted straight into the ground.

Norina called out to the cuckoo, looking for it greedily. "*I got here first! Where are you, merlo?*"

Nevia called it too. "Look over here. Come on, little bird, I was the first to hear you!"

The first time an unmarried girl heard the song of a cuckoo, it was said, she could ask it how many months or years there would be before her marriage.

Norina took off her barrette and shook free her curls. Nevia showed off with her cheerful smile. She was looking around, as if searching for her girlfriends, but her timid glance was directed toward the group of boys.

Norina had already been looking over there. She'd been counting all the deadbeats who were an annoyance to the People's Committee. Among them was the boy known to be the biggest deadbeat of all: Franco Bacàn de Buroli.

He was rolling a cigarette, sitting on the wall, his legs dangling. His thick and curly blond bangs covered some of his face. He was wearing work boots.

His full name was Franco Radonich. A while back, she'd seen it appear in the local newspaper, *Nostra Lotta*, except there it was spelled in the Slavic way, Franjo Radonić. The paper also used Slavic spellings for other names, first and last. Next to his name, there was a list of dates: the mornings where he'd been seen with a cigarette stub between his lips, twiddling his thumbs. People said he was *morlaco*, from someplace else, that he came from somewhere beyond the Quieto River valley, even if they didn't know exactly where. Everyone knew him by his Istrian name, though: Franco Bacàn.

The word *bacàn*, which meant "a lot of noise," suited him best. He brought merchandise to sell to women, leaving at dawn from Buroli, after spending a long, festive evening at Sior Toni's osteria. Like thunder, he'd bark out his prices and snatch the money—Ha!—with his big, thick hands. He'd count it and recount it, breathing fire if someone tried to cheat him.

"Pagliacco," a clown—that's what Norina's father would say, and he'd say it in Italian, especially about Franco. And then, in Istrian, he'd add, "*Pedocio refà*"—nouveau riche, a show-off. In those days, though, everyone also knew that people like Franco Bacàn were useful to have around. The gossip was that at night he brought wine from the farmers to sell at Sior Toni's, in order to diminish the stock at the warehouse or to subtract it from their obligatory share at the co-op, the *zadruga*.

Norina didn't know if her father also supplied wine to Franco, because in public he would disapprove of "that brigand," shaking his head and stroking his mustache. But he did deliver his large, golden grapes—their sweet juice squeezed to the last drop to make Malvasia—to someone during the night. And then, on the first of May, her father, too, had hung a woolen flag out of the window, with ITALIA written on it—the country he wanted to keep as his own. And so, her father, too, had been forced to hide under the bed for days, like a brigand, until young men, with no official identification, came to take him away. Those boys were the same age as his daughters; he had seen the day they were born, then baptized, and watched them grow. But still they had shown up at his place, as if they were in charge, with a beaten-up van to bring him back to the factory.

And so, when you took everything into consideration, someone like Franco Bacàn was useful to someone like Norina's father, although there was no question that, if Franco ever tried anything with his daughter, Franco would get skinned alive.

At the San Martino cemetery, Franco shook his hair back and lit his cigarette butt. He looked around, squinting those close-set eyes that everyone in Buie, upper town and lower, recognized— their strange gray-blue color was like no one else's, changing as it did with any variation in the weather. Norina was one of the few brave girls who managed to look straight into them.

Lately they'd been running into each other early in the morning, at the market. Norina would walk slowly past the marketplace stalls. Franco would straighten his back, take a long drag on his cigarette, and stare at her, without a care in the world. Norina welcomed his glare; she wouldn't stop, but she did slow down, as her heart leaped and tumbled. Those eyes would follow her shamelessly all the way down the street.

At the San Martino cemetery, Norina looked at him without blushing. He turned up the corner of his mouth, but she walked on by, so she wouldn't seem too brash.

Sitting next to Franco was Mariano, someone who wasn't a deadbeat at all. Norina turned her head away haughtily. Mariano began staring at her, smoking that new brand of cigarettes, Morava. He was wearing his Sunday best; the hem of his pants had been lowered three inches.

"Ha!" Franco jumped down from the wall, pointing at Mariano. *Look at this guy, he likes slogging stones around . . . And bums like us should get punished because of him?"*

His full name—Mariano Potleca, though everyone called him "Stretch"—had appeared in the party newsletter too, though his name was used as a counterexample to Franco. Mariano had done his share of volunteer labor, without ever wearing a satisfied smile on that face of his, with its bony cheeks and big forehead, topped with a clump of hair shaped by sugar water.

Mariano had worked odd jobs for people like Norina's father. He had volunteered, thinking it would be good for him too. Not everything the new authorities did seemed wrong. Someone had to watch out for the poor and unfortunate. About those Slavs who were in charge now, he didn't know much. He didn't speak "Slavic," as he put it, but his neighbors did, and so did a lot of his new colleagues at the Proletarian. Such things had never been a problem. The city was Italian, the countryside Slav, and he wasn't from either. He came from Stassion, a neighborhood down below, just outside the town walls, and he didn't have any land.

"*Ha, look at this mona, what an asshole!*" Franco threw an arm over Mariano's shoulders, teasing him.

Mariano gave him a violent tug, to free himself.

"*You asshole!*" Franco raised his fists and threw himself at Mariano, making him stumble, but only a little—Mariano was a head taller than he was.

One of the girls shrieked. Livio Barbo, who lived in Sucolo, got between the two of them and pushed Mariano away. Livio had just come back from a long stay at the sanatorium in Trieste, and he didn't want to ruin his Sunday. Others rushed up as well, trying to convince Mariano to let it go. Weren't they all there to have fun and celebrate Livio's return?

"*You're nothing but a pajasso!*" Mariano shouted, walking away.

Nevia was holding tight to her sister's arm. Norina felt like laughing; her father and Mariano were agreed about this "clown." Though she also knew very well that her father wouldn't let her marry anyone like Mariano either, someone who came to work in his fields for hourly wages and now toiled in the factory woodshop.

"Let's go, 'ndemo, you motley crew, 'ndemo, let's play bocce. It's better than this." Livio Barbo grabbed a couple of the bigger boys by the arm. They all wanted to go have a glass of Malvasia at *Sior* Toni's. Better than hauling stones and pushing wheelbarrows for free!

Franco went back to the wall next to the other boys, where his impudent attention began to linger over Nevia's bow. Norina flinched. All their care in getting ready, only to have that bow admired by the wrong person. Franco, mockingly, turned up a corner of his mouth. Nevia blushed bright red. Norina glared at her in response. The younger sister excused herself, whispering that she had to go home and finish the mending. She said goodbye to her girlfriends and went off quickly on her way, without looking back.

Norina held on frantically to a stone sticking out from the low wall. Then she excused herself with the other girls as well, saying she had to join her sister. But as she left, she turned the other way, alongside the city walls.

She went back past the Duomo, then the school, before noticing that someone was following her. She turned into a cool, narrow backstreet. She turned a corner, where a small alcove opened up, covered in luxuriant, blooming wisteria. When she was sure it was him, she turned around at last. Then she began to run.

Norina and Franco were sitting at the base of a fig tree in the *Sotto la Losa* neighborhood, where the farmland and brushwood end in a cliff. Franco would stretch over toward Norina, and she would pull back; laughing, she would move away from him, just to make him try again.

"*If you let me touch your leg, that means it's love.*"

Someone else would have promised to do what was expected. In such hard times, though, it seemed better to leave promises to the speechmakers' megaphones. That's what Norina thought, anyway, though she did take Franco's comment as a promise: that means it's love.

Not long after, Norina hurried her way home, with her lips still burning, her lipstick gone, devoured by all the kisses. *Amor, amor, amor,* she kept repeating to herself, gasping, with her hand on her chest—not in order to calm the commotion within, but to convince herself once and for all that it was really true. And it was. The love she'd waited so long for had come. Even for her.

There was no one out and about who might see her. There were no voices coming from the houses she passed, not even a curious old woman looking out from a window. The doors were closed; the courtyards were empty. It had already become a ghost town.

Norina came back for lunch later than she'd ever been. Nevia looked at the ground, and her mother folded her hands. Her father tapped a fork nervously on his empty plate. For Norina, there would be no God, and no saints. Or grace, or pardon.

From that day on, according to her father's adamant verdict, she would not be allowed to leave the house. But she rebelled.

She hurled forks and spoons against the bolted door. She messed up the bed linens, the mending, and the piles of fabric, and she ran up and down the stairs, beating a broom against the handrail. Enough noise to wake the demons of hell.

Then a period of unexpected calm followed, during which Norina seemed to give in to her father's decision. In reality she had put her trust in the impermanence of those times.

Her mother concentrated her attention on Nevia, because summer was passing quickly, and Livio Barbo di Sucolo—now that he was back from the sanatorium, and after some initial revelry—had settled down and started to court (of all people) her Nevia.

"For heaven's sake, mother!" Nevia implored desperately. *"You want me to marry that snout?"* Nevia said she would never be able to love someone with a giant pug nose like his.

But her mother responded stubbornly, a haggard look on her face, *"In time, you won't even see a nose, but land—that doesn't go away."*

Livio had orchards, vineyards, olive groves.

At night, even with the scorching heat, Nevia would close the shutters, so that all of Buie wouldn't hear Norina's sobbing. With her heart full of pain, for herself and for her sister, she would tell Norina, "It won't last."

And, in fact, it didn't last. The days flew by quickly, up to October 1954. The government of the Free Territory of Trieste was dissolved, and Zone B was handed over to Yugoslavia.

In Buie it seemed as if the end of the world had arrived, and no one any longer worried about two girls, like Norina and Nevia, who still hadn't stopped sighing, laughing, and crying over love.

Many of the houses emptied out, as if they'd been surprised by a blizzard, an out-of-season *neverin*. Whoever wanted to repatriate to Italy, to Trieste, had to line up at the town hall and surrender their property. Families broke up. Friendships crumbled like pastry crust. The ties that had bound a community together were cut. And the oaths and promises that had sung *amor, amor, amor* snapped, like so many desiccated branches.

CHAPTER NINE

Travel Permit

MARCH 1955, SPODNJE ŠKOFIJE/ALBARO VESCOVÀ

(YUGOSLAVIA)

THE TRUCK STOOD motionless, crushed under the weight of two large bed frames; two mattresses rolled up together; the tall mirror with a bronze spiral frame, which the girls didn't want to leave behind; Nevia's sewing machine; three wooden chests full of linens; and a great deal of nice clothing for all seasons, as well as everyday clothes, along with some fabric and sandals that were still new. Her father's scythe hung there crookedly, though what he planned to do with it in Trieste, no one could say. These were the sole personal possessions the Benci family brought along with them. Everything kept together in a precarious equilibrium, items chosen carefully and then piled haphazardly. The hammer's final blows secured a tarpaulin over the truck and signaled their departure.

Early that morning, Norina had looked out at the horizon toward Umago. Judging from the threatening, bluish clouds, bad weather was brewing over there. Across the countryside the air spread crystalline and clear, apparently making a promise it couldn't keep. You could see the fields, and even the lines marking where they began and ended. That one belonged to the Barbo family. And it would remain theirs. That other one belonged to the Vascottos. And the Vascottos had already gone. That other one, down there, was the Bencis'—surrendered formally to Yugoslavia, along with the rest of their property. It would be taken by someone.

Norina's father had made the cows go out of the barn. He'd given each of them a big slap. Before putting down his hoe, he had walked unsteadily through the vineyard, stabbing at the new shoots. They had already been left untended. Then he told himself, "*You've gone mad.*" And he left it alone. He'd thrown the hoe down into the wire rows and stormed off, without bringing the cows back to the barn.

The truck tottered over the uneven cobblestones. It made a last stop in the Sucolo neighborhood, almost wanting to delay the inevitable. Livio Barbo was waiting there, standing motionless. Orietta ran to his side, wiping her hands on her skirt and tidying her hair. Livio would stay in Buie, with a few others. He would marry Orietta, who was the same age and also wasn't leaving.

Norina and Nevia's father stepped out of the truck. He seemed smaller, perhaps because he was in his Sunday best, the dark jacket and pants from his wedding twenty years earlier. He gave the young man a big hug, expecting to hear him say, "Addio," or "I forgive you."

Livio's eyes were shining. He, too, would have appreciated receiving a consoling word, or an apology, because now his life would be more solitary. But it's always those who leave who think they're worse off. As they passed by his house, Livio sent the trucks off with a wave. Few of them exchanged pleasantries or promised to come back. Who knows. Maybe someday.

When the two men's embrace ended, Orietta came up to Livio, as if she wanted to take him back for herself—the sort of gesture that in normal times wouldn't have been allowed for any couple that wasn't fully anointed as husband and wife. But by now the times had changed, and even the priest was gone. Those two would be married in a civil ceremony, or by a Croatian pastor.

Norina, sitting in the cab, held on to a fistful of dirt that she had dug up with her hands from around the *rosèr* that had grown up between the walls and stones in front of their house. Her mother checked to be sure the gold was still hidden in her blouse, then leaned out the window and stroked Orietta's bony face, caressing again and again the waves of her still-uncombed hair. "Dear Orietta" was all she could manage to say.

Orietta had been in the group of girls that day when Livio Barbo had returned from the sanatorium and Franco and Mariano had come to blows. It was the last day Norina remembered as happy, where she had left home with a light heart and confident step, wearing her first spring dress and the new sandals from Trieste, even if the People's Committee had yelled, in red letters, denouncing the deadbeats who dressed up for the festivities.

Norina had been locked up at home until the London Memorandum was signed. It dissolved the postwar stalemate, giving Trieste to Italy and most of Istria to Yugoslavia. From that point on, no one worried about her any longer. In the streets, at the town hall, in the houses and the fields there was a swarm of people that belonged to a community about to split in two. In that frenetic, confusing movement of goods, property, people, and documents, Norina lost sight of Franco. He had gone looking for her, but that was before, just before the tempest descended upon Buie, forcing the town to its knees.

He'd come one night to whistle and throw pebbles at the shutters Nevia had sealed. Norina had tried to wrench them open, but managed only a crack; she peeked out and then decided to fling the window wide open.

"Watch it—if Father comes up here, he'll go after me too," Nevia had whined.

Ignoring her sister, Norina sent out some kisses, so timidly they might've seemed some sort of wave. Across the street, leaning on the wall of a house, Franco Bacàn laughed.

Perhaps Franco had also come back as a challenge to Norina's father, taking the bull by the horns. That way, Franco could say around town that he was the one who took her father's golden Malvasia and sold it, for whatever it was worth. But Norina didn't care about the wine. She only cared about the kisses that had flown back and forth. Franco took the toothpick out of his mouth, brought his fingers to his lips, and "Ha!"

Eventually, though, Franco left. Gone in the general confusion. In a way that let him leave, disappear, without all sorts of pleasantries. Some were saying around town that he'd gone to Trieste by himself, without his family. That he'd decided on Italy, even if he was *morlaco*. All you needed to do was declare yourself Italian; even someone like Franco Radonich or Radonić, an intruder, a troublesome but necessary presence, could do it.

You could get on a bus, taking next to nothing with you, except for a travel permit, granted without much red tape. In part, this was possible because at times, granting a transit pass meant getting rid of someone for good. And that might suit everyone just fine.

Norina wondered if she'd ever see him again. And the question tormented and consumed her.

Nevia raised a hand to wave to Livio, smiling at him. His face darkened. And Nevia's smile became bitter—her mother had been right. "*The nose, you don't even see the nose.*" Now that Livio had stayed, and they were going away, his nose didn't seem so big anymore.

Their father climbed back in, slamming the door shut with a dull thud, and started the truck. Livio Barbo and Orietta, from the Sucolo neighborhood, waved a white handkerchief. The truck wobbled down the final descent. After the curve, Buie disappeared.

Their journey continued across the plain. Their truck came across others hurtling in the opposite direction, light and empty. They hit their horns twice and sped away. They were on their way to pick up other people. The Bencis answered with their horn, without slowing down again, clinging to one another inside the cab packed full with their possessions. Going forward, it felt as if they were the last ones left, just the four of them.

Benci Pietro, son of Nicolò.

Benci Ederina, wife, née Bibalo, daughter of the late Vincenzo.

Benci Norina, daughter of Pietro.

Benci Nevia, daughter of Pietro.

They weren't a large family. After the first two children, there had been no others. There were no longer elderly family members to take care of. They'd buried Grandpa Nicolò in November. He had let go just in time, and one day, perhaps, they would be grateful to him for that. Hard to say for sure now, but in the future all doubt would disappear. Doubt about who might be right and who might be wrong. Who went away, leaving everything, and who stayed behind, holding on to everything, only to divide it up later with whoever showed up.

The Bencis repeated to themselves over and over these words: Nicolò is dead. Only you four are left: Pietro, Ederina, Norina, Nevia. Nothing will ever be the same. What do you do? Stay there just to hold on to a tomb? What do you do? Stay there and then regret that you didn't leave like all the others? What do you do? Do you want to live like foreigners in a new country? Or do you want to live like foreigners in a country that, for now, you think you have the right to call your own? No, not your own. You're the ones now who belong to it. By right. They let you come in. They let you cross. Go to Italy. Now or never.

At the checkpoint, they stopped in front of a long crossing gate where a Yugoslavian army patrol was posted. On the other side were the Italian border guards. Women wrapped in headscarves and men in elegant overcoats smiled in silence, waiting for their relatives.

Old road signs stood out against the gray sky. JUGOSLOVANSKE VOJAŠKE OKUPACIJE—LINEA DI DEMARCAZIONE. Yugo-Slovenian military occupation—limit of the occupied zone.

The world had been divided in two. The four of them were at a crossroads. The world, however, wasn't prepared for this sort of intersection. It would be better to slice it up, and then stitch it together with barbed wire; that way, you would have to decide which side to stay on and where to go.

There was also a new language—"demarcation line," in English—which seemed not to have sound or weight. But they were wrong. Though Trieste had gone to Italy, and the English and Americans had left, that language would make itself heard in their homes and in their lives.

Their father got out of the truck and buttoned up the collar of his coat. He seemed to have gotten even smaller. He handed over their travel permit—No. 6214—to a young man, thin and dry as a sardine. No "*buongiorno*," no "*dobar dan*." That day wasn't good for anyone.

The thick, humid haze pestered both people and things, clinging to their hair, their clothes, their scarves and hats. Everything seemed unreal.

This document hereby authorizes BENCI Pietro, son of the deceased Nicolò—born in Buie in 1908, profession: agriculture, residence: Buie, possessing Identity Card No. 54873, issued by the municipality of Buie—to transit through the checkpoint at Albaro Vescovà en route to Trieste.

Beyond that travel permit, beyond its wording, all the rest would open—the rest that would take the place of all that the Bencis had left behind them. It wasn't a new land. It was the land they had no longer. It was a giant world they didn't know, a world that inspired dread but also the illusion that they had returned to their homeland. They had wanted this. They knew that—it was even written on their travel permit: "This document is valid through 4 April 1955 for ONE crossing[s]"—they would have to stay there.

Norina's eyes grew wide. She observed the slow movements of the *milissioner*, the soldier who, scowling, studied their travel permit and inspected their permit for transport of personal possessions. Their mother hid a bit better the jug that she kept between her legs. Nevia placed both of her hands on the dashboard. Norina let the fistful of dirt fall onto her good coat, the brown soil now sweaty from being held throughout the whole journey.

The city could not yet be seen. They'd placed their expectations, dreams, tears, and anger there. Yet even Trieste now, under the cover of fog, was snubbing them, holding herself at a distance—beautiful, arrogant, and indifferent.

Their father got back in, and the *milissioner* closed the door of the truck with a sharp thud. He touched his visor, without changing his expression. Four squeaky sweeps of the wipers cleaned off the windshield. The truck began to move, and the crossing bar was raised.

CHAPTER TEN

To the Other End of the World
AUGUST 1956, PADRICIANO/PADRIČE (ITALY)

FOR NORINA AND Nevia, the first name for their new world was refugee camp. That's where they put the Istrians, in long rows of wooden barracks, left behind by the British and American military, along with the rancid odor of their living quarters and the smell of the soldiers' feet.

The barracks were identical in appearance, except for the numbers on the doors, the identifying mark that would allow you to say, just as they used to in the fields, "Look, that barracks belongs to the Vascottos. That other one, down there, exactly the same as the first, belongs to the Potlecas and their boy, Mariano. When it came down to it, they didn't want communism either. Across the way, where you see the other row of buildings, there's Baba Antonia; she used to go back and forth by bus to Trieste, for business, and now she's ended up in Trieste too. *Ciapa su e porta a casa*, as we say. Take that and deal with it. Two barracks farther down it's the Benci family, with two of the most beautiful girls in all of Buie. They've been here for a year and a half. They don't have the time now to put their best dresses on and curl their hair. They take the bus at dawn and go to work in the city. The older girl works at the Mercato Coperto. The younger one works as a maid in a private house. The tall mirror with the bronze spiral frame, which they brought to Trieste as a keepsake, ended up in a Porto Vecchio storehouse. They wrote their names and where it came from on the back, in white chalk. That way, they'll find it again someday. Still farther down, by the brick buildings for teachers and clergy and the carabinieri police headquarters, is where the Milossa family lives. Opposite them, they put the Bibalos, together with Franco Radonich. The rumors were right: he had gone to Italy, and the Bibalos don't have any kids, so they gave Franco a cot. Franco is giving them gray hair and rotting their teeth, even if he's barely ever around. Well, guys like him discovered Italy instead of *la 'Merica*: the life of a refugee as idler. One ration card for the canteen, plus an ID card for refugee status, then a government stipend, some time at the tavern, and everything's good."

The block with Norina and Nevia's barracks was separated from the block with the Bibalos by a straight gravel road that divided the refugee camp in two. It led up to the canteen, there where the forest grew thicker; in the opposite direction, it ended at the metal gate, covered with barbed wire, and the county highway. From there on was an expanse of fields and sinkholes, their borders marked by dry stone and brambles.

If it weren't for the bounded, rectangular space occupied by the barracks of the refugees, the countryside there would have seemed continuous with the one left behind; the camp was an

FEDERICA MARZI

ugly appendage joined to a small town, a town like so many others, where they spoke Slovenian and made dark, sour wine, and where their houses clung to a small church and central square.

From the moment they'd arrived, Franco had been ignoring Norina. His hair was long, below his ears. Norina's had grown too, but she wasn't bothering with it; she would just tie it up under a scarf bought from her first paycheck. If they happened to meet in one of the lanes between the barracks, he would avoid her, muttering a greeting and turning away. As if he were annoyed. Or else he would turn up a corner of his mouth, his eyes would narrow and darken, and he'd continue on his way, without a word.

Sometimes Norina would make up an excuse to go out—she had a stomachache and needed the bathroom, or she went to fill her mess tin with mush—to scan the camp, looking for him. And often she'd find him, but with other people. He would be smoking and talking, flicking his cigarette butts and taking no notice of her.

Whenever Norina would go to the baths, or to visit Baba Antonia with Nevia, if she happened to come across Franco, she would pretend not to see him, and he seemed to be fine with that. When she took the bus back from the city, she'd get off a stop early, so she'd have to walk by the tavern. She'd look inside, quickly and discreetly; the windows were open, and someone was always going in or out. That someone was never him. She might think she heard a "Ha!" from inside, and for her it always caused the same skip of her heart. For an instant she felt alive. Since, as a woman, she couldn't go inside, she'd limit herself to a sigh, then tie up her scarf more tightly and hurry back into the refugee camp.

Norina didn't understand Franco's callousness toward her, but she attributed it to the new life they had there. In fact, many things might have stayed the way they were, although they hadn't: the now-chipped porcelain plates; the pages of Florence Montgomery's *Misunderstood*, soaked and stuck together, and now leathery and illegible; blankets that didn't keep them warm; nice dresses that were getting worn out; their dialect, blending together with other Istrian speech patterns that were similar but not the same. And her former neighbors from town had now been mixed with people from the coast; the Malvasia from this new soil didn't taste like it used to; Nevia was still sewing, and she kept getting better at it, but she no longer made anything for herself or Norina. And Franco, who had once promised to love her, now behaved as if she no longer existed.

Norina lost her sense of time passing. It was as if she always had plenty but didn't know what to do with it. Everything was suspended in days that dragged past with no difference between them. Yet the time did pass, and after spring came the muggy summer, and after fall came winter, and a deep freeze, worse than usual.

The frozen weather of February 1956 surprised Norina. Even if nothing had really changed in their wooden barracks, with its inadequate electric heater, at least their living quarters had stopped smelling like a barracks each time she came in. But doubts had remained. Doubts that the odor had soaked into her clothes, into her skin and hair, and had become her own.

Norina was shivering. The temperature was fifteen below, and it was numbing her fingers, even under two pairs of gloves. Nevia's face had turned gray; she seemed reserved and distracted.

She would come home irked by the riches of the house on Via Bellosguardo, pulling out the pearl barrette from her hair, as if the refugee camp suited her less than the others.

When the snow reached their knees, Norina and Nevia didn't go to work, because public transportation had come to a halt. The camp looked haunted. Icicles hung from the roofs of the barracks like pointed teeth. Their leather boots weren't waterproof, and the floor of the barracks was soaked. Some of the blankets had to be used to block the windows, so that the heat wasn't all lost. The Bora wind from the northeast knocked and rattled at the glass like it was possessed, and the floorboards creaked all through the night. Nevia spiked a high fever, and Norina wiped her forehead with a sponge soaked in vinegar and water.

And that was nothing compared to how children suffered the cold. Fathers would shovel clear their front doors, but the snow would return the following night. A ten-month-old baby from Grisignana, living just three barracks down from them, died from hypothermia. That was the worst moment of all.

Dear Mother, dear Father, dearest sister of mine, we're dying here, from cold and from heat. We're all dying here. But I don't want to die, I want to live.

When their suffering got to that point, Norina understood that love couldn't exist without land. That all you could do is drag yourself onto new ground. She understood that you'd have to give up many things. The beautiful dresses from before. The white sandals brought by Baba Antonia. She understood that you'd have to forget the fragrance of wisteria climbing up the stone walls, the smell of the countryside in the mornings, the spectacle of the land sloping down to the sea.

Except for Franco. Not him. Norina couldn't get him out of her head.

Night after night, he appeared in her dreams, with his up-beat chatter, and after waking up she might feel lighthearted, but then an anxious thrum would slip into her chest. Those strange-colored eyes, which would narrow sarcastically, made her smile dreamily as she packed endives and radicchio into a crate. She winced, though, when she remembered his hand flat on her leg. For Norina, it was impossible to believe that everything which had happened between them no longer meant anything at all. And even if everything now said just the opposite, she wouldn't give up hoping. She was blind and deaf. She was lovesick.

Nevia seemed to be a shadow. She seemed to disappear from her, from their lives, silently swallowing its bitter portions. Signora Venier had hired her because she was an expert tailor. But the dresses Nevia sewed for her were used only for one season and then quickly gotten rid of, given as charity to the poor. So many poor girls like Nevia had come from across the border; she had seen the work of her hands thrown away, but no one ever gave her anything for free.

At the refugee camp, everyone paid great attention to whatever the Italian government did or did not do. The border was close by. Norina and Nevia, too, were consumed with fear at the prospect of being excluded once again. One international dispute was all it would take for the line, in a single night, to come their way and pass them by, pushing them back into Yugoslavia again. Or maybe they were the ones who, not paying attention, might go beyond that line cut into the earth, beyond the signs posted in the woods warning you to stop, because the international border was there, even if the thick undergrowth here was just as thick over there.

Norina listened closely to the accounts from elderly women in the baths about cases where people from Isola had tried to cross, only to be taken back by the military police. And also about a boy from Verteneglio, who by mistake had found himself on the other side. He'd been brought to the police station in Capodistria, and from there he hadn't returned.

She heard the men from Pirano talking in the canteen about the Canadian Embassy or the Office for Assisted Passage in Australia. Norina didn't know if Nevia was listening too or what she was thinking about. Her sister ate, sitting stiffly in silence, with her eyes lowered.

But there was also good news—about who was born, and who got married. Life moved on. And there was sickness, and mourning. There were some who found an apartment to rent in the city, like the Bibalos. With no children and with Franco Radonich to bedevil them, they made do with a cockroach-infested hovel in Via Belpoggio. And there were even some who got jobs. That burly boy from Isola, the one who was a little slow, received an anonymous letter. He was asked to appear at the port, for a position of assistant chef. It was a real job, and he got it, setting him up for life.

And then, well, that was it. There were others who still had nothing and kept their mouths shut, their lips sealed and dry.

Norina, too, had become withdrawn, worried. She was always on the alert. She felt like something was about to happen, but she didn't know what.

Dear Mother, dear Father, dearest sister of mine, perhaps the others will say terrible things, that you should be ashamed of me. I ask your forgiveness from now on. Forgive me if you can.

The camp was immersed in a gloomy silence from the moment the gate closed with a metallic thud. In the mornings, even before the sun, a dense hum of voices would rise up.

In June, the heat returned, lessened in the mornings by the breeze from the woods.

In August, the heat hit its peak, and the camp woke up with the sharp cry of a woman coming from the Benci family barracks. That cry spread through the lanes between the barracks, turned the sharp corners and started down the parallel sets of paths. Two women whispered to each other at the door to the baths. Then they all fell quiet, and an unusual, grim silence ensued.

The shout was followed by words that were clear, though few, revealing the truth and the shame of a family that had already been bled dry of everything it had, already been left with only a small core, just four people, with their elders all dead and their tombs far away, with two grown girls, both of an age to marry but unmarried, who worked instead of their father, and who continued to have nothing.

The mother cried on her knees, making a useless gesture, as if pulling something out from her chest. The father

FEDERICA MARZI

stayed standing at her side, his arms hanging down, bruised and speechless, as if someone had cut out his tongue.

Norina had been the one to find the letter. She had noticed that the bed was empty, though, oddly, the covers were in place. She'd found the sheets of paper on the chair, next to the gas stove.

Before her eyes the tiny, slanted letters shifted, superimposed themselves, one on top of another. For an instant, Norina could no longer see anything. But then she understood.

Her father had snatched the page from her hand.

Dear Mother, dear Father, dearest sister of mine. I'm going to the other end of the world, with the *Flaminia*. We arrived in the camp in springtime. Then another spring and now summer, but other than the heat that came after the cold, for us nothing had changed.

Norina turned white.

Her mother's cry traveled in waves from one alley to the next. Unkempt women and children stuck their heads out of their small windows, alarmed. Some began to ask what had happened; others answered with invective, a curse.

Dear Mother, dear Father, dearest sister of mine. Signora Venier has close contacts in the Office for Assisted Passage in Australia. She tells me that I'm a very talented tailor, and if I work hard, they will give me money and a house in the biggest city in the country, Melburn. They even showed me a photograph. It looks like a very beautiful house. I had a medical checkup, and they said that I'm fine and that I can go. Two years, and then I'll come back, I swear to you. I can't explain everything to you, but I have you with me, deep in my heart. I will help you, I promise.

Her father checked beneath the mattress to see if the money and gold were there. They were. Then he sent Norina to look for Nevia, just as, once before, her father and mother had given Nevia the task of bringing Norina back home. They sent her into the city, as if all that she needed to do was to turn the corner and go through the *Sotto la Losa* neighborhood.

Norina dressed quickly, but she forgot to put on her slip. She only realized it when she was already outside, hurrying to the toilet with her purse on her arm. Her hair uncombed, like a sleepwalker, she went past a group of women and men who were speaking under their breath, elbowing each other to be quiet. Norina thought it must be because she had forgotten her slip and hadn't combed her hair.

At the Maritime Terminal, she felt a stabbing pain in her temple, so severe that she could no longer see or move. And yet somehow her thin body tried to slip into the crowd. In between sweaty men shouting and waving their arms, and between mothers holding their little ones close, or others, blowing their noses. In between old people looking stoically ahead, wiping their foreheads with a handkerchief, next to a couple embracing, beside women hiding their faces on their husband's (or fiancé's) shoulder, and alongside entire families waiting expectantly—from the oldest to the youngest—as if they were marching together. Norina took several steps forward, not knowing where to look, where to search. She stopped in front of a thick wall of bodies.

The giant ship loomed over them, taller than the palazzi of the old town, the *città vecia*.

When the whistle blew, everyone began pushing and crowding forward. Even the *Flaminia* itself rocked under the weight of its human cargo.

Norina pushed with her fists and got shoved in return. She stood up on her toes, looking everywhere around her. In the multitude of heads and hats, she noticed a thick head of chestnut-colored hair that fell softly back onto a pair of delicate, straight shoulders. They belonged to a woman who stood and stared at the ship without moving. Norina felt as if she recognized that small white collar, set over an old dress, to make it look new.

She shouted loudly. Two men in front of her spun around, staring at her and scowling, but the woman didn't turn. Norina called again. Someone pushed her, making her stumble forward a few feet. She stood again up on her toes and desperately shouted out her sister's name. The woman turned around. Her eyes were small and faded. She was older than she had seemed from the back. She held a handkerchief in front of her mouth, sobbing. It wasn't Nevia.

The *Flaminia* began to move, the crowd rocked back and forth, and Norina was crushed within it. Yet another whistle and a puff of smoke, and the emigrants were departing. Crowded together on the ship's bridge, they began to wave their hands, their arms, and their handkerchiefs. Coins were raining down from the steamer. Three young men, with hats pulled down over their foreheads and cigars in their mouths, were holding up a banner: "Mother arrives and the children leave." As the ship moved away, Norina saw families with serious expressions, couples that hugged each other exuberantly, and other young people. But she didn't manage to spot a young woman alone, leaning up against the ship's railing.

CHAPTER ELEVEN

The Point Isn't to Go, It's to Stay
FALL 1956, PADRICIANO/PADRIČE (ITALY)

NOTHING WAS LIKE before. In the refugee camp, after Nevia's departure, not even getting up in the morning was the same. Sleeping wasn't either, though that was something Norina was only able to do off and on, holding tight, tossing across dreams on the surface of slumber. One night she had an especially nasty nightmare.

The casks were lined up, stored in the *stanzia* of Sior Toni, though his farm had gone to ruin. Norina was wearing the dress with flowers that Nevia had sewed for her. She was running barefoot through the field, and the moist ground buzzed below her feet. The grass scratched her calves, and the meadow was covered in red poppies and chamomile, bending in the breeze. Lush rows of grapevines that no one pruned were turning into bushes. Norina leaned over a cask full of murky water and saw her image, blurred, covered in reddish-purple and blue speckles. She didn't see anything, but she felt a hand grab the back of her head and force it down, inside.

She woke up, unable to move, her heart pounding and a disgusting taste in her mouth, as if she had actually tasted that water. The first sounds of the day could be heard from outside: someone walking by perhaps, a dog barking in the distance, or possibly the drone of a motor. She listened to her mother breathing heavily and a whistle in her father's throat, and terror gave way to misery.

And yet that day still needed to begin. A little milk still needed to be heated up. Hurrying to the bathroom, wrapped tight in a shawl. Getting dressed, reluctantly. Pulling up her woolen stockings. Taking the bus into town. Feeling her stockings itch and feeling the cold anyway. Getting lost in the dull gray that clung to the windows. Coming to the last stop and fumbling through the bustle of the city. Then back again at the barracks, amid eyes that avoided others' and mouths with little to say at day's end. And watching her mother getting rid of Nevia's dresses from Buie, a few at a time, but then in secret opening up the trunk where they still kept the sewing machine, as if it were still good for something.

There had been a short letter from Nevia. Only one. Repeating, "Two years, and then I'll come back. But I might come back sooner, you know, as soon as I can." She said that she was in someplace called Bonegilla. Nothing else about her health, about why she wasn't in "Melburn," about the job she'd been promised (and where was that job now?), about the money she'd promised to send. The little news she gave would have to suffice.

For Norina, though, it wasn't enough. Nevia had climbed aboard that steamship—a mix of hope and despair, human cargo and export goods—to go far away, toward a different life. Norina went forward into her days and duties feeling herself flattened by the hand that, in her dream, had pushed her head into a cask of murky water, in a field flooded by violet light.

Working, helping the family, saving up, getting out of the refugee camp. And above all, finding a husband. Her mother would waste words on nothing else. Norina would nod her head yes, then shake her head no, and would then turn away, to look somewhere else.

Her mother worked in a home that belonged to two wealthy women from Trieste. Her father slaved away on construction sites as the city rebuilt. In the evenings, he suffered from terrible bouts of coughing due to the dust and cold that got into his bones, and from the work that his farmer's arms didn't know, and didn't want to do. To keep from thinking about it, he started smoking.

Once, after dinner, he seemed to be suffocating. Her mother ran to call for help. Baba Antonia rushed over, with a brown glass vial in her hand. She raised her finger in warning, with the verdict, "*Look, what you've got is asthma. You need to see a doctor and find a job inside.*"

"*It's just a scratchy throat,*" he retorted, exhausted after spitting into his handkerchief. "*A real son of a bitch!*"

"*Let me see.*" Antonia looked at the handkerchief, raising her eyebrows. "*Just what I said. Look, this is nothing to joke about.*"

Her mother grew pale, but her father acted as if it were nothing. A stubborn man, he would go nowhere near treatments or doctors. In this moment, he would say, we need to collect our pennies and find an apartment in the city. In one of those neighborhoods where they were building condominiums like honeycombs, one apartment on top of another, with a common yard. They might even have a balcony. On the top floors, there might be a view of Porto Nuovo. That way they'd be looking out at the same old sea, except from the opposite shore.

"*C'mon, get up,*" ordered her mother, just back from Trieste. She shook Norina's motionless body, which turned listlessly toward her. She'd spent the entire day curled up on the cot. "*You can't keep goin' on like this.*"

Her mother took off her coat, ready to fight, at least for the future of the one daughter she had left. She didn't believe anymore in Nevia's "two years, and then I'll come back." Two years were an eternity. And what would have become of them in two years? Even if it would cause her pain, her mother sealed off the half of her heart named Nevia and opened up the half named Norina. It was difficult to live with only half a heart, but she had to.

"*Get a move on. Go and ask Auntie to check you out. You look like a stick.*"

Her mother complained about Norina's yellowish complexion, the circles under her eyes, her striking skinniness. Something needed to be done. Norina needed to go see her aunt.

"*Ask her how to get some color back in those cheeks.*"

Norina obeyed her mother. She went outside, past the open doors of the empty barracks that the Delises and Visintins had left behind, after they moved to Trieste. Next door was Baba Antonia's place, with the lights on. Her aunt never went out anywhere, except to use the bathroom. As for praying, she didn't, and she didn't go to Mass. She lived on the good, thick milk from Padriciano that the tireless women and girls from the camp would bring her, before using the occasion to ask her about remedies or cures.

Norina knocked timidly on the door. The flooring creaked. Antonia was sitting in a chair near the small window. There was no table, and the absence of such an everyday object was striking. She was sitting straight up in a black dress that left her knees bare; heavy woolen stockings covered her legs up to her knees. On her thick neck, wrapped in black, she wore a mother-of-pearl brooch that she had never taken off, not even during the exodus.

"*I never want to see them again,*" said Norina, throwing at Antonia's feet the sandals that she had once bought for her in Trieste, back when her aunt would take trips over the border: on the way there, shopping bags stuffed with Istrian produce, on the way back, bags bursting with goods from Trieste to sell in Zone B.

With eyes like a monkey, Baba Antonia inspected Norina. "*Sit down,*" she commanded.

Norina found a chair.

"*Your father?*"

"*He's still coughing.*"

"*And your mother?*"

"*Better.*"

"*And you?*"

"*I have dreams. Bad ones.*"

"*How bad?*"

"*Really bad.*"

In the most recent, she and Nevia were together again in Buie, back in their bedroom. Norina had hugged her sister, caressing her hair. It was soft and fluffed up, as if from the wind.

Baba Antonia said, "*Nevia will have all sorts of problems ... We can't do anything more for her. Anyway, you need to think about yourself.*"

Norina shook her head in distress. "*But that's not where it ends.*"

She didn't know how to say it, but in this dream her hands had come closer to her sister's neck, encircling it, squeezing tightly. The worst part was the throat ... it made a sound. The small bones broke under her fingers the way bones in chicken broth crumble in your mouth, so that all you can do is spit them out. Norina felt scared to death, but she didn't want to stop.

"*Listen to me carefully,*" her stern aunt interrupted. "*Quit feeling sorry for yourself. Nevia left, and she's not coming back.*"

"*But she wrote that after two years ...*"

"*And how quickly will those two years pass for her? Do you even know where Australia is?*"

"*The other end of the world.*"

"*And so?*" Antonia pushed her. "*People who go that far don't turn back. Stop thinking that you should have gone instead of her.*"

Norina bit her lip, as if she'd been caught in a trap. "*But what can I do?*"

"*You have to figure that out for yourself.*"

With a thin, fragile voice she admitted, "*I wanted to go away too.*" Because that was what she wanted. "*But how can I, with my folks so old?*"

"*Going away, going away!*" thundered Antonia. "*What for? Didn't we all go away already? Drive this into your head! The point isn't to go, it's to stay.*"

To stay, but to do what?

Norina lowered her eyes, so that she wouldn't aggravate her aunt. But even more, so she could search for the words that

FEDERICA MARZI

would help to express the real pain she had within. She never found the courage to speak the name of what was causing her to suffer. A name impossible to accept, belonging to a face that resisted showing itself, even in nightmares. Because even there it would have created a scandal.

"*Franco,*" Norina said at last, and she felt herself blushing.

"*Who?*"

"*Franco Radonich.*"

"*De Buroli?*"

"*Yes.*"

"*What about him?*"

"*I was attracted to him,*" Norina admitted, with a sob. "*But I swear it was love.*"

"*When?*"

"*In Buie.*"

"*What, then, two or three years ago?*"

"*Oh, I don't know, Auntie. It was before all the troubles.*"

"*Look, now, I've heard stories about that one.*"

"*Me too, but I don't know if I should believe them.*"

"*Well, there is a lot of gossip.*"

"*What if it's true?*" Norina wrung her hands, waiting for her aunt to tell her the truth about gossip that had been running through the camp.

"*To me that's what they said.*"

"*What?*"

"*That he'd gone away,*" Antonia told her. "*On that ship.*"

Norina stopped breathing. Gone away. On the same ship as Nevia.

"*And they say that he's in Australia too.*"

He's in Australia too.

Norina stared at her aunt, her mouth open wide.

"What are you saying? That's not possible."

"Yes, it's true."

Suddenly a memory popped into Norina's head—the time she surprised Franco and Nevia behind the washrooms. But she would never have thought that they could possibly... That they would have wanted...

Nevia had been leaning on the wall. Franco had his hands in his pockets as he walked back and forth. It was a hot day. The sky, on fire from the sunset, seemed lower.

Norina had left the canteen, and after she noticed them, she hurried, almost running toward them. When they saw Norina, Nevia and Franco moved farther apart.

"Don't say anything, for God's sake!" Nevia said, putting her index finger to her lips. Norina had grabbed her sister's wrists, as if she wanted to break them. Nevia didn't fight back or push her away; she hadn't even cried.

Nevia did say one thing. That Franco had asked her to put in a good word for him with Signora Venier. That he had debts or something, who knows what. That he needed money. But she had told him that she couldn't do anything for him.

And so what?

And so, Norina wouldn't allow herself to think, she refused to believe the two of them, Nevia and Franco, could have left together.

"Yes, it's true," Baba Antonia repeated, sternly.

So, that was the truth.

Norina collapsed onto a chair. *"I feel like I'm dying, Auntie."*

"Unfortunately, no one dies from love. Pick yourself up."

"I can't do it."

"You have to."

"But what will I do with myself now?" Norina's voice cracked in pain.

"For now, take those papusse scalcagnade and throw them away." Norina hurriedly picked up the pair of sandals. *"And go home now. I'm tired."*

"Can I have something to help me sleep?" Norina implored her.

"I don't have anything left, can't you tell?" Baba Antonia shouted, slapping her hands on her knees. *"Nothing more than gossip."*

"Something so that I manage to sleep at least a little."

Antonia closed her eyes. *"All right, come back tomorrow. And don't forget the milk."*

"Goodbye, Auntie."

Norina closed the door carefully, so it wouldn't make noise. She wrapped her shawl around her. The Bora was back, the winter wind that howled and made their doors and windows clatter, sweeping up piles of dried leaves, lifting and turning over everything left lying around.

She kicked an empty can, and before going back inside, she pinched her cheeks to give herself some color and make her mother happy. She dried her eyes and tucked the sandals under her coat.

Mariano was sitting in front of his barracks, with his elbows on his knees. He was smoking. Norina sensed he was watching her discreetly. Even though the camp had put everyone on the same level, Mariano still felt the lingering deference of a time when some people were above the others. He stopped puffing on his cigarette. She pretended she hadn't seen him.

Only many days later did Mariano find an excuse to say hello to her and ask how she was doing. And tell her some things that he might have had in mind for quite some time. And explain to her that he'd been attending night school to study surveying. And that there was plenty of work on construction sites, that all you need to do was look for it, and that he, at least, wasn't afraid of hard work. That he'd gotten used to the brutal tiredness that came over him every evening. He was lucky. Every evening he slept like a log, and until the next morning, he didn't think anymore about it. And then about the house. He would also have told her about the house he wanted to plan and build with his own hands. Two stories, outside the city, on a low hill like those in Padriciano, near the oak forests bordered by dry stone walls, so it would be like they'd never left. Even that could be a good place to live. In Trieste, other people like him had found more than whatever they'd left behind. It was still possible to dream with your eyes open, not just at night, when dreams could only be bad.

Norina wouldn't have stuck around to listen, but Mariano still would've continued to speak to her about dreams, about houses, and about life, which at a certain point would change, even for the two of them.

CHAPTER TWELVE

Upheavals

AUGUST 2004, BRISTIE/BRIŠČE (ITALY)

IN THE HOUSE in Bristie, built exactly where and how Mariano had imagined it, the photo of Simon arrived many years later, as an attachment to a short email. They were all staring at the screen. Amila and Mariano were sitting close together. Norina was standing behind them, her cold hands resting on Amila's shoulders.

Simon was in Singapore, waiting for the connecting flight to bring him to Europe, and then, after a second transfer, to Trieste. He'd sent the photo of himself so Norina would be able to recognize him at the airport.

Mariano didn't immediately click on the attachment. He moved the cursor back and forth. Amila encouraged him to open the photo; they could save it afterward. He nodded but seemed as if he wanted to think a bit more about it.

Finally, he decided. "Here he is!" he said.

The background went black, and then the long-awaited nephew appeared.

The printer began to hum, and then the close-up of a smiling blond boy with glasses and a graduate's cap appeared on a sheet of A4 paper. That was Simon.

In the room, strangely for August, a chill set in.

Norina stood motionless, clenching her eyebrows together, by instinct, tightened near the point where the pain was whenever she got a headache. It didn't take much effort to recognize those closely set eyes.

Even hidden behind a pair of thin, scholarly glasses, the eyes stood out as undeniably gray blue, a strange icelike color, something that no one else in their family had, let alone anyone in Buie. Maybe those eyes, too, could change shades with the weather and throw out darts, casting a lifelong spell over you.

Ha!

Maybe those eyes, too, could shine or darken, just like that— which was, by the way, downright awful.

Simon had Benci cheekbones, like Norina's father. His thin lips stretched into a satisfied smile, yet it didn't seem at all arrogant. He had light, delicate skin. His face inspired confidence, not simply bluster. There was also something restrained about him, which was, when it came down to it, just as Norina had imagined him. That clashed, though, with those eyes, and their obvious origin.

Simon was Franco's grandson, at least by blood. *But blood doesn't lie.* Norina had always known this. But she had never realized that Simon would have inherited Franco's eyes. Seeing them now was a problem. And finding them reflected and magnified on a computer screen, one that nobody there had the courage to turn off.

FEDERICA MARZI

Mariano stared at the screen. There's no way that certain thoughts didn't cross his mind, that Mariano didn't understand. But such things weren't easy for him to think about either. Amila took the photo from the printer and turned toward Norina.

"Your nephew." She offered her the photo, with a smile.

Norina grabbed it, without taking her eyes off the screen, and she let her arm fall down to her side. She didn't need the photo. At the airport, she would have recognized her nephew even among a thousand other blond, Istrian Australian boys with glasses.

"*I'm going to the woods,*" she said, out of the blue. "*You all do whatever you want.*"

She needed to be alone. She stuffed the paper into her pocket.

She gave a command to Luli: "*Get up, we're going.*" Lying on the carpet, the dog only raised an eyelid, then closed it again.

"At this time of day?"

"*Today we're getting some fresh air.*"

"But without eating anything?"

"*Me, I'm not hungry.*"

Mariano saved the photo in a file, without saying another word. Norina clapped her hands twice. Luli got up, reluctantly. The long, muggy days, along with the violent thunderstorm the evening before, and the fright caused by the hail and thunder that followed, must have tired her dog out.

Norina crossed the deserted county highway and stopped in the small square. On the wall of an abandoned house, she noticed some shaky handwriting, with some parts covered over:

And thus, once again it was necessary to speak of deadbeats.

But the politicians, deadbeats, and bosses had already robbed her of her youth once. They had dealt their blows, and the earth had shuddered in response. Some made choices adapted to these circumstances. Franco and Nevia had freedom under their feet. Their gaze had managed to focus on the horizon, while their future rolled out, following the wake of the ship they'd taken. For everyone else, attempts to stand on their own had been useless.

The day when Franco had kissed Norina, when they were together in *Sotto la Losa*, had been one of the last happy moments of her life. Back then she was still an Istrian girl, standing straight and proud, free to walk over the cobblestones of Buie, which her feet, wrapped in sandals of the latest fashion, knew by heart. Norina had loved Franco. He had promised to love her. His awful reputation should have kept her away from him, but those had been uncertain times, and things happened which never had before.

It had never occurred to Norina that only one side of love could fade. For her, it was all the fault of the "political upheavals." Those had changed everything. Istria, first occupied, then handed over to Yugoslavia, the refugee camp, and the mass exodus for a new continent—and for love, well, nothing more would be done about that. The political events had been the cause of her misfortunes, including the end of her love affair. If Buie had been given to Italy, nothing would have happened as it did. And that is what she had never been able to accept.

"Upheavals." That was the expression Norina had heard on the TV news. It must've buzzed around her ear like a fly that escaped from an open window, then came back to pester her again. The meaning of that complicated word had become clear to her, all at once, as she looked at this stupid graffiti. Definitely the work of one of those troublemakers from town.

Norina turned onto the path toward Monte San Primo, which went through the forest of pines, beech trees, and oaks. Luli walked close to her, listlessly. The grass was tall and dry. That stretch of woods seemed more wild than usual. The lush tops of the pines brushed one another, renewed by heavy rain the night before. The rocky path, in contrast, was already dry. The rain was too violent; it didn't seep down into the guts. Pity for the soil.

Norina stopped at the spot where, a few days earlier, a suspicious fire had ignited. It was the talk of the town. She studied a fallen, charred oak. Luli smelled it and peed. On the trees still standing stretched long, black burn marks. The leaves had dried up into clumps. The rain had washed over everything, but it hadn't given new life to those trees.

Norina continued on in silence. She walked a bit slower, but she wasn't able to slow her thoughts. Her old fixations once again forced her to confront everything that had happened, in her family and in her life. Simon's photo was devastating and terrible proof of the fact that Franco had gone away, that he had left for Australia with Nevia, and that he had gotten her pregnant. Franco, the only man Norina had ever loved. Love had shown its face only once in her life and had chosen not to reappear. As time passed, Norina had instead seen everything around her dry up, wither, and harden. Her youth had remained a dense and throbbing knot, inside an empty womb. And that love, which had chosen not to return, had by now grown old, at least as old as she was.

Norina had spent two years at the refugee camp waiting for her life—a husband, children—to arrive. She was a girl; what else could she want? But the problem was that she had waited too long. For Nevia to come back as she'd promised, as she'd written in her first letter. "Two years, and then I'll come back." And for Franco, in some way or another, to let her know he's alive, assuming he was still alive.

Nevia had let her sister know that she'd married Carmine, assuring her that he was a good husband and a hard worker. She'd sent them the birth announcement for Ann, Nevia's first child, when the child was already two years old. She hadn't even sent a photo—of Ann, of the two of them, or of the three of them. As for the money she'd promised to send, it hadn't arrived, not even a little. *Gnanca par forbirse el dadrìo*—not even enough to wipe your bottom.

At the camp, their father would count on the fingers of both hands, trying to fit the nine months of Nevia's pregnancy into the sequence of months and years gone by. The sums didn't come out right. He would scratch his forehead and keep smoking. He'd complain about having to put up with those immigrants from the south, the *cabibi*, with all their gossip. Would Nevia really be coming back and bringing that whole tribe with her?

FEDERICA MARZI

And so, Pietro would begin muttering again. He'd put a fingertip up to his lips, moisten it, and continue counting. His hair had turned gray. He would cough and spit. And he'd tell himself they weren't going to trick him. *Sure, in school, I was a dope. But they're not going to treat me like an idiot.* He still knew how to count. And the months and years didn't add up.

And with that, he would slap his hands on the table, down his glass of wine, and go to bed, while Ederina would cry softly to herself, bent over her sewing. Although she'd erased her favorite from her heart, she had begun again to wait for her younger daughter. Norina had always known that, for her mother, she would never be enough.

After Nevia's promised two years had passed, Norina decided to write her a letter. She'd asked when Nevia planned to return, and if she had news about Franco, if he, too, was in Australia. Where he might be. Nevia would have to tell her the truth; that was all she wanted. All that mattered.

Nevia mailed a padded envelope for her sister to a box at the central post office. Norina sat down in the square, on the steps of the fountain. The scooters and cars sounding their horns mixed with the splashing of the water.

"My dearest Norina."

Norina flattened the sheets of paper on her legs and greedily began to read.

"Yes, it's true. Ann is Istrian, like us. She's ours."

So that's how it was. Ann was Franco's daughter, though he'd never recognized her as his. Franco was no longer in Melbourne. He had gone back to Europe, swallowed up in the random movement of events, or perhaps pushed by his own rush to take, leave, and go.

But, for the love of God, Nevia urged Norina never to reveal this secret to their parents. They'd die of heart attacks. Yet it was time that at least someone in the family knew. In case something happened. It was better this way.

As for everything else, well, Carmine acted in every way like a real father. Over there such things were possible. No one judged you; instead, they offered to help. Carmine was a calm, generous man. Too talkative, but, well, so be it. Her place was by his side. Even if he had nothing in common with them, and he would never think of going to Trieste, no more than she would think of going to Calabria. So they would stay where they were. Nevia dreamed of owning her own dressmaker's shop. Why not in Melbourne? No place was better; here it was still possible to dream.

Norina had always expected she would be crushed by the truth, already imagined so often. But when she saw it in writing, all she felt was the icy impulse to tear the letter to shreds. She stood up, flattening her skirt. And, walking up Via Roma, she made the decision to marry Mariano. As soon as she'd returned to the camp, she knocked on the door of his barracks and told him yes. Mariano lifted her up, twirling her around in the alleyway. He had wanted to celebrate and buy everyone drinks at the tavern, but Norina came down with a nasty migraine and had to go straight to bed. They gave her parents the news gradually, and they all began looking for an apartment in the city. Outside the refugee camp, with the four of them, they'd be able to make it work.

From time to time, in the evenings, when Mariano would come close and his intentions were clear, Norina would again have the same violent headache. She would then ask everyone to leave her alone in the master bedroom, darkening it like a version of hell. Mariano would leave her in peace and prepare some broth. His mother-in-law would grumble about being left to twiddle her thumbs, but he would say that a husband's duty was to take care of his wife.

Norina hadn't revealed Nevia's secret to anyone. Mariano had never asked questions. Only Pietro had drawn his own conclusions. His fingers didn't lie—Ann was illegitimate.

That was the hardest blow for him. Ederina, in contrast, minimized it all. *You're crazy*, she told him. Secretly she was still waiting for her daughter and granddaughter to return. But they never came back.

And so Norina had to take care of her parents by herself, right up to the end. Pietro died in a calamitous fashion, falling down the stairs. For Ederina it was cancer, after three months of agony. Norina managed to speak with Baba Antonia; though not a close relative, she was the only one left.

"*You didn't listen to me,*" Antonia had told her, bluntly, at the end of a long conversation, sitting down at the table—the right way, with an embroidered tablecloth, and in her own house. "*You're not living your own life. And you know you're not. But you chose this, didn't you? So then, wipe your nose. No one will thank you, but at least you'll live in peace. And you can't put a price on peace. You're a good girl. But you shouldn't forget to let yourself be a bit happy too.*"

From that day on, Norina always got up early on Sundays. She would ask Mariano to take her on trips. To Grado, Aquileia,

Tarvisio, Udine. To see Italy. She would tie on a nice scarf and put on her sunglasses. Mariano couldn't be more happy about it, and he'd go to great lengths to please her. They bought themselves an automobile. It was wonderful. Their sky-blue Fiat 850 could take them wherever they wanted to go, even great distances.

In the evenings, they'd return home tired but happy, as Baba Antonia had instructed. Norina would come into the bedroom after taking a bath. She would wear a lace chemise that she'd sprinkled with eau de cologne. She would let down her hair, which grazed her shoulders. Straight and thick, with fashionable bangs. Mariano would hold her tightly in his arms, but then, in the eyes of that big, sturdy man who never let anything or anyone beat him, a trace of disappointment would appear. Norina wouldn't have been able to explain it. Something in him was too tender, something in her still too coarse, and the two just didn't mesh. It didn't work.

At times Mariano would make her moan loudly, when he was more daring in bed than other husbands with their wives. The women didn't speak of it, but Norina could guess it from their unsatisfied faces. Sexually fulfilled, Norina would throw herself back on the mattress, red-faced and breathing heavily, staring at the ceiling. Was this the happiness that Baba Antonia had spoken of?

It seemed possible, and, indeed, Norina had made clear her desire to have children. So everything had changed, because at last there was a goal, and it wasn't simply love. That would be her salvation.

But the children never came. Not even after the second and third consultation with a specialist. Norina would vomit like a volcano and rush to the hospital. She would return home as empty as a tin can. For her there was no enduring form of happiness. And during precisely the same period, Nevia sent the birth announcement for the twins, Maria Vittoria and Louise. Happiness continued to turn only in one direction.

Children, the most normal thing in the world, had been impossible for Norina and Mariano. Even the doctors had told them that. Nature had wanted it this way. Nature, that sees and foresees, but often does so at random, without anyone getting anything out of it. Deep down, Norina had always known the two of them weren't made for each other. According to her, nature got it right.

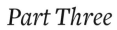

Part Three

CHAPTER THIRTEEN

Today's the Day
AUGUST 2004, BRISTIE/BRIŠČE (ITALY)

NORINA WOKE UP before everyone else, impatiently and happily inspecting every room, opening all the windows. Daylight was coming later each day. Summer was rushing toward autumn, not the most beautiful season, but one that Norina preferred. It was cooler; you needed a light sweater with long sleeves, which was a comfort after all that heat. She made a quick trip to the bakery, after which her Panda was filled with the sweet smell of chocolate brioche. She turned around at the gate, drove in reverse up to the edge of the woods, and then backed in to park in front of the garage. She got out of the car, holding the two paper parcels like they were gold.

Everything was set, then, up to the oak tree, anyway. Norina suddenly stopped and stared. She saw the tree's canopy moving, as if something were shaking it from within. It might be swallows, the flock that stops, pausing in the yard during early October, before heading south. That was the most beautiful moment every fall. And it was her best oak too, robust and older than she was. The only tree left from the grove cut down so they could build their house. It was a tall tangle of coarse wood and leafing branches. The symbol of home.

Norina heard a noise, and, suddenly, the branches shook again. That definitely couldn't be the swallows. It wasn't yet time for them anyway. She moved forward cautiously. She noticed a ladder on the other side of the chain-link fence; leaning on it, at the top, was a worn-out pair of leather shoes. She looked up. Adriano chopped into a branch, and the sharp blow of his hatchet shook the canopy. He threw the branch down. He grabbed the top of another branch, one of the branches of Norina's oak tree, extending majestically also across the other side of the fence.

"*Adriano!*" she shouted, grabbing the fence. "*Come down from there, manigoldo!*"

That scoundrel's utility vehicle—an old Piaggio Apé—was full of boards, empty crates, iron bars, and, on top of it all, a pile of wood from Norina's oak.

"*Leave my tree alone! I'm telling you, I'll call the police!*" That was what she'd always thought of doing. "*And the Mental Health Center! That'll be the ruin of you!*"

Adriano let go of the branch.

Norina felt a tap on her back. She jumped.

"Hello, Auntie!"

Simon didn't have glasses. He wore jeans with no belt, drooping below his waist, and a black T-shirt with a big and illegible slogan written on it. He'd come outside in bare feet and with a drink in his hand. A tattoo with green tongues ran from his wrist along his arm. On the other elbow there was a smaller tattoo, a sun with pointed rays in the same green. Simon smiled at her, serene.

At the airport he'd appeared with a baseball cap and a duffel bag over his shoulder. He'd smiled at her, saying, "Hello, Auntie," in just the same way, cheerful and relaxed, in a melodious voice.

Norina had never thought about how her nephew would greet her, or what he would call her. Or how he would sound—that his words would have a slight Istrian accent. Or about that "Hello, Auntie," with his hand never moving from his shoulder strap. Hearing him say the most obvious of things really hit home. "Auntie"—she was his aunt, or, technically, his great-aunt, even if they'd never seen each other, and they'd lived on opposite ends of the globe. And the most natural thing, which is really the most strange: in the end, Norina had embraced him—like someone she cared about, like family.

Even now, under the oak tree, his "Hello, Auntie!" caused her to feel confused, off-balance. She offered him the pastries from the bakery. He thanked her and took a sip of his Coke.

Since the night before, Norina had been looking in his eyes without finding what she looked for. Because Simon's eyes were no longer like the photo. The color was, yes; that was him. And every so often Norina seemed to recognize a hint, a wrinkle, or a twinkle that belonged to Franco, but then it all disappeared and those were again the eyes of a boy with a nice voice who called her "Auntie." And as for body language, he didn't have Franco's frenzied gestures at all. He was slow, measured, attentive.

Simon looked around curiously. Norina glanced over at Adriano with suspicion. He had climbed down and taken the ladder away, and he was locking the tailgate of his Apé. Simon went to the fence and turned up his angular face toward the leafy canopy. He scratched the back of his neck, puzzled. His hair was shaved short; you almost couldn't tell anymore that he was blond. He was tall, but not so tall as the rest of their family, those beanpoles and *morlacchi*.

A scooter arrived. Amila got off, removing her helmet and shaking her hair. She greeted them with a wave of her hand.

"What are you all doing out here?" she asked, merrily.

Norina had a long face, and Simon was looking at her, quizzically.

"*Adriano is skinning my oak tree!*"

"What? Where?"

Norina pointed to the broken branches.

"Well, as tree pruning goes, that's not an expert job," she commented, sarcastically. Then she looked at Simon, greeting him in his language.

"Who's that bloke?" he asked her, in English.

"What?" Amila felt confused.

"My aunt's very upset 'bout him."

Simon spoke English with a British-sounding accent, but his polished words, smooth like bubbles from a glassblower's tube, were cut through as if hail had rained down on them. Once on a school trip, Amila had been to Murano and seen a glassblower at work. But she'd never heard anyone speak English with that accent.

"Auntie, what was he doing to you?" he asked, turning to Norina.

So then, Simon understood Italian, and even the patois Norina spoke—a language that was hers alone, that no one else in town spoke. Except that, when he spoke Italian, Simon's words seemed vacuum-packed; they creaked a little, even though they felt natural, like something carried with you from the cradle. There was even a trace of his aunt's accent, but spoken without really knowing the words.

"That man owns the land here," Amila explained. "From time to time he does annoying things, but he's harmless." Adriano was leaning on the back of his Apé, one leg crossed in front of the other. "Well, you see how it is. We're in woods full of rocks and sinkholes. And plus, he leaves his stuff lying around everywhere." Amila pointed to the moss-covered hull of a boat leaning on the fence. "And your aunt, understandably, gets fed up."

"I see," Simon nodded, starting to speak English again, the language where he seemed most comfortable.

"*Look, there he goes again!*" Norina hissed. Adriano was trying to strike a match, without success. "*He's going burn me down! Who lit that fire in the woods, anyway? Who?*"

The suggestion that Adriano had started the forest fire was really over-the-top, so Amila burst out laughing. Simon laughed too.

Amila only now noticed how he was dressed. She got a better look at his tattoos, and she also noticed his bare feet, under the frayed legs of his jeans. She wouldn't have been able to explain why, but she hadn't imagined him like this. He wasn't quite the same as the photo, at least as she remembered it. That guy seemed fastidious, and instead . . .

"Is there a road back there?" Simon asked.

"That's the highway. Just behind the woods." Amila added, lightly, "Look, you just have to get used to it. Here it's like being downtown. Even if all you can see is fields and trees, cars go by day and night."

"Oh well, I sleep like a log."

"So, it's okay then."

"Yep, all good."

Norina nodded. While Simon and Amila traded their "yeps," "okays," and "oh wells" at the speed of light, Norina looked first at one of them, then the other, like she was watching a game of tennis.

"Anyway, my name is Amila, and you're Simon, I know. So then, are you ready for the big day? Today your aunt is taking you to Trieste."

"Trieste?"

"Yep, sure. We are in Trieste!"

"Trieste... oh yeah!" Simon repeated, happily.

"And Mariano?" Amila queried.

"*Look over there!*" Norina pointed at her husband, who was waiting, looking out the window. He greeted them, waving in their direction to indicate they should all come inside.

After less than an hour, though, Norina had begun to squint and her face grew tense. The wrinkled furrows around her mouth deepened. All symptoms of a migraine, another of the sort that she often had. She leaned her head on her tightened fist. Luli had put her head in Norina's lap. From time to time, she would whimper, and Norina would pet her in response. The two of them seemed to speak to and understand each other.

Amila, who was worried, sat in front of her in the kitchen. She'd put water to boil on the stove, so she could make tea from the mint in their garden, which usually helped. Waiting for the migraine to get better, Simon and Mariano had gone upstairs to look on Google Maps for the family house in Melbourne. But it wasn't getting better.

"*No,*" Norina said, as she blew onto her steaming cup. "*Today of all days, we didn't need this!*"

"It happens because you get too stressed." Amila set her phone down on the table.

"*That's not true at all. It's because the others stress me out. And now what?*"

Amila sighed. "Try taking 500 mg of Tachipirina."

"*But where's the Novalgina?*"

"In the medicine cabinet, I imagine. But it lowers your blood pressure, so you shouldn't be taking it."

"*For me, Tachipirina doesn't do anything.*"

"Why? Isn't it bitter enough?"

The wrinkles in the corners of Norina's mouth deepened. "*They're pills, not drops.*"

Amila shook her head, got up, and went to get the medicine. She'd been coming to the house for two months now, but to her it seemed much longer. She and Norina had gotten used to speaking to each other with saucy, affectionate familiarity.

When she offered Norina the small pharmaceutical package and a glass of water, Norina indicated she should put everything on the table and take a seat. Luli was snoozing with her muzzle lying over a paw.

"*Listen to me now,*" Norina commenced, in a serious tone.

"Oh no, time to head for the hills," said Amila, trying to lighten things up.

"*Look, not now, not today. It's not time for jokes.*"

"Okay, okay. I'll settle down."

"*Someone needs to show that boy around.*"

Amila's expression changed. "Who, Simon?"

"*I certainly can't leave him in the house all day long!*"

Amila shook her head, resolutely. "But Norina, I have an appointment, I can't."

"*Why not?*"

"I told you that, at the latest, I could only stay until two."

"*So go take him someplace until two.*"

Amila looked at her phone. It was almost eleven. "But there's not enough time!" She gave a worried glance at her messages. Another one had just appeared.

We'll be at the small port at three. Perfect time for a swim. The water's great today, the current's not strong at all.

No, not this time; Amila just wouldn't be able to make Norina happy. Even though Norina had never asked for something extra before, and she'd always been very fair about defining the parameters of Amila's job.

"*You can take him in the Panda,*" Norina insisted.

"But it takes a half hour to get downtown," Amila protested. "And plus, there will be all the beach traffic, and then the same thing on the way back."

"*You can take the high road.*"

"That's even longer."

Norina looked at the clock. *"It doesn't matter where. Just until two, as part of your regular hours."*

"But you could go together tomorrow! Look, if it will help, I'll come back."

"No, I need help today," said Norina, resolutely. *"Today's the day."*

Too bad that for Amila as well, today was the day.

Everyone was about to arrive for her as well. Papà Željko was ready to go. Mamma Selma and Majda were packing their bags, and they'd be taking the bus. Her sister had sent her a text from Sarajevo: We're coming home, sister!

She said that she'd had it up to here with aunts and uncles and parents, and with not having any friends. During the summer Amila stayed in Trieste, Marijin Dvor had become a cave for Jurassic-era types who talked only about Yugoslavia. Even Olga left for Vienna earlier than usual.

Amila rubbed her thumb; she could feel it burning. Norina finished drinking her tisane.

For her too, this was the last precious day of summer—the season that for an entire two months had been her own, just what she'd wished for.

The days had passed quickly. Many of them had been solitary, spent on her favorite beach, where the stones were hollowed with holes and the wall of woods dropped straight behind your back. Sometimes she'd permitted time to pass without knowing how, easing the heat by taking one swim, then another, until the hours quickly turned into sunset, the most beautiful hour of all. Amila would come out of the water into the fading light with goose bumps.

From time to time, she had called Olga to check in, and Olga would ask whom she went out with. Amila's answers would be evasive: with some girlfriends, most nights. Olga would be astounded. What are you talking about? To her it seemed impossible that Amila still hadn't found a boyfriend, that she didn't like someone.

Amila had met groups of tourists and local beachgoers. She'd chatted with plenty of people, the sort of beach conversations you have when stretched out on a towel, so soaked in salt that it never comes out. She had studied. She'd also written articles for her eco magazine—for fun, though, without worrying about having to do better, just taking it easy for once.

Toward the end of August, a boy did surface. He was from Trieste, and older; he worked in a bank, just like Olga. He was at the Deutsche Bank branch in Trieste, she at the Raiffeisen Bank in Vienna. To Amila, the coincidence seemed both curious and a good omen. These were the last days of his vacation. He came down the path alone, with a backpack on his shoulders, just like she did.

They had neighboring towels, and he'd found an excuse to open a conversation with her. What are you reading that's so interesting? What do you study?

They had talked for a whole afternoon, about the sort of things that happen at the seaside, things forgotten immediately by the time you are on the trail back to the coastline road. But they had also told each other about the things that happen in life, when everything goes back to normal, far from the sea.

He'd looked at her, with confidence in himself. Intention was apparent in his eyes. And Amila hadn't minded at all. Quite the opposite. At last she was experiencing what she'd wanted

FEDERICA MARZI

to feel. Her heart had started to beat loudly, promising to her that this time it would be different. That this was the situation she'd been waiting for. That he was the one.

When she told him her name, the boy had asked, without worrying, about where she was from, complimenting her because, as he put it, you could never tell from her accent and her perfect Italian—better than most of the Triestini. Amila had laughed, but she also started stumbling over her own words.

Then he asked for her telephone number. That was the clear sign Amila had been waiting for. Perhaps the sign of a beginning. Love could begin at the end of the summer too; so far as she knew, there weren't any rules against it.

He invited her to come back to the beach for a party. He would arrive in a boat with some friends. Amila had said yes, but she let him know that she could only come there in the afternoon. Because that was the day she'd also promised to Norina. Simon's first day in Trieste.

"Today's the day," Norina repeated, as if Amila hadn't quite gotten it on her own.

"Put the drops in the water and drink it down," Amila said, trying to take her time. "Otherwise the headache will never go away."

Norina squeezed the bridge of her nose tightly. *"Do this for me."* Her eye, trying to stare at her, made its usual twitch to the side. *"Just for once I'd like everything to go smoothly,"* she said, as she swallowed the contents of the glass. *"Please,"* she asked again, with measured sweetness. *"Just for today, and just until two."*

Amila sighed and felt herself nodding, agreeing to the very last thing she would have wanted to do that day. "Okay, but only until two, and not a minute longer."

"*You're a sweetheart.*"

Finally, Norina unlocked a smile of gratitude from the look of pain disfiguring her face.

CHAPTER FOURTEEN

"Yellow"

AUGUST 2004, TRIESTE/TRST (ITALY)

REALLY, THOUGH, THAT trip to Trieste should never have happened. From the very start, Amila screwed up everything. She took the scenic route, so they'd start off well and get it done quickly; then, of course, there was a traffic jam between Miramare and Barcola. But the intended effect, at least, was achieved—the panorama.

Simon, intrigued, was observing whole herds of bodies in bathing suits basking in the sun or swarming on the sidewalk that ran along the sea between kiosks and fountains, behind an oleander hedgerow.

"I'm guessing that in your whole life, you've never seen anything like this. For the Triestini, this is the main beach."

"Oh," Simon commented, hiding his thoughts.

Once again they weren't moving, just sitting behind a long line of cars.

"You know, it's really not that bad. You just have to see it from their point of view."

"Do you go there?"

"No, never. Years ago, I would have liked to, but I couldn't."

"Ah."

On the waterfront, in the center of the city, Amila had trouble finding a parking space.

Before getting out of the Panda, she warned him, "I'm sorry about this, but I've got an appointment at three. So I can't take you around to see everything. Anyway, Piazza Unità is worth more than all the rest of it."

"Okay."

But when she suggested going to the most ritzy café, with a view of the sea, Simon's nose wrinkled. "Looks a little pretentious," he commented, unsure what to do.

"All right." Amila realized what a silly idea she'd had. "Let's go somewhere else."

She took him to Cavana, in the so-called *città vecia*, the old town, which made a better impression on Simon. He studied the palazzi from top to bottom, stopping in front of a building with an entryway door supported by columns.

"What is it?"

"A nice old palazzo. C'mon, let's go!"

They crossed the street and pushed on up to the public library and Piazza Hortis. The garden there was just the refuge they needed from the heat, which had returned, taking them by surprise. But there wasn't anything scenic. Some shrub gave off an annoying, saccharine odor. Cats scratched themselves against the dusty hedges, and pigeons drank from a blackened fountain. Not a living soul there except them, and they managed to find a clean bench, unsoiled by pigeons.

Amila tried telling another story, to make what would have to be the last stop of their trip interesting. "Italo Svevo wrote in this library. Maybe you've heard of him—the famous twentieth-century author?"

She went on, adding everything she'd learned in high school, but at the level of a CliffsNotes summary, something she never would have done at school. She hoped Simon liked it. And he did seem to be interested, too interested, in fact. At this rate, Amila would never make it on time to the beach.

When she started to move, Simon was quicker than she was. He stretched a bit and then offered to get her an ice cream from across the street. It was lunchtime. She couldn't let him go without eating. What else could they do?

"What flavor would you like?"

"Whatever."

Simon didn't move. Amila was getting everything wrong. Trying to make it quick, she made everything take longer than ever. "A scoop of Nutella swirl. Or else pistachio."

Simon came back with three scoops for her, and three for himself, with whipped cream on top. That's what happens when you talk too fast. Mamma Selma always told her the same thing: other people won't understand you. Or they'll get the sense of what you're saying wrong. Norina scolded her too: "*Such a hurry! After a while, I don't understand a blessed thing.*" Well, at least he got the flavors right.

"How do you like staying at Norina's?" Amila asked, to make the time pass. It would take at least a quarter of an hour for them to finish the ice cream.

"Oh, it's fine. Except for not being able to sleep last night."

"The jet lag, I'll bet."

"Yep." Simon stretched his legs. He was wearing Converse All Stars too, except his pair was black and looked like they'd been through a war. "But also because of those dolls staring me down all night long."

Amila burst out laughing. She imagined Norina's dolls, with their gloomy glass eyes, lined up on the shelf over the bed, making faces, scandalized at that unexpected guest with tattoos on his arms, sleeping under the pink bedspread that smelled of fabric softener.

"But didn't you say you sleep like a rock?"

"I do, but without dolls."

"Oh, sure. That must've been really tough!"

"Tonight, though, they're going under the bed."

"But in the morning you'll have to put them back. All of them. Otherwise, you'll answer to Norina. With those dolls, she doesn't play around!"

Simon laughed.

"Along with those adorable dolls, what made you decide to come to Trieste?"

"Well, I'm traveling around Europe, and I wanted to see the place where my grandmother was born."

"Norina's sister?"

"Yes, Nonna Nevia."

"And what does all this seem like to you? Who knows what you were imagining, right?" She kept on, without even waiting for an answer. "Of course, we all romanticize our city—its multiculturalism, the Hapsburg empire, a border city, blah, blah, blah. We're in love with it."

"Sure, I like it too."

"But you haven't seen anything yet! As a tour guide, I'm not very good," Amila said. "Look at that place where I just took you!"

"It wasn't so bad."

"Yes, it was."

"Well, okay then, it was. But it was interesting. Just a little different."

"Different from what?"

"From how I imagined it."

"Which was?"

"Different from the stories my grandmother told me."

"And what did she tell you?"

"Oh, story after story after story. She never talks about anything other than Trieste."

"And she's never coming back?"

"No."

"Why not?"

"She's old, and it's too far away. When she was younger, she had other problems, and so . . ."

"But your grandmother and Norina weren't born in Trieste, were they?"

"No."

"So where was it?"

"In Buic."

"Where's that, in Slovenia?"

"No, in Croatia, but near the Slovenian border."

Everything, it seemed, was always near a border. Amila remembered when Papà Željko tried to reassure the family about their decision to stay in Trieste. He came up with the same story about borders. At least they'd be staying nearby, so they'd be able to keep an eye on their old country as it fell to pieces. Mamma Selma, though, had argued with him: "Why, the border next to Zvornik wasn't enough for you? No matter what, we're condemned to live close to a border!"

"But, before, it was all part of Yugoslavia," Amila corrected Simon.

"I know, I know. But when they were born, the Italians were there."

"That's true," said Amila. She'd finished her ice cream and was trying to remember something Norina must have told her, something when maybe she wasn't really paying attention. This stupid rush. Anyway, Norina always talked about Istria, and said that she was Italian, so it was coming back to her homeland. For Amila, that seemed to be the boiled-down story of Norina's life.

Now, though, putting two and two together, it was like saying Italy plus Yugoslavia plus all the new autonomous republics, a sum that you could also do backward, or change the plus sign to minus, so she'd understood how she and Norina shared a common story. Norina, too, had left some place behind, and maybe she, too, had a twisted relation to the transformations of a country that had been, but was no longer, that had become something else, cut according to the crossing of old and new borders. The country left behind.

"Does your grandmother ever speak about this Buie?"

Simon burst out laughing. "Oh yes, much more than Trieste!"

"So then, you're definitely in a tough place."

"Exactly."

Exactly. Except now it had gotten so late, Amila would have to speed to get Simon back. She chose the high road, as Norina had advised, even though it was longer. Simon was talking; Amila concentrated on driving. And then Coldplay.

A radio station was playing "Yellow," which came out crackly on Norina's ancient car radio.

"Awesome!" exclaimed Amila, as Chris Martin's acoustic guitar took the lead, and then Jonny Buckland's powerful rhythms wove in.

"The best," Simon added, echoing her.

"What, you like them too?"

"They're my favorite band."

"No kidding?"

Amila continued to have that song in her head later, even when she left the car in front of Norina's garage. In the meantime, she sent a text and got on her scooter, happily starting down the road from Santa Croce to the coast.

When she parked, it was already past four. She found a gap in the line of cars, their metal red-hot from the sun. She jerked her scooter up onto the kickstand. It was a bit late, but she'd made it. She glanced at her phone. There were no new messages.

As she followed the path down the hill, the words of that fabulous song came to mind again: "I swam across / I jumped across for you." The watery expanse below came closer and closer. The rays of the sun split it in two, with points of fire spreading over it.

'Cause you were all yellow.

Amila tidied up her hair, stopped to spread Labello balm over her lips, and continued on even more quickly, with her backpack hanging down one side, her helmet and jacket under her arm on the other.

Down below, the boy who she was supposed to meet at three, at the small marina, would be waiting for her.

And, in fact, Amila found him there.

And it was all yellow.

She found him there, but she couldn't find the courage to take the last stairs and go over to the sailboat moored by the fishmonger's stand. Amila stood back against the low wall, trying to breathe more slowly. And, in her head, for a moment, "Yellow" clicked off.

The boy was sipping something, relaxing with his arm stretched along the edge of the boat, just on the edge, but next to him was a girl in a bikini. He was talking to her with the same attitude that, on the beach, had made Amila understand he'd been making a move on her. His usual routine?

His tanned arm seemed to nudge itself toward the girl.

Amila instinctively scuttled backward up the stairs, like a crab. Then she stuck close to the wall, one slow step after another. She was covered in sweat.

She stopped at the fence by the first small, freshly cut field. She still managed to see down below, and the scene wasn't changing; if anything, the boy seemed to have moved even closer to the girl.

Amila turned and climbed back up the path, choking more than breathing. She paused to catch her breath, leaning on the terraced wall of a field left fallow. The tall, dry grass seemed to swallow up the wild olive trees.

That boy had been a disappointment. But not even the disappointment he'd caused was really worth it. Even if Amila could feel the tears welling up in her eyes, he shouldn't have been that important. She looked down one more time. The sea seemed more green than blue; the pebbled beach stretched almost to the barrier reef. There was an unusually low tide. The bathers were small and moved slowly. The city around the bay seemed to be a sculpture made of white and red bricks enveloped by a light haze.

Amila sighed. At this point, only her cousin Olga could have helped console her. She was the only one who knew how to solve her problems of the heart. She imagined Olga narrowing her eyes and inspecting her with that seemingly innocent smile, then puffing hard three times on her cigarette underneath what they called the "weeping plane tree" of Marijin Dvor. She would have straightened her hair, tapping the ashes firmly. Finally she would have asked, "What did you say was the name of this idiot?"

"Guido," Amila would have confided in her. The boy was named Guido.

At that point, Olga would've lost it, and her crystalline laugh would've burst forth.

"Guiiiiido!" she would have shouted, with her cavernous voice turned to those heavens surrounded by the courtyard walls. "*Puši kurac*, Guido!"

Literally, that Guido should smoke his own dick, that's what Olga would've said, as only she could say it, with one of those uniquely Bosnian curses. And she would've been right. Because sometimes you have to call it as you see it. And in certain circumstances, Bosnians, well, they definitely weren't subtle.

And as for Guido, Amila hoped he would, in fact, smoke it all, right down to the filter, whereas she felt a bit like laughing, but then again like crying, and a surge of nostalgia washed over her.

Her summer had ended with a clamorous defeat. She felt like an idiot for not going to Sarajevo for even a single day, not even for a quick visit, to pass a little time with Olga and Majda and make Mamma Selma happy. And all that in order to find at the end someone like Guido.

She felt as if too many absurd circumstances had played her for a fool. Because rather than a nice sail on a boat, she'd spent the whole day running between the rocky cliffs, the city, and the sea. And instead of being with Guido, she'd spent it with Simon, who had nothing to do with it and who, for her, was just work. Through no fault of his own, that Aussie nephew of Norina's was the cause of this whole debacle. All the better, anyway, if Guido was that sort of guy.

But what could she report to Olga about this vacation she'd had?

She'd never have the courage to tell her the truth. That is, once again, everything had gone up in smoke, and this time Bosnia had nothing to do with it. Everything had happened in Trieste, in Italy, where she'd stayed, after putting her foot down, after staging her little revolt, where she'd broken the family contract about vacations, and also not giving a damn about that empty apartment in Zvornik.

Italy was, therefore, a country where not everything worked out. But that was obviously something that Amila shouldn't ever say. Not to Olga, and not to anyone else.

CHAPTER FIFTEEN

That Takes the Cake

MAY 1996, TRIESTE/TRST (ITALY)

AFTER SO MANY years in Trieste, Amila knew how to speak her mind and hold her head high. She'd struggled to make things turn out right. But it didn't take much to ruin everything. Any minor mishap, a slipup with an idiom, say, or simply telling someone her full name, and things suddenly got worse.

Italians had no trouble pronouncing her first name; unlike some Slavic words, it wasn't missing any vowels, and its syllables were divided the same as in Italian. A shame, though, that no Italians were named Amila. She felt like she needed to apologize, to justify her own existence.

A teacher in middle school kept calling her Amina; his memory lapse seemed incorrigible. As Papà Željko always said, "Never correct the teachers. They're sensitive creatures. Believe me, I've got insider knowledge." So Amila let it go. Teach was nice, a good-natured, chubby guy. So she always answered when called by her new name, as if she'd been given it at baptism.

But then there was her last name—all the instructors found it impossible to pronounce. Whenever they took attendance and got to her, they'd stop in their tracks. "Hadžigrahić, Amila" was the name on the list, though the secretaries had omitted the accents, changing the sound of the letters. Italians pronounce their consonants the same way each time, except they don't pronounce "h" at all, because Italian doesn't have that letter. So her name became "Ad-zee-gra-ick." Yet another baptism.

Only once was she asked how to say her name. The woman who taught English at the high school slid her glasses down to the tip of her nose and looked Amila straight in the eyes, ready for dialogue. She was really good at first. "Ha-jee-gra-hitch," she said. She was someone who knew languages. But then everyone in class started laughing. In that free-for-all, there was no time for learning Bosnian family names.

Only Mrs. Sandra—in her blue smock, corpulent and uncombed, rigid and severe—explained things clearly: "This is Italy. We don't have accents like that. You should stop using them."

That had been her first baptism, the one that mattered, administered in fourth grade at Jesolo. Amila learned to do everything without accents, even when she wrote her name on exams. When she introduced herself, she'd use her new last name, pronouncing it as they would.

But she didn't know what to do with her first name. She had to leave it as it was, since everyone said it correctly, almost naturally. If one of her schoolmates was named Jenny or Sharon, no one batted an eye. But when they heard the name "Amila," you could see their doubts—and their effort to contain them.

She could feel herself under examination, even if the inspection of her face, her clothing, and even her Italian didn't yield anything unusual. And she would always be the first to give in.

"I'm Bosnian," she'd say, calmly, and then count off in her head the inevitable ten seconds of silence.

One, two, three . . . there would be some measure of relief, since they now had a category for her, even if they were sorry she came from a country that was so unfortunate. She was sorry about that too. But Amila was strong—she wouldn't be defeated by her country, by the pity people showed her, or by the names she was given. Or by testy teachers—or her school, naturally. Where everything had begun.

"I've decided, you know. I'm changing schools." That's what she told Lazar, her forever friend, the boy who would later become a sort of boyfriend—that one time they'd dared to pull down the zippers of their jeans.

The day when Amila made her pronouncement, they were near the end of the second year of middle school. Lazar would grow another four inches and be nearly six feet tall. He had broad shoulders, like someone who played basketball, which they both did. He wore glasses with thick, unfashionable frames. They were in Piazza Garibaldi, sprawled out on a bench in the corner. Behind them, the usual dirty pigeons were cooing. In front of them, in the middle of the square, a vendor was selling fabric, lace, and doilies, all crammed haphazardly on the hood of an old Honda. Amila and Lazar had their hands in the pockets of their jeans. They looked at each other and chewed their bubble gum.

"Why do that? Switch before the last year? Why bother, when we're on our way to high school?" Lazar must've had a crush on her, but Amila had never noticed. Just like her.

"Yes, but I'm not going to go to the vocational school."

"No, you're too good for that."

"I'm bored, you know that, don't you, Lazzarone? We don't learn anything." Amila blew a big bubble until it popped.

"But what the f…"

"Hey, before you start cursing, have you taken a look around?"

The men in the square had formed groups by language: Serbs or Albanians. Their work day was over. They were smoking and chatting outside the bars. The Chinese were staying inside their stores. Senegalese women, wrapped in loud stoles, were sitting on benches, rocking baby strollers back and forth. The sun was setting behind the tall palazzi, casting an amber light over the flowering plane trees. All around was the din of cars idling at traffic lights. A golden statue of the Madonna towered over the pedestrian island where they stood. The statue seemed to be signaling someone to stop, but it wasn't working. Everything was in flux, a chaotic mass of people, things, and pigeons.

"Well, darn it, Furlan will definitely be disappointed. You're her favorite student." Lazar had stayed as he was, without moving.

Amila leaned forward on the bench, in order to make him look at her. "Sure, but I'm tired of all her films about immigrants, gay rights, and fair trade."

"But she's great! And it's definitely better than all that stuff we read from textbooks."

"But you get it, right? I want to go to college."

"What good will college do you, if it doesn't teach you who you are?" Lazar had become completely red.

Amila burst out laughing. "Wow, what big speeches! You're really smart, you know, Lazzarone. You should come with me to the new school."

"I'm fine here. And besides, I don't want to leave everyone behind."

"But Nenad went to Germany."

"That's different. His father got a job there."

"Well, look. I'm the only Bosnian girl in class. I'm on my own anyway."

"Alex's mother is Bosnian."

"Actually, I think she's Croatian."

"So?"

"So, I'm fed up with being stuck in a ghetto."

"It's good here with us."

"But it isn't the real Italy."

"Oo la la, the Real Italy! And then what? What are you going to do in this Italy of yours?"

"I'll have a better life." Long ago, her father, too, had promised her that.

"And then?"

"And then, well then... You really just don't get it!"

"And you do?"

"You did just say that I'm intelligent."

"No, you're the one who said that to me. I only said you're good in school."

"So then, we're even."

"Perfect."

"Gimme five!" Lazar held up the palm of his hand, reluctantly. "Now, though, wish me luck. Tonight, I have to get my father on my side."

"Why?"

They'd both gotten up from the bench; it was time to go home. "I still haven't said anything to him, and my mother definitely won't like the idea."

"So, it's not for sure, then, that you're changing schools?"

"It's for sure, Lazzarone, one hundred percent," Amila responded, keeping him at arm's length and smiling at the challenge.

However, in the Via Pascoli apartment, when Amila announced her intention to change schools, what happened was precisely the opposite of what she had imagined. It was Selma's face, not Željko's as she had imagined, that brightened up, as if good news had arrived—she even forgot to put a hand over her mouth to hide her blackened teeth. People would usually blame her dental problems on the war, but Mamma Selma would shrug and explain that, at the end of the eighties, she'd had some fillings done with an amalgam of silver, mercury, and lead. That was the usual thing in Yugoslavia, and that was what had blackened her teeth. She had one of them fixed each month, on payday, and so this story had been going on for quite a while. First they would do a root canal and then put in an implant. And then they had to pay for the crown. That was expensive, and so Mamma Selma had begun cleaning houses. "For the last time in my life," she would say, even though this last time would last for eternity.

For Papà Željko, it was a bitter pill to swallow, since it meant that his salary wasn't even enough to cover dental care. That wasn't a happy time for him in Trieste.

But her parents had a strange ability to keep an even keel. Always. For example, Selma would find renewed enthusiasm whenever Željko started to lose his sense of humor. So, she would issue warnings: "Be careful—if you don't stop, I'm sending you to clean houses too. And just so you know, Željko Hadžigrahić, I'm doing this for me, not for you. I haven't come all the way here just to watch you pout. Listen, I can always go back where I came from!"

It was paradoxical, obviously, but it worked. Because it always ended up with the same story: the fact that they'd come to Trieste, but that at any given moment they could also always leave, as if their lives could never be something permanent.

The entire family was together again, around the walnut table with a centerpiece, their forum for discussions and important occasions. And Amila's news about school seemed inevitably to force each of them yet again to vote for or against staying permanently in Italy.

"I chose for myself the best academy in Trieste," Amila explained, mumbling her words, a bad habit she also had in her other language.

"I don't agree," objected Papà Željko, firmly. "In your class, for honors students, they already study Latin. Tell me what other middle school in the city does that."

"Papà, in this school, we're all immigrants."

"That's the school of the future," he responded, unfazed.

"Then why are all the Italians in this neighborhood fleeing?"

"That's not my problem."

"But it's mine. The classes are too easy."

"Look, kiddo. You aren't in a position to judge the level of instruction. You're an excellent student. That school needs you."

Her father believed in social justice, and in the evenings, he was tired because he also worked for the union, even though Mamma Selma always warned him against it, telling him not to get mixed up in the politics of a country that isn't yours and not to steal time from your family. Meaning from her.

"Now that takes the cake!"

Mamma Selma had taken control of the debate without a need to groan or put a hand over her mouth. Her fists were squeezed tight on the table, and she sat straight as a soldier. Everyone had turned toward her, even though she stared straight at Papà Željko and wouldn't look away.

"If she likes to study, let her go to a good school. That's why we're here, isn't it?" Mamma Selma seemed happy to go back again to what they'd always been: a family dedicated to education. "And you, a teacher, should be better informed about schools in Trieste. But you never wanted to get involved. So then, Amila knows what's best, since she goes to school every day."

So, the light in Mamma Selma's eyes that Amila had noted at the beginning of the discussion hadn't been a mirage. Her mother was giving her clear support in favor of Trieste. But Papà Željko was determined, shaking his head no.

At this point Amila had only one last ace up her sleeve: Bosnia.

This was another well-worn ploy in their family: Italy, Trieste, their new home. The country where they'd chosen to stay,

FEDERICA MARZI

to live. Did they love it? Yes and no. And they could always refer to that other country, that lingered as an imaginary being, an alternative memory, a life that they hadn't had, but that could always exist.

"Listen, in Zvornik or Sarajevo," Amila said decisively, "you would never have sent me to a school like that."

She had emphasized the that, ready for potential rebuttals from her father. Which might have been: "That's simple. In Zvornik or Sarajevo, there are no immigrants. There are only *dijasporci* like us returning to our homes, more advanced than everyone else, because we've studied in half the countries of Europe."

But her father only stroked the base of his nose, his glasses propped up on his forehead. Maybe he thought his Amila had grown up too quickly. Because of the war, of course, as he'd often said. And, in part, that was true. Amila wasn't even thirteen, yet she was challenging him like an older teenager would, striking a hard blow to his sense of social justice, the cause he was most proud of. And not because of the war, but because it was her life, and she wanted something foundational, something that she, too, could be proud of.

Luckily, Majda jumped in to defuse the situation, shaking her index finger in the face of everyone. "Listen, all of you, you know that none of this will work with me!" Everyone had turned toward her. "The immigrant school suits me just fine. I'm not moving; I'll stay there."

Though she wasn't even eleven, Majda was declaring her neutrality. She was in favor of a living wage and the *dolce vita*, wherever she ended up. She, too, had taken quick steps forward for her age. But Majda took things easier, perhaps because she had her father's Roman nose and her mother's big eyes, and she wasn't like Amila, who instead seemed the daughter exclusively of Željko. And anyway, Majda mostly just resembled herself. Plus, in their family, someone would always come up with the right move at the right moment, so that everything would settle down to normal.

Papà Željko had also listened thoughtfully to Majda's outburst, without the flicker of irony in his eyes that usually prefigured a joke he'd use to close the mouths, and the debates, of the women in his family. Instead, he simply stood up from the table and limited his reaction to the sentence shared by all the defeated fathers of the world. "Do what you want," he declared, with a lack of conviction.

Amila, Majda, and Selma shared a look, exulting in their conspiracy.

So it was decided. Amila would change schools. And for once she would be able to do something very simple, like stretching out her hand toward a dream that spoke of staying, not of leaving, of belonging and stability. A dream that was on the right side for once. And that's where she wanted to stay.

CHAPTER SIXTEEN

Burqa
JANUARY 1997, TRIESTE/TRST (ITALY)

IT DIDN'T TAKE long for Amila to learn that for every step forward there was another step back, and for every dream you achieve, another stays buried in the back of a drawer. And that the better education she wanted came with a price, which wasn't cheap.

One night at dinner, after being at the new school for a few months, she reported, "Elisabetta Sancin asked me if I was a Serb, Croat, or Muslim."

"It won't be too hard to know what to say, I imagine," Papà Željko quipped, slurping loudly from his spoon.

He'd come back late, after his turn staffing the immigrant help desk at the union. Amila had served him a bowl of hot broth. Mamma Selma was ironing. Majda was sitting on her knees at the small table in the living room. She always did her homework at the last minute.

"Sure, but you should've seen the face she made!" Elisabetta's eyes had gone wide, scandalized, as if it couldn't be true. Really?

Elisabetta, her only friend? "And then she asked me if our ancestors were Arab."

"Oh, *sant'Iddio*!"

As they left school that day, Elisabetta kept her distance, saying goodbye to Amila with a vague smile, one which, instead of hiding her feelings, made clear her embarrassment and concern. All because of Amila's religion.

"Why don't you tell her that you come from the Emirates, from Saudi Arabia, or Afghanistan?" Željko responded, after a minute or two. "You know, 'those people' are coming in from so many places."

"Papà!"

"In fact . . ." Her father left his spoon on the plate and was leaning back comfortably in his chair. "Let's get your burqa out of the closet tomorrow, so we can make Elisabetta happy!" Then, with gusto, he bit into a piece of bread he'd bought next door, from the Turkish shop. They sold good *somun* there, but he was also fine with any sort of *hljeb* or *hleb* from the Serbs on the corner. Or bread rolls, small loaves, or *struzze*. Although the real day to celebrate was when Mamma Selma made the bread.

"It's all Calogiuri's fault," Amila explained. "In her class, she said there'd been a bloody civil war in the former Yugoslavia."

"Well, let's just say that it didn't exactly begin under the banner of Brotherhood and Unity between Peoples," Željko retorted.

Mamma Selma was ironing the sleeve of one of Željko's shirts again and again. She was nervous.

"What does Calogiuri teach?" Papà Željko asked, calmly, as he served himself some *pita*.

"Italian history and geography."

"She's a substitute teacher, isn't she?"

"She says that she's not substituting for anyone; she's just a temp."

"And who isn't a temp, these days?" her father continued, laughing as he chewed.

"Papà, stop joking about everything!"

"Yes, enough of that!" Mamma Selma echoed, concentrating on her shirt, which she smoothed out energetically, using her hands.

"So what do you want me to do?" Irritated, her father put his napkin down on the table.

"Go there and talk to her, and explain our history."

"Can that be done in fifteen minutes? Some things are just too complicated, my girl, and impossible to understand, especially for a substitute teacher of Italian."

"Anyway, you have to come and tell her something; otherwise, I'm finished. You can't imagine how they look at me now. She needs to sort things out. She has office hours on Fridays, from 11:00 to 11:54.

"Hmmm . . . in that school, they're very precise."

"Because there are so many students, she says she can't give more than five minutes to each parent. And she says they don't pay her overtime. So you have to get there at 11:00, or earlier; otherwise, there will be a line and you won't get in."

"You're joking, kiddo, aren't you? This is that great school you decided on?" So now the discussion was getting serious.

"It wasn't up to me to choose my schoolmates and substitute teachers!"

"Aren't we always the lucky ones?" Mamma Selma commented, with one of her melodramatic asides. "And now? What can we do?"

"I'd like to change classes. Is that possible?" Amila was hoping that her mother would side with her.

"Listen, we're about at the end of our rope with you." Mamma Selma was nervous and tired, like everyone. "And leave your nails alone!"

Amila had definitely picked the wrong night.

"Wait, wait." Her father interrupted the squabbling, so that he could think things through calmly, which meant, for Amila, that more troubles were on the way. "What could I tell the principal about why I'm asking him to put you in another class? I certainly couldn't say that you don't like your Italian studies teacher."

"But this teacher is an idiot! Surely you won't tell me it's normal for teachers to be idiots. Or maybe you will, since you're one too?"

"I stick up for you in my own house, but elsewhere..."

"If you tell me again that we need to behave, I swear I'm going to scream."

"No, no..."

"A lot of help I get with assimilating!"

"I am helping you. Adjust to what your teachers want and how things are here," her father said, reaching for his newspaper.

"Leave your father in peace! And you leave Amila in peace!" Mamma Selma yelled, from behind her ironing board.

"I'm done. I'm out of here," Majda announced, taking advantage of the moment to sneak away, notebooks under her arms.

"Where do you think you're going?" Mamma Selma scolded her.

"To watch TV in your room."

"And who gave you permission?"

"There's too much confusion in this house. You all talk at the same time. It just creates chaos. And it gets boring."

"But not too much for you to finish your homework."

"Oh, it's so boring that even your distraction helps me."

Mamma Selma accompanied Majda out, like a prison guard. So now Amila had to manage her father on her own.

"Papà, you can say I haven't managed to fit in, which is the truth."

"Didn't you get invited to a birthday party this Saturday?"

"Yes, Elisabetta's. It's the first time I've been invited anywhere, and it's practically the end of the term."

"Well, that's a step in the right direction, isn't it? Are you going?"

"Yes." Even though, after what had happened at school, Amila was no longer so sure.

Ready to finish the debate, Željko asked, "So, tell me, kiddo, this Calogiuri, does she teach Italian well, or not?"

"Usually," Amila said with a shrug.

"Humph, well, that's her job. And what grade did you get on your last homework assignment?"

"Seven and a half. But Calogiuri says she never gives more than an eight."

"So it's an excellent grade."

"But with that I'll only get a seven on my report card!"

"Such drama! There's always room for improvement. And how much longer will this teacher be around?"

"Until June. I told you she's a temp, not a regular substitute."

"Good. That means the lesson plans won't be interrupted." Amila snorted loudly in reponse. "Come on, June will be here soon, and your schoolmates will forget long before that. And you'll have plenty of friends, you'll see. And in high school everything will be different."

"Sure it will."

"Look, kiddo. You have to learn Italian from this teacher. Forget about everything else. It's Dante, right? Not Andrić. Him you can read on your own. That's better, anyway. That way, you'll have your own ideas about it, not just the ones the teacher rams down your throat."

"More great advice about teachers from a teacher!"

But her father didn't take the bait. "Eventually, you'll better appreciate more or less everything, including our own history." Željko opened up his newspaper.

"By the way, if that's the issue, I've already read Andrić."

"Oh, you have? What, in particular?" he asked, surprised, setting his paper on the table.

"'A Letter from 1920.'"

"When was this?"

"It's in one of your books, one of the ones you recommended I read."

"In fact."

"Yep."

"Great, kiddo, you did the right thing. Though that one's not exactly age appropriate . . . But fine, did you like it?"

"I don't know. There's too much 'destiny' in that story." Amila had pronounced it "destino," in Italian.

FEDERICA MARZI

"Hmmmm… 'destino' is a difficult concept. Where did you learn about it?"

"At school, of course!"

"Aha! You see, eventually, investments do pay off."

"Just the same, I don't like all that stuff about destiny."

"You're only in ninth grade. You wouldn't understand." Željko had picked up his newspaper again and was glancing through the headlines.

"Papà?"

"Yes?"

"Listen, I understood perfectly."

Perfectly indeed. Amila understood so well that she even knew her year at school would be as she predicted: a disaster. She continued to be the only foreigner in her class, and during the whole second term she never stopped feeling like a freak. She wasn't close to anyone there, and all her friends from her old school, except Lazar, thought she'd become stuck-up. And so they didn't invite her to parties anymore either. She didn't end up going to Elisabetta's birthday party, telling Mamma Selma she had a stomachache.

In June, the eighth-grade class dinner before the exam period presented another occasion for socializing, one where no one could be excluded or absent. Papà Željko ordered her to go. He did it without ever imagining that it would be the first time his daughter would be ashamed of him. She would be ashamed of herself too. After all, what sort of person is forced to experience such things? Shame had taught her to value such experiences differently. To value herself differently too.

Amila stayed pretty quiet throughout the dinner, but she literally felt herself sinking when Papà Željko picked her up, and, in her eyes, he behaved like a stereotypical immigrant, going around the entire table to shake the teachers' hands and thank them, as everyone watched him out of curiosity. The other parents just gave a quick, reserved wave, slipping out the door with their children following behind, with the excuse that their cars were double-parked.

Calogiuri was the one who managed to salvage the situation, since, just as "destino" would have it, she was seated very close to Amila. That hated instructor of Italian stood up and shook her father's hand, flashing her horselike, toothsome smile. With her smoker's voice, she said, "That girl has talent," while Papà Željko oozed pride from every pore. "At first I thought she wasn't sure of herself. But then her writing blossomed, and I rewarded her with an eight on her report card—coming from me, that's the same as a ten. Send her to college. I predict a very bright future for her."

"Yes-yes, yes-yes, yes," Papà Željko said, nodding again and again, as if no one in his home had ever studied anything.

But that's how her father was made. He believed in respect—for teachers, adults, children, women, and other cultures. He was a complete original; even at a class dinner, he had to do it his own way. Because it was normal that a father, even if he was a teacher himself, would go to thank the teachers, and, if anything, it was not normal when all the others didn't do the same. Željko had given her a good lesson on what it means to be equal or different. And everything in life is useful. That's what her father would always say.

FEDERICA MARZI

CHAPTER SEVENTEEN

Mašala, Kćeri

AUGUST 2004, TRIESTE/TRST (ITALY)

AT TIMES, AMILA felt as if she'd learned to speak from Papà Željko alone. As if she had a father tongue, instead of a mother tongue, along with the gift of gab that in their family she was famous for—it would manage to accommodate itself to all sorts of languages. Željko seemed able to read her thoughts, and he would always push her to analyze deeply the meaning of words. Above all, follow the argument, he'd say, so that everything will turn out for the best.

They were in the car together. "And what about the apartment in Zvornik?" Amila asked him. It was time to face serious issues, the sorts of things that could go really badly for her

"Well, I guess, it all turned out well." The night before, Papà Željko had gotten back from Sarajevo, and now they were waiting at a red light in Piazza Libertà.

"Meaning what?" Amila insisted. She had the right to know.

"We got an estimate for remodeling the place," Papà Željko explained, pushing his glasses back on his nose. "It costs a lot less than here, of course. It won't be more than fifteen or twenty thousand marks. And then we'll need to buy furniture, or at least furnishings for the bathroom and kitchen. We'll see how it goes."

After two months her parents still hadn't decided to do anything in particular with the old family place. What had they been doing all summer? Had they just been amusing themselves, fantasizing about major renovations of a house in Bosnia that was currently unfit for habitation, while planning the whole time to continue living in a rental apartment in Italy?

Her father shook his head, a sign of his doubt and uncertainty. No one had been contemplating spending every summer in—or worse yet, moving permanently to—Zvornik. Amila shouldn't worry about that. But this story would still continue to drag on, and that, for her, was definitely not welcome news.

When the light turned green, Papà Željko drove on. They pulled into a parking space between the train station and the bus terminal. Amila noticed how her father might be losing his hair, with gray threads sprouting up here and there. He seemed eager to see Mamma Selma again, even if it had only been two days, not years, since they'd been together in Sarajevo.

For the past summer Željko had skipped his work at the union and stayed as long as possible in Bosnia, in order to focus on the apartment in Zvornik. Following their usual practice, he'd made a trip back by car alone, so that he could transport a new water heater and kitchen countertop for the Via Pascoli apartment, since they cost less in Bosnia. He took some suitcases too, and various provisions to tide them over next winter.

He was tapping his fingers on his jeans, waiting for the bus to arrive. This familiar impatience made him still seem young, despite the years, his gray hair, family tragedies, and all the long trips.

When Mamma Selma and Majda emerged, wearing sunglasses, in the middle of a group of women who commuted across the border for work, Amila was the one who first caught their attention. Mamma Selma shouted out a lively, joyful "Ohhh!" and gave her a big hug. She touched Amila's face and shoulders, as if she wanted to make sure her daughter was still whole.

"Look how beautiful my daughter is! That tan looks wonderful on you!"

Amila had actually gotten several shades whiter, one for each day since she'd last been to the seaside. It was so difficult to look like someone else.

Selma let herself get wrapped up in Željko's arms. She gave out another "Ohhh!" and squeezed up even closer to him. The love her parents had for each other was strong, even crushing. That might be why Majda had turned out so superficial, whereas Amila was always so demanding and impossible to satisfy.

Majda exclaimed, "Hail, Earthling!" and kissed her sister on the cheeks. She put her arm next to Amila's and declared, "Chocolate with whipped cream. So, big sister, you've had a good summer?" But Amila didn't take the bait.

"Well, so then, how is everything?" Selma started off the conversation, while Željko was backing the car out of the parking space. Up to that point, they'd only heard bits and pieces by phone about their reciprocal vacations. And now Mamma Selma was eager to tell her everything. About the repairs made to those two buildings in Marijin Dvor, about the renovation of the National Library, about all the neighbors who sent their best greetings, about their relatives, about the new bakery on August Braun, where their *burek* was the world's best. She was skillfully managing to avoid saying anything about Zvornik. But that was a tough subject for all of them.

"How is Norina?" she asked, finally, as if that must have been the real center of Amila's summer.

"Good, she's good."

"But your job hasn't ended by now?"

"Well, no. But today they've invited me to lunch."

"Hmmm . . . what's that about?"

"They're having a sort of celebration. Her nephew from Australia has come for a visit."

"Australia? So, you should go!"

My God, Mamma! Amila felt like shouting out loud in the car. She would have liked to shout that, for all of July and August, she'd gone every day to a beautiful beach, something that none of them had ever done, even though they'd lived for years in that city. And she'd have liked to explain how suddenly everything had vanished, the end of a love that had never even begun, and that made going back to normal even more impossible to endure.

Papà Željko hit the horn, to make the car in front of them hurry up, because he didn't want to miss the light on Via Milano.

"What a comment, Mamma! You two just got here." That was all Amila could manage to say, with a hint of resentment that Selma seemed not to notice.

"Ahhh!" Mamma Selma declared, rhetorically. "Just so you know. You'll get nothing for lunch today from me except some bread with a little *pašteta* spread on it. You've been warned, guys! I've been traveling all night, so what do you expect?"

Papà Željko winked at Amila. Lunch had already been prepared.

"*Pašteta*, bleah!" Majda protested.

"You be quiet! It has iron in it," Mamma Selma reprimanded her younger daughter warmly. "And iron is something you have to have."

Mamma Selma was having a lot of fun playing her part. That's always how it was, after she'd had her fill of Bosnia. A moment of happiness. She was still somewhat able to tap into her long-term memory of movable borders. This was her unique way of tuning in to the frequencies of Trieste while still feeling a bit of Sarajevo.

"As far as I'm concerned, you won't see me all afternoon," Majda announced. "After an entire summer of suffering, I deserve some vacation too!" She was already texting her friends.

"Well then, I guess I will stop by Norina's after lunch, since you all are so busy," Amila said. "If I don't, I think they'll take it badly. At that place, they don't have many celebrations."

"Give her our regards," said Mamma Selma, with that characteristic good humor that let her be flexible about everything.

"Let's just hope you don't also send her your boxes of *pašteta*!" declared Majda, laughing out loud.

Using the mirror in the car's sun visor, Mamma Selma inspected her appearance. Satisfied, she closed the visor and laughed shrilly, showing her teeth, just like in the old days. She no longer needed to hold her hand over her mouth.

Amila left her mother and father stretched out on the sofa. Majda had gone out immediately after lunch, taking advantage of Mamma Selma's momentary distraction, which would last no more than a day. In short, either they needed to make up for lost time, or they were relishing their return, only because they'd just gotten back, but everyone had something better to do. Not fitting in with either camp, Amila hopped on her scooter and took off for Bristie.

The minute she stepped inside, she understood that the place where she'd worked all summer was no longer a hideaway for two lost souls; it had become a real home, full of sunlight. It was a special day, a holiday, at Norina's too.

Amila was welcomed in as if she were family. Positive energy flowed from one end of the table to the other. Mariano's eyes were shining. His glass was lined with a halo of the sharp red wine which, on another occasion, he had told her was called Terrano. The tablecloth was sprinkled with crumbs, the napkins balled up. Norina extended her arms and stamped a wet kiss on Amila's cheek. She and Mariano shook hands. Simon was sitting with his hands folded behind his neck, rocking his chair back and forth. Anika got up from the table and hugged Amila with affection, insisting that Amila take her place since she was just leaving. But Amila didn't fit in there either.

Heading for the kitchen, Norina called out festively, "*Dessert's on the way!*" She asked, in a singsong voice, "*Who's going to help me?*" Simon quickly set his chair back down, stood up, and followed her into the kitchen. Luli popped up from under the table, wagging her tail; maybe she thought they were going for a walk in the woods.

"How are you all doing?" Amila asked.

"Better than ever!" was Mariano's response, as he gestured for her to sit down. "And your family? How was their trip?"

Mariano didn't have his walker behind him. His pant legs were rolled up to his knees, exposing his thin bare calves, rutted with blue veins. His swollen foot was bandaged and resting on a flip-flop.

She'd always really liked Mariano. A gentleman with his old-fashioned, brown sports coat, wending his way through the world with his tall, bony, lopsided body. And he was interesting to talk to. Even if he rarely went out, he knew a lot about what was going on in the world. He'd tell her about what he was finding online, the most disparate sorts of information, from water found on Mars to the origins of Firefox, from Marlon Brando's death to global warming. Politics, in contrast, just made him mad.

He was interested to hear about Amila's studies. What was "deep syntax"? he'd ask her. He'd struggle to understand the branching diagrams Amila drew for him, even though that was the subject she liked least. He, instead, was curious about it because it was technical and would require sketching out straight lines and squares on paper, as he must've done in his former job.

Mariano read her articles, proud of her when they went longer than a page, a little like Papà Željko, who would never read them just once, whereas Mamma Selma only cheered when her name was printed in boldface type. But when he was done reading, Mariano would sink down, slumped over in the glare of his twenty-inch screen. Amila thought he spent too many hours that way, while one floor below Norina watched, completely wonder-struck, the sort of TV variety shows and politicians that her husband railed against.

But now, Mariano was back from his solitary activities in front of the screen. Norina's dessert smelled good. Even if it had risen a bit more on one side than the other, it garnered as many admiring glances and excessive compliments as ever. Its steamy filling was made from the large, round, red prunes from Anika's tree. Norina must have worked hard in the heat to prepare her special tart, *polentina alle susine*; whenever she was in front of a stove, she'd hunch down and wipe the back of her hand across what she called her *mostaci*.

Simon continued the conversation they'd begun in the kitchen. He explained that Melbourne was good for work and school, but people lived in enormous homes outside the city. Norina looked around, cautiously measuring the size of her living room. Simon set up his camera at the far end of the table; in his hand he had a remote control. Amila stood to the side, but Mariano took offense. "Over here, c'mon!" She accepted his invitation and took her place next to Norina, who stood straighter and smiled. Simon's head slipped in between the two seniors, who were just brushing against each other. He put his arms over their shoulders.

When they looked at how the sequence of photos came out, Amila said, "I like this one." Norina seemed not to agree, and when Mariano suggested they send it to Nevia in Australia, she said, simply, "Good," one of her comments that finished any discussion, and got up from the table. She had to take Luli out, at least for a short walk; otherwise she'd be peeing on the floor. The group split up. Mariano decided to move to the couch. Simon followed him over, but Mariano didn't need to lean on his arm.

"Do you smoke?" Simon asked, looking over at Amila, the last one left at the table.

FEDERICA MARZI

Amila looked up from checking her watch. "Sometimes." Practicing with Olga in their Marijin Dvor courtyard gave her the right to say so.

From the back pocket of his jeans, Simon extracted a pouch of tobacco, filters, and rolling papers. "We're going out for a bit," he announced.

Mariano nodded, but added, "Do it before your aunt comes back."

Amila and Simon sat down on the wall under the oak tree, where there was already an ashtray. They leaned back against the fence. The soles of Simon's untied All Stars reached the thick, rough trunk of the tree; the soles of Amila's identical shoes—though hers were pink—were on the ground.

"Where are you always running off to?" Simon asked, smiling and rolling a cigarette.

"Somewhere."

Given the questions he asked of her, it seemed as if Simon was up to speed on a lot of her business. Clearly, Norina had told him that Amila got money for doing odd jobs and cleaning, and for spending time with Mariano—a sort of home care worker. Although Amila always avoided using that awful term, and she knew Norina definitely didn't call her that. Norina found other words. At best, she'd declare, "You blessed girl!" Out of all her baptisms, this was one of the best names they'd given her, in part because it felt like a dialectical offshoot from her mother's language, since her favorite expression, after *sant'Iddio*, was *mašala, kćeri*.

Simon had to know that her name marked her as a particular species, and that she wasn't actually Italian, even if, so far, his questions hadn't touched on the subject.

"And where exactly is somewhere?" Simon said, offering her an especially thin cigarette.

"Oh, down at the seaside."

"Is it beautiful, like it was at Barcola?"

Amila laughed. "Nooo! Completely different."

"Where is it?"

"Only ten or fifteen minutes from here."

"I'd like to see it."

Amila instinctively shook her head and said the first thing that came to mind. "I don't have my bathing suit."

"We could take a walk instead." Simon squinted a bit and puffed out some smoke. "It's not all that hot."

Amila hadn't been back there after the last time with Guido, who must've finished his vacation and returned to work. Though she hadn't heard from him.

After her brief walk, Norina approached them. "*Since when do you smoke?*" she asked Amila, giving Simon a look of reproach.

He put out his cigarette quickly. "Auntie, would it be okay if I went with Amila to see the beach?"

"*Where to?*"

Amila stubbed out her cigarette in the ashtray, petting Luli. "Down at Canovella."

"*Mamma mia, how many years has it been since I went there?*"

Simon invited her to join them, but Norina shook her head. They could take the Panda, though, if they wanted.

To Amila, Simon seemed like a nice guy, easy to talk to, just the sort of guy she usually met: a potential friend who didn't know anyone in Trieste and was looking for something to do. Which suited her fine.

When Simon started the car, Norina and Mariano waved to them from the window. It was the first time Amila had seen them at the window together for a ritual send-off, like an old couple who still had a life to share. However good or bad it might be seemed less important. Because for the first time, they were really a pair, not just one times one, which always and barely equals one.

CHAPTER EIGHTEEN

Zemlja

AUGUST 2004, CANOVELLA DE' ZOPPOLI/PRI ČUPAH
V NABREŽINI (ITALY)

WHEN THEY GOT to the end of the path, Amila's hesitation about returning to Canovella dissolved, and her mood brightened, as it always did when the sea was there. Indian summer would soon arrive, which meant autumn was coming, with its narrow windows of sunny days where hopes and expectations were high. Simon stopped below a large plaque in the wall. He looked up at it with the curiosity of a thoughtful tourist. Amila read the verses to him out loud:

*Naj kdorkoli kdaj te vpraša,
kdo živi na zemlji tej,
vedi: zemlja ta je naša,
tvoji dedi spijo u njej,
zanjo bori se naprej!*

"What's it about?"
"It's about earth."

"Do you mean about 'the Earth'?" Simon asked, using the English word.

"No, it's about who lives on this land."

"About the land or the country?" he asked, again in English.

"No, *zemlja*. It's something different."

"What, exactly?"

"The lines are from a poet of this region, Igo Gruden."

"And what does he say?"

"That his grandfathers are resting here, and that one needs to struggle. For their land."

"That's your language, right?"

So Simon did know about her other language, the one that interfered with her Italian.

"No, it's Slovenian. But we also say '*zemlja*.'"

"This language suits you."

No one had ever said anything like that to her. But then, Simon did say things naturally, even when they were over-the-top. He seemed to glide over his words or take them from somewhere else, out of context. His eyes had an unusual color, a blue marked with vague, transparent flecks, that made him seem sincere.

"C'mon, let's go!" Amila urged him on.

Simon followed her down the pathway left free of beach towels. "But isn't Serbo-Croatian your language?"

"Or is it Croato-Serbian?" she teased him. "Careful here. We have to go behind the reef, or else get into the water."

Simon took his shoes off, but he didn't roll up his pants, so they got wet. They stopped in front of the lacy ridge of rock barely visible along the surface of the sea. The sun was about to dip below the hazy line of the Grado lagoon, pierced through by orange darts. The crowd bunched up at the entrance to the beach had begun to thin out.

"Until the war, Serbo-Croatian was a single language. After it, you went home with four, at a bargain price: Bosnian, Croatian, Serbian, and Montenegrin," Amila explained, counting them out for him on her fingers. "Such a great deal. Now we get to put all of them on our cvs." She laughed.

"And you speak all of them?"

"Of course! There are a few differences, but we definitely don't need subtitles to understand each other."

"What's the name of the city you come from?"

"Trst," Amila told him, having some fun. "That's what it's called in Bosnian, Croatian, Serbian, Montenegrin, and also in Slovenian," she explained, again using her fingers to count them out.

Simon didn't get the joke.

"C'mon! I mean Trieste!" Amila gestured for him to follow her.

They walked side by side, with their shoes in their hands. Amila recognized the familiar form of the porous, rough stones pressing against the balls of her feet. She'd been walking over them all summer long. But Simon was somewhat unsteady.

"I was asking about your other city."

"The city that used to be mine, in other words."

"Yes."

"Its name is Zvornik." Amila quickened the pacc. Here the stones were big, and the tree trunks washed up onshore had lost their branches and ended in a tangled knot of hardened roots.

"Where is it?"

"In Bosnia."

"Yes, but where?"

"In the east," Amila answered, reluctantly. "Near the border with Serbia."

"What else is nearby?"

"Bijeljina, for example."

Simon hadn't heard of it, but he persisted.

"Okay, look, if you're asking about another city, now famous for its macabre horror show, yes, we were also not far from Srebrenica. About forty-five minutes by car. I do come right from the heart of the tragedy, assuming you could ever say there was a heart in that part of the world. Are you happy now?"

Amila began to walk hurriedly. Simon caught up with her; she felt bad for having lashed out at him. "Don't worry about it, really. These discussions always end with everyone feeling bad, but I've gotten used to it." Except that Simon hadn't actually felt bad, at least not in the way Amila was thinking. It was as if, behind that troubling place-name, he'd been looking for her. It also wasn't entirely true that she had gotten used to it. It was hard for her to name certain things or have a joke ready to defuse the situation, as Papà Željko always did.

Mamma Selma would protest that he always laughed at serious things, since she preferred to err on the side of drama. Though she too often ended up seeming somewhat comical. Turning tragedy into melodrama.

"Here we go. This spot is really nice."

Simon looked up. A rocky spike stood out from where the thick brush dissolved into beach.

"Wow!"

The beach was interrupted a little farther on, next to a villa, and then continued along a small asphalt road, hemmed in by cliffs and nearby a tall wall. Amila rolled up her jeans to her knees and went into the water.

"Do you ever feel like going back home?"

"I'm there now." Amila splashed at him. "This is my home."

Simon stepped away from the splash as he entered the water, balancing himself so he wouldn't slip, but he managed to get his jeans even wetter. "I'm asking about your other home."

"That's a complicated story. For many years, we spent our summer vacations in an apartment we'd rent in Sarajevo."

"It must be a beautiful city."

"It really is. But in the meantime, we also managed to get back our first apartment, in what used to be my city. We had to file official petitions and get government approval. And now we'll have to spend a lot of money to remodel it. So it's back there, empty, and in poor condition, and my folks aren't sure what to do with it. Neither my sister nor I want to live back there."

Earlier that afternoon, in her room before Majda had gone out, Amila had quietly asked her sister how Zvornik had seemed to her. Majda had made an ugly face and answered, "Like a Bosnian city." And then she'd left, slamming the door behind her.

Amila and Simon stood in silence, looking over the water, leaning against a tree trunk that had been smoothed and whitened by the sea. Offshore, the multicolored buoys of mussel farming bobbed up and down. In the distance, an anchored merchant ship looked like a toy boat.

"How did you get to Italy?"

"As a refugee."

"That must've been hard."

"Well, you know, we're a hard bunch."

Simon smiled, thoughtfully. He threw a stone into the water. Then he picked up another one. He rubbed his thumb over it, tracing the variegated textures cut into it by the sea. The tide was coming in, the waves breaking on the water's edge, not far from where they'd left their sneakers. The stirring of loose pebbles lent the scene a soothing sound.

"So what about you folks, in Melbourne? You're all good there, you've managed to fit in?" Amila asked him.

"Yes and no," Simon wavered, "like everywhere else in the world. We're doing okay financially. "

Her cousin Olga would always say that too, but she didn't feel at home in Vienna.

"I'm Australian; I was born there." In English, he added, "That's all," and threw another stone in the water.

"And your parents?"

"They're both Italian."

"What are their family names?"

"My father's is Monforte. My mother's is Benci." For Simon, the Italian family names naturally had an English twist to their pronunciation. One of the two was also written, without the twist, on the nameplate over Norina's gate, below the broken surveillance camera.

"Isn't Benci also Norina's family name?"

"Well, yes. And it's my Nonna Nevia's too."

"But why does your mother have it?"

"Because my grandmother wasn't married to the man she had her with."

"Who was he?"

"Someone from their town, from Istria. He got her in trouble and then took off. Where to, no one knows."

Amila's eyes opened wide. "Not even your grandmother?"

"Well...my grandmother talks about everything, but never about this. And my mother never really talks about anything."

And then Simon told her a story in English, though Amila wasn't sure she got it all. It began with San Nicolò. As Simon explained it, San Nicolò would appear in December, but he wasn't anything like Santa. He would arrive with a sack of presents for the good kids and a sack of charcoal for the bad kids. At least that's what his grandmother used to say.

"San Nicolò de Bari, the holiday for scolari. If Teacher wants to hold class, we'll knock him on his ... Do you know that one?"

Amila shook her head. She'd been too old for stories about San Nicolò when they got to Trieste, and, besides, her parents didn't even know who he was.

One year, Simon explained, when he'd been six or seven, they were all at Nonna Nevia's house to get their presents from San Nicolò. The women of the family were in T-shirts in front of an empty fireplace. The men were out smoking on the porch. The children were in bed. Following their family tradition, they opened an old cookie tin full of photos. Nevia liked to arrange them, one next to the other, as if it were a jigsaw puzzle. This time, rather than spreading them out on the long glass table in the dining room, the photos passed from one hand to another.

Ann stared at a photo of Zio Mariano. "Why the hell was that guy hugging you?" she asked. Except that young woman hugging Mariano, posing next to their sky-blue Fiat 850, was actually Norina.

Next Zia Maria Vittoria tried to get Nonna Nevia to talk about her boyfriends. "How many boys did ya have, Mummy?" His grandmother didn't reply. And Ann threw a fit.

According to Ann, Nonna Nevia had kept every photo of Jesus, Mary, all the saints and name-day saints, all the throngs and battalions of uncles and cousins and grandchildren—from Calabria, all the Buiesi in Melbourne and even in Sydney. Every relative who she'd been able to find or whom she wrote to in Trieste and Istria, every year, for every major holiday. Nevia had collected photos her entire life, she had reassembled what was left of Istria, everyone who had moved to Trieste or emigrated, but she didn't have even one single photo of the father—Ann's father, whose name was Franco, not Carmine, even if no one knew who Franco really was.

Simon was hiding behind the glass door the whole time. Shivering from the cold.

"Oh, shit!" Ann shouted out, when she noticed Simon. She hurried over to him and dragged him to bed, pulling him by the front of his pajamas.

And that's how Simon found out his grandmother's real story.

"My mother is chronically depressed. Though when it comes to me, she's hysterical and obsessed."

"Maybe because she never met her real father?"

"Who knows."

"Do your aunts and uncles know anything?" Amila asked, after a pause. "They must have met him."

"I don't know. He was from another village, but I only know that because a woman close to my grandmother told me."

"And who is she?"

"Someone else from Istria. A neighbor."

"Why did she tell you that?"

"Um, well, because I asked her to."

"Why?"

"Listen. . ."

"Yes."

"No, really listen."

"But I have been listening!"

"Yes, but then you start talking too fast."

"I know, everyone tells me that."

"If I tell you a secret, do you promise not to tell anyone else?"

"A secret?"

"Yes."

"You have a secret?"

"Do you want to hear it or not?"

"Yes, of course."

Simon paused for a moment, then said, "Well, I've just gotten a degree in law, but I no longer want to be a lawyer. It's only what my mother wants. And my father, who follows her like a puppy. Even if he is always away for work."

"Oh," Amila responded, though to her this secret didn't seem so important. "So then, what will you do?"

"Become a lawyer," Simon said with a laugh. "And a writer," he added, embarrassed at his confession. "I'm writing a novel."

"Really? That's great." Suddenly she stopped. "Wait a minute—what is the story of this novel about?"

"My family."

"The story of your family?"

"More or less."

"By any chance, is that why you decided to come to Trieste?"

"In part, yes. But I also want to go to Buie."

"But does anyone else know this?"

"Of course not! Are you crazy?"

"But why, out of all possible subjects, do you want to write this story?"

"Listen…" Simon held back a smile. "Because I know almost everything, and I just want to be done with it. But there's one part still missing."

"What part?"

"My grandfather." Now Simon was serious. "I have to at least try and imagine him."

For Amila, this seemed like it might be interesting. Everything suddenly seemed interesting to her. The twilight was lighting up everything around them.

Simon pointed toward the villa. "What's over in that direction?"

"A lot of cliffs and the FKK beach."

"What?"

"F-K-K. Freikörperkultur. What you call a 'nudist beach.'"

"Could you repeat that?"

"Repeat what?"

"That German word."

"Freikörperkultur."

"You say it so well that it doesn't even sound German."

"Of course not," Amila laughed. "I attended the best school for languages in the whole city!"

"Yes, of course," Simon said, in a mocking tone. "I'll bet you were the smartest student in your class. The best, obviously."

Simon knew a bunch of details from her personal story, and Norina couldn't have told him all of them. He saw them on his own, and he saw them very clearly.

Amila pursed her lips, as a way of ending the conversation or protesting, but she felt thrown backward by a wave of warmth and astonishment.

"Look, why don't we just go there?"

"To the nudist beach?"

"Noooo! To Buie."

"What would we be doing there?" Amila was truly surprised.

"Looking for my grandfather."

Amila burst out laughing. "You're crazy! Stark raving mad!"

Simon was asking her to go to Buie, but Amila couldn't tell if he was also asking her to go out with him. Maybe it was something more, maybe something less, but everything corresponded perfectly with all the other oddities and sensitivities of Norina's adored nephew. Olga would have complimented her, given her a slap on the back; she would have said that one nail drives the other one down, and that, all summed up, her summer in Trieste hadn't, in fact, been a total waste. But this wasn't the sort of situation like those her cousin imagined. Amila didn't really know exactly what sort of situation it was, only that it was taking place on some entirely different planet, but maybe for precisely this reason it seemed even more wonderful to her.

CHAPTER NINETEEN

Where the Past Touches the Present
SEPTEMBER 2004, BUJE/BUIE (CROATIA)

"IT'S LIKE YOU want to reclaim the Istrian part of your identity, right?" asked Amila, slamming the door of the Panda.

"Why, do you want to reclaim your Bosnian identity?"

"How is that even relevant? Mine was officially assigned. I was born somewhere else."

"Well, that's true. And anyway, no, not really."

True. Complicated origin stories weren't always possible to comprehend or rehash, untangling them like threads from a knot. Especially when those origins were no longer on firm ground, when they were hidden in a dark, dangerous place that called to you, at times seeming inconvenient and annoying, at times vital and necessary. Amila was well acquainted with all that.

She was walking next to Simon, feeling upbeat. It was a beautiful day. In the end, Amila had decided to seize the moment, and she'd gone with him to Buie. They told Norina that they were going to the lagoon of Grado. But actually they were climbing up the shaded, cool, and narrow streets of the city where she was born.

They reached the Duomo and stopped underneath its Venetian bell tower. A light breeze wafted through the sun-filled square. They looked around; no one was there. Simon handed Amila an old guidebook. On the dark green cover was written "Iugoslavia."

The fusty old name, written in Italian, made her smile. "Where did you dig this up?"

"Oh, I found it at my aunt's house. But I also have this."

Simon opened up a notebook and showed her a map on A4 paper, downloaded from the internet, marked up with a felt-tip marker, with crosses next to the names that had been circled and written down. He put his camera on video mode. He was making a video as a surprise for his grandmother, though he did realize that her generation still thought of photos as something that needed to be "developed," and he knew that photos were the only form of memories she collected.

"Do you remember?" said Simon. Amila nodded. Those photos from the old cookie tin. "Well, I want to bring the missing pieces of the puzzle back to her."

He focused the lens and pointed his camera at the faded lettering on a building: SCUOLA ELEMENTARE E MEDIA. The light-colored shutters, their paint peeling off, were opened a crack, as if time—which had ceased to move, congealed inside the empty, abandoned classrooms—still wished to peek outside. A group of children appeared, chasing after a ball. They were cheering each other on, speaking words that sounded Venetian and Croatian. Their dialect was the same as Norina's;

in this place, it seemed fitting, an echo of the narrow streets, of the stones and cobblestones, torn loose in some spots. Here, their speech sang with a lively, happy sound that Norina had lost. In Trieste, her language had been roughened and bastardized by mixing with the local dialect.

Simon showed Amila the itinerary he thought they should follow. They would have to go down along the city walls in order to find his family's former home. A woman with long, blow-dried hair appeared behind them.

"Ten kune to visit the top of the bell tower," she proposed.

"We're not tourists," Simon responded.

Amila explained that his grandmother had been born there. The woman asked about first names and family names, but then shook her head. Her Croatian seemed to echo the intonation of the Italian dialect they'd heard—two languages within a single accent.

The stones of the city walls encircling the historic center of town were punctuated with small windows and loopholes. Amila stepped up to one. The countryside below stretched out to the horizon.

"Where is Trieste? Over there?"

"No, I think it's over there," Amila said, pointing straight ahead, beyond the hills, toward a mountain carved up into small squares of different sizes. Below it you could make out more clearly a group of apartment buildings.

"Uncle Mariano must have lived somewhere down there," said Simon. He looked at the map again to be sure and mentioned a train station, though you couldn't see one. He focused his lens and took some more photos.

Ahead of them, peering out from behind some other homes, there was a house split in half, with no roof and the interior gutted. Laundry was hanging out to dry on a line fixed to a hook in the rubble: life popping up again, like an impudent clump of grass wedged between the stones. There were a lot of those.

Nonna Nevia had told Simon to go toward the section of the city called Villa, that he couldn't go wrong, even though on Google Maps it was marked as Belvedere and San Martino. The blue, bilingual street signs had place-names in both Croatian and the old names, with their mixed origins. It was the houses, however, that most visibly registered the time that had passed, or that remained contained within their walls. They seemed unstable, clutching onto each other as they did, flanked by cobblestones that broke apart in some spots and were patched together here and there with a quick layer of cement or smooth, slippery stones.

According to Simon, they should be looking behind the oldest palazzo. Nonna Nevia used to say that hers was "the house with the small tree of roses." They stopped in front of a four-story building. On each floor, the windows grew smaller and smaller. The last of them, directly under a protruding gutter, were not much bigger than skylights. The dark, wooden entryway door, surrounded by a simple stone cornice, opened onto a dusty and worn brick walkway that led to a stairway. Next to the door, out of a flowerbed embedded in the wall, a tall bush of climbing roses unfurled, creating a thick cover of fuchsia-colored flowers. The final, festive bloom before autumn.

"My grandmother asked me to see if they were still here." And they were still there. This was the house.

FEDERICA MARZI

With one foot, Simon stepped into the entryway, then quickly stepped back. In front of him was the house he'd imagined and searched for, that might have existed, once upon a time, the house of ifs and buts, of whys and who knows. Simon felt he was at a precarious, wavering crossroads, where the past touched the present, imagination imposed on reality, and heredity's forking paths led to the future. There he was, stunned at having at last arrived.

"What will you do with all of this?" Amila asked, unsure about breaking the silence. "Are you planning on putting it in the novel?"

Simon nodded.

"Who is your protagonist?"

"My mother. She'll be the one who returns, instead of me."

"To look for her father?"

"Um, yes." Simon smiled. "But also to tell her mother's, my grandmother's, story."

"So, tell me, does your mother find him?"

"Well, that depends."

"On what?"

"I suppose it depends on what I find out."

Simon again hesitated. Then he got to work and took a great number of photos. Eventually he decided to leave behind the house that, in some sense, belonged to him.

"C'mon, let's go," he said, without turning to look back.

Trg Slobode/Piazza della Libertà were the names on a plaque in the place they were now, surrounded by remodeled homes with colorful walls and pitched roofs. Another plaque said *Ulica pod Loðom/Via Sotto la Losa. Mater Misericordiae.* The wall next to the church was scrawled with graffiti: *Long Live Tito!*

The writing had faded somewhat, but its provocation was still clear and timely. Amila smiled at this involuntary twitch of Yugo-nostaglia.

Simon had other landmarks to consider. *Piazza Le Porte* and *Sotto la Losa*, he repeated to himself, looking at his homemade map. But the new city, in part disinhabited, had inevitably been written over the former city, which remained whole only within his grandmother's memory. Not far away, a marble plaque commemorated the victims of fascism and the militants of the L P L.

"What does that stand for?"

"*Lotta Popolare di Liberazione*, the People's Fight for Freedom," Amila translated, relying on her second memory, the memory held in reserve, where phrases reminiscent of "*Narodno Oslobodilačka Borba*" still lingered fuzzily from her elementary school lessons.

"Look, there's even one named Potleca, like my uncle!"

"Yes, there is," Amila responded, struck by the coincidence.

Via Sucolo was still there, with the same name, and Livio and Orietta Barbo were there too, waiting for them.

"My grandmother would say Livio had a big nose, and that was why she didn't want to marry him. But she also said if she had, she would never have gone to Australia. I've never been able to tell if this is something she regrets or not."

Livio looked tall and thin; Orietta had long, wavy, copper-colored hair, which made her seem younger than him. His face seemed well proportioned, and his nose wasn't so big after all, just a bit pug, perhaps. They welcomed the two visitors into their living room on the second floor, as if they were long-lost

FEDERICA MARZI

relatives. The contacts Nevia had maintained for fifty years had held up well, even across such differing and distant worlds.

The ties were sealed with a round of homemade grappa, which Amila and Simon barely sipped. They weren't used to this ritual, but they couldn't refuse. Livio and Orietta laughed, as if they'd happened upon two tourists with delicate digestion.

Livio insisted on getting up-to-date about everyone: Nevia, Norina, and Mariano. They talked about children and grandchildren, about their jobs and their studies, about uncles and grandparents, and especially about their health. Nevia had terrible asthma, Simon explained. Mariano had developed an ulcer, and was in need of a hip replacement, and Norina . . . well, no. Norina was doing just fine.

Orietta laughed, shaking that head of hair. The two of them were doing just fine too, she assured Simon, except for some rheumatism that came along with the humid weather. She spoke while she set the table with their holiday best. She'd made fusi with a thick brown sauce of capucci cabbage with prosciutto, even if it wasn't dinnertime.

Livio sighed. "Incredible how much time has passed! We look at you all from here, and you all look at all of us from over there; we think about sending our regards, and so it goes," he said, referring to the sea washing up on their two opposing shores. Over there their gazes peered out, tunneling through mountains and lands to look for one another, as if Nevia had never gone to the land down under and could be found on the other side of the peninsula.

Livio spoke with pride about his olive orchards and vineyards. His hands were accustomed to working the land. Even at his age, he was still at it. They sold their wine and olive oil to Italian and German tourists, Orietta told them, happily. And lately also to the Slovenians and Czechs. "Who could have ever imagined?"

When they had the opportunity, they rented out rooms, since their pensions weren't enough to pay for everything. Livio wasn't all that enthusiastic about the democracy that had come after Yugoslavia. "Men are still beasts. As soon as they get ten, they want fifty, when power changes hands, and after that, when power changes hands again, they want to get more than a hundred."

"Why didn't you two also leave?"

"Leave for where?" Livio asked. "This is our home. On some other land, we'd no longer live as equals—that's what we thought at the time."

Simon fell silent. Then he cleared his throat. "And Franco?"

Amila lowered her eyes.

"What Franco?"

"Franco Radonich," Simon answered, ready to go straight to the point.

"Who? Franco Bacàn?" Livio corrected him, surprised at the question.

"He was from here too, wasn't he?" Simon said, almost as if he needed to justify his question. "Nonna Nevia mentions him sometimes."

"Really?"

"Well, he was another Buiese who left for Australia."

"But, bless you, my boy, he's been back here for years!" Livio said.

Simon turned white.

"Yes, that's true, but not for so long," Orietta corrected him. "It must have been just before the war."

"You mean he lives here?" asked Amila, impulsively.

Livio stayed silent, as if he had some questions about her but was keeping quiet out of discretion. Probably he assumed she was Simon's girlfriend, a bit exotic, given that she was Bosnian—from the name, he would know that. So she must be the girlfriend of the grandson of the woman whom, at one time, he had hoped to marry, but who had then moved away.

"Franco isn't from here. He's from Buroli," Livio clarified, speaking in a distant, reserved voice, as if he would like to banish Franco beyond the city limits.

"What do you mean?" Simon glanced quickly over at Amila.

"*He's certainly not living in Buroli these days,*" Orietta said to Livio, switching to dialect.

"*God knows!*" Livio answered her, before turning to Simon, who seemed to have frozen. "*Listen, son* . . . Everything around here is one big scandal."

"He had some problems," Orietta explained.

Livio nodded.

"What problems?" Simon asked. A corner of his mouth began to quiver.

"*Aaaah, schei. That's always the reason!*" Livio answered, emphatically.

"Money," Amila hurriedly translated, in a whisper.

Simon looked over at her, confused, but he didn't give up. "Problems, in what sense?"

"Problems," Livio repeated, impatiently, making a gesture to say, Leave it be—this is our business, local stories, things you others couldn't possibly understand.

Amila's cheerful curiosity had evaporated. Instead, she was beginning to worry. This definitely wasn't good news, even if Simon's long-lost grandfather might be living in his home village.

To change the subject, Orietta said, "It's a shame, though, that Norina and Mariano don't come back anymore to visit," remembering when their two old friends would return to Istria to visit their family graves. Now it was Nevia who took care of them, from afar, in order to make sure they didn't go to rack and ruin and the State didn't get rid of them entirely. Each spring, she sent money to pay for maintenance and for their efforts. Just then Simon remembered that he was supposed to deliver an envelope for next spring.

"Can we go to see them?" he asked.

"Of course you can! Finish eating, and we'll take you there," Livio answered, once again in good spirits.

At that, Amila and Simon realized that the cornucopia on the table before them was for them, and that the conversation about Franco was over. Livio and Orietta sat down to watch them as they ate.

At the door of their home, Orietta pinched Simon's cheeks. "*Look here, Nevia's boy . . . and what a boy!*"

Simon laughed, out of embarrassment.

"It seems we're always having to say goodbye to one of us who's leaving," Orietta added, with a tinge of nostalgia. She gave a hug to Amila too.

Livio offered to take a photo of them outside in the piazza. As a souvenir. Simon adjusted the camera and wrapped his arm around Amila's shoulders. She leaned her head toward him.

"Ready? Cheeeess..."

Livio snapped only one photo—and did it before the "cheess." Then he walked with Simon and Amila toward the cemetery, passing through the new part of the town. They came to a quiet place with tall cypresses and a view over a wide expanse of countryside. In the lawn were rows of white, gray, and black stone slabs, with the usual mix of Italian and Croatian names. An oval, black-and-white photo was set into a plaque of white stone: a man with a solemn face, a thick, dark moustache, his head set into his square shoulders.

NICOLÒ BENCI
61 YEARS OLD
DIED 12 NOVEMBER 1954

HIS FAMILY AND RELATIVES
AS A SIGN OF THEIR GREAT LOVE
LEAVE THIS
REMEMBRANCE

"This was Nevia's grandfather," Livio explained, "so he was your great-great grandfather, we should say. At least he stayed here. At home and in peace." Next to Nicolò, there was a photo of a woman who was so beautiful, she seemed like an actress from another era. "His wife."

Simon contemplated in silence these images of his ancestors. He didn't lay a hand on the camera around his neck. Amila felt herself wavering, even if she had accompanied Simon to support him in this strange adventure with the past. Perhaps it was due to the expression of condolences written on the tomb, words she knew were rhetorical, though no less beautiful for that. Or the message of "great love" carved into a stone that someone continued to pay for, from an ocean away. Or perhaps what moved her were the stories etched into these mute faces, separated forever from their emigrant families. Or the restless eyes of Livio and his worn-out hands—hands that kept their grip on the land where he'd remained, though more alone, without the others. Amila didn't have graves she could return to visit. The old graveyards had been destroyed, and the new ones were lost in a field sown with white stelae. Though that was a place where she had never been, and had never wanted to go to. Whenever she got really angry, Mamma Selma would accuse her of having grown up disrespectful. But that didn't change Amila's feelings about graves.

Livio brought them over to another marker.

HERE LIES THE MORTAL REMAINS
"BABA" ANTONIA BERNES,
LOVED AND MOURNED JUST AS SHE WAS
A MOTHER
1905–1983

The words referred to a black-clad woman with a grim face; a brooch pinned to her collar; thick, wrinkled eyebrows; and deep eyes that dominated in their severity.

"Ah, this was one of Nevia's aunts, or, more precisely, one of her poor mother's cousins," Livio said, pulling up a tuft of grass. She'd left the refugee camp in Padriciano and gone back to Buie—the only one to have done so.

Livio explained that, as long as Baba Antonia had lived, Norina had come back regularly to Istria. She had been very fond of her aunt and wanted her to have a grave that was just as nice as the rest. That time, Norina and Nevia had disagreed about money, or some other damned thing. But that's how Norina was—even if in the end, in recent years, it had been Nevia who shouldered the expenses. Norina had cut all her ties. Even with graves.

Simon stood tense and still, his lips slightly parted. Amila suddenly felt like taking his hand. It was sweaty, but he let her hold it, gripping hers tightly. And there it was: now they were truly close. Within their common story of shifting borders.

Livio walked with them back to the traffic circle, so then they could go to the parking lot, and he could go back up, inside the city walls. One at a time, he gave them a hug. Then, calmly, he said, "Come back again next year, if we're still alive. All the best!"

CHAPTER TWENTY

It, Too, Was Somewhere—It Was Real

SEPTEMBER 2004, BUJE/BUIE (CROATIA)

"ARE YOU OKAY?" Amila asked. They'd parked the Panda outside the city walls, on a ramp hammered by the sun. Their seats were scorching hot.

"Well, I guess we're going to this Buroli, right?" Simon said, looking straight ahead.

"First I need to hear that everything's okay."

He turned toward her. "Okay."

Amila pursed her lips and shook her head.

Simon opened up a map and propped it up on the steering wheel. "It's just ... really, who would have imagined it like this?" He adjusted his glasses, so he could better read the map. He seemed confused.

"Are you really sure you want to go there?"

"Absolutely." The corners of his mouth tightened.

"Orietta, though, did say your grandfather might not still be living in that village."

"Exactly, maybe not. So anything's possible."

"If he is there, what do we do?"

"I don't know. We'll talk about it later."

"No way! Let's think about it now." Amila stiffened. Where the hell was he taking her? "Just in case you don't remember, Orietta also said your grandfather had been in some trouble."

"She was talking about money, right?"

"Exactly!"

"But he's my grandfather!"

Amila gave up, leaning back in her seat. In this moment, she thought to herself, she didn't understand Simon at all.

Yes, Franco was his grandfather. But what did that really mean? He was the man who had dumped his grandmother and left his mother fatherless. He was a complete stranger and could be anyone. What's more, something serious must've happened. What was Simon setting himself up for? And just because, as he put it, he was doing it for his novel.

"I'm sorry, but what does it really mean, anyway, that he'd been in trouble?" Simon chided her, looking for an argument.

"You could have asked Livio."

"Couldn't you see he didn't want to talk about it?" Simon said. "Look, I've studied law, and I've seen people with plenty of troubles. They're no different from anyone else. And if I don't hurry up and write my book, I'll see plenty more, for the rest of my life. So I might as well start with someone from my own family."

Amila didn't find his attempt at humor funny. "At the very least, we should think of something, so he doesn't slam the door in our faces—look at how we're dressed!"

Simon looked at his black T-shirt, perplexed.

"Trust me," Amila said, "I have good instincts here. I've got a journalist's nose."

"Why, are you a journalist?"

Amila avoided his gaze. "Not yet. But I'm going to be."

"Now you tell me?" he responded, offended, as if she'd been hiding something from him.

"Yes."

"But aren't you in college?"

"Sure. But I also write for a newspaper. A small one."

"I see . . . It did seem strange . . ."

"What?"

"That you seem to understand everything."

Amila laughed. "People do tell me that."

"What do you write about?"

"Natural food, beauty and health treatments, homeopathy, bicycle lanes. Things like that. But I'm still just a volunteer, and it's a long road . . . Look, how about we get going? I'll tell you about it later, or some other time. I'm boiling in here."

"The only thing I really want now is a cold Coke."

"Finally, a good idea! Let's stop somewhere and get one; then we can think about next steps."

"Okay," he said, making peace. He put his face up to the map and followed a series of roads with his finger. "There it is, there!" he exclaimed, putting his finger down on a point packed with names in tiny print. "It's written there."

Amila's face moved in, and her chewed-up index finger brushed against Simon's.

"Buroli. That's right, isn't it?"

"I think so. Can you follow on the map?"

"First the Coke, though."

Simon started the engine, and they were off. "Just think!" he exclaimed, in a lighter tone. "A writer and a journalist. We make a great team!"

Amila didn't fully understand if he was suggesting a "dream team," as he might have said, given his rather original manner of speaking, or if he had something different in mind.

They continued along a downward slope, followed by a series of curves. Then the farmland began, and the soil changed colors. The ground was a rust-colored red, in sharp contrast with the lush vineyards, weighed down with clusters of amber and purple grapes. In that direction, looking across two borders, one between Italy and Slovenia, the other between Slovenia and Croatia, the sky seemed more vast and clear.

They changed direction. The car bounced over the broken asphalt, lined with stones of karst covered in dirt. They turned onto nameless, narrow roads shaded by oak trees. Two stone houses, one in front of another, signaled that they were about to go through a village. All the road signs continued to point in the opposite direction: Buie, Umago, but no Buroli.

They stopped at a roadside *konoba*. They went in; the tavern was dark, its decor rustic. Fishnets with starfish and a *Playboy* calendar were hung on the plywood walls. Many of the benches were set upside down on the tables. The air was filled with the sharp smell of ammonia.

The man who served them was overweight; he rubbed his hands on his black apron, speaking in dialect. Simon rolled a cigarette. He offered it to Amila, but she shook her head no, so he smoked it himself. In a corner of the bar, there was a group of old

FEDERICA MARZI

men wearing work clothes. The center of their table was presided over by a pitcher of red wine, that clear, dark red that must still be called Terrano, or Teràn. They were playing cards and, from time to time, looking over curiously at the outsiders. The owner, his arms folded behind the bar, added his running commentary on the card game, in the same dialect he'd used with Amila and Simon, seasoned with a few salty curses in Croatian. The speakers mounted in the corners of the room rehashed old Italian pop songs.

The atmosphere made Simon and Amila feel like they'd stepped into another world, a place where it seemed you might see the world differently. And not just differently, better. Everyone here shared a sort of off-kilter Italianness. People from the borderlands, mixed ethnicities, the products of old and new population shifts. All of them had stopped in to spend some time in an unnamed bar in the Istrian countryside, in the middle of nowhere. A landfall of castaways, people who happened to wash up, who got thrown overboard, who had roots in the air, or were transplanted. Yet even this was somewhere. Even this was real.

Simon smoked nervously, without saying a word. From time to time, he gulped down some of his Coke. He continued to study the map, meditatively.

"So then, what are we doing?" Amila asked him.

He lifted his head. "Let's ask where Buroli is. You should do it, since you speak better."

"I don't think we should. These are villages. Everyone knows everybody."

"So let's go," Simon decided.

"First you need to tell me what we're planning to do. Go and meet a man who might not even know that he has a daughter?"

"I think so. I think he knows."

"You think so? And what will you say to him?"

"I'll speak with him."

Amila shook her head.

"Look, I do want to go there." Simon took out his wallet and got the owner's attention. "If you want, wait for me here. I can go on my own." He downed the rest of the soda.

"Is that what you want?"

Simon shook his head.

"Then I'm coming with you."

Simon smiled at her. He paid up and left too big a tip.

They continued on in silence over roads that were all the same, through woods and over dirt roads, so that they had the impression of going in circles. It was impossible to follow on the map the miniature labyrinth of roads that crossed, vanished, then popped up again. And sure enough, they came across a stop on the state highway where cars and campers sped by a campground with little multicolored flags waving over its entrance. On the coast there was more wind. The sky seemed to stretch before them, its color faded. But then, after a few more turns, there it was, at last, a sign that said BUROLI, covered by a branch, at the entrance to a small hamlet. Simon slammed on the brakes. They might have already passed it by, without even realizing.

They parked in an open space, near a dilapidated house and next to another, just painted, though it still had a flat roof and a balcony with no railing.

They continued on foot and saw other houses, made of stone. Some were older and smaller, with a garden. Others were modernized to the point that they seemed artificial. Many of the courtyards were covered by the wide, leafy canopy of a mulberry tree. Cars with German license plates were parked next to their gates. Chickens ranged freely, scratching the soil along the sides of the road, in front of storage sheds and stables. Then a field, a lot filled with old automobiles and tractors.

Simon hurried over toward two young men wearing mechanics' overalls. They were leaning on the hood of a white Zastava, talking and smoking. Amila stayed behind.

He went right up to them and got straight to the point. "Hey there. I'm looking for the house of Franco Radonich." What sort of lawyer would this Simon have made?

The two looked him over from head to toe, without responding. Then they looked at Amila, whose heart was beating rapidly.

One of the guys, cautiously, crushed his cigarette butt out on the ground before saying, "Who are you two?"

"Relatives from Italy."

The one who'd stopped smoking turned as if to question the other, who shrugged. Then he pointed with his chin, to indicate the direction they should take. *"Up there, made of old stones, the last before the woods."*

The guy lit a new cigarette. Simon had him repeat everything. The guy pointed to the houses that weren't the right one. "One, two, three, then up, over there, on the side, after the end of the village."

The house they'd been directed to was a composition of irregularly shaped stones and sharp rocks that seemed to have pushed their way out by force. It had four windows with dark-brown wooden shutters, recently repainted. The shutters were closed. As was the door, surrounded by a stone arch. Closed with a deadbolt and a big lock. The front lawn had not been cut. On one side, the woods got thicker. There weren't any cars parked outside. There was a low gate, also closed.

Simon just stood there, chewing his lip.

"Oh well. It would have been too easy to find him like this," Amila said, brushing his shoulder.

Simon pulled back abruptly.

"What were you thinking?" she said, resentfully. "Were you expecting to just show up on some random day and find your grandfather, right there in his old house, in this ghost town? And that then you'd immediately write a bestseller and gain worldwide fame?"

Simon pursed his lips but didn't say anything.

"Okay, c'mon. I'm sorry."

"It's annoying in a way I can't even explain," he responded, staring at the house. "It's like we're so close, you know?"

"Though maybe we aren't. Who knows how long it's been since he lived here. Who knows how far away we are from him now." Amila looked around, to see if there might be someone nearby. But there was no one. "Do me a favor, though. Don't take any photos, okay?"

Simon took the camera from his neck, gave it to her, and jumped over the gate in a single leap. Determined, he walked up to the door and knocked loudly.

"What are you doing? Have you gone crazy?" Amila shouted. "I'm leaving!"

Simon turned to go around the back of the house.

Amila went to the Panda parked in front of the ruined house, with its broken shutters ready to fall off. Metal fencing covered the window openings. She looked around, afraid that someone might appear. Simon came back without saying a word, without even looking at her. He opened the car door, and they got inside. He put his hands on the steering wheel. He was breathing hard.

"So?" Amila asked, after a brief pause.

"So nothing." Simon continued to look straight ahead. He put the key in the ignition and put his hands on his legs. He breathed deeply, trying to calm himself, gripping his jeans tightly.

"Listen, it really had to turn out like this."

"No, not like this." Simon turned toward her. "But thanks anyway. You're pretty badass, you know." He took off his glasses, placed them carefully on the dashboard, and pulled her over to him.

The long, heartfelt kiss took Amila by surprise. This was not a moment for kisses. In a situation like this, really? She would have expected almost anything but this. But this was, after all, what she had wanted, right? And so she squeezed her arms tightly around his neck and pushed her tongue into his mouth.

They looked at each other, surprised, as if they needed to catch their breath. Simon started the engine. Amila was shivering a little. They began to leave, but then Simon pulled over again where the shoulder of the road widened.

"Okay," he said. "End of the story with Franco Radonich."

He held her tightly and kissed her again.

"Okay. Beginning of the story with Amila *Hajigrahitch*," he said, pronouncing her name better than anyone else—almost perfectly.

They laughed. And kissed again. Everywhere.

Really, everywhere. On a beach covered in smooth stone slabs that dipped into cool, crystalline water, the water of another sea. Stretched out with their jeans rolled up to their knees in a small, solitary cove with smooth white stones, in the shade of giant tufts of cane rooted in the red soil. And then while wandering through fields that looked out over the sea, land left fallow, punctuated with dark-purple, fragrant flowers. And where there were massive rock cliffs, protecting them from eyes other than their own. Where a breeze came down from the forest of pines with their wide, green heads, stretching out toward the sea. That was on a small cape, and the same northeasterly wind, the Bora, that blew over Trieste must have made them grow that way. Crookedly over roots held tightly in the earth.

They kissed a thousand times during that day and then again in the evening. Everywhere.

Amila felt her body breathing, opening, and growing. Everywhere. It no longer mattered to her in what point or place of the world they were, or if the ground shook or was solid. It was as if they were there, yet everywhere. And that—for her, for once—was enough.

CHAPTER TWENTY-ONE

There Are Rules for Love
SEPTEMBER 2004, TRIESTE/TRST (ITALY)

NORINA SLIPPED HER bare feet into her gym shoes and wrapped a shawl around her shoulders. She went into the yard after dinner, after she'd washed the dishes and waited for Simon to go out. It was getting dark earlier and earlier; you had to get used to night falling like a rock. She preferred to keep the light outside the garage off. She looked around cautiously. Behind the hedge of myrtle, she heard the loud snorts of a hedgehog that passed through every evening. She continued to listen. The hedgehog fell silent. It must've sensed her presence and rolled itself up, the single, piteous means of defense that it knew. Norina took a handful of Luli's kibble from her pocket and left some near the flower bed. She continued on, through wet grass that tickled her ankles. She stopped next to the fence. The silhouette of the roses, which were spectacular in the daylight, seemed ghostly in the dark. The weeds had grown back, thick and tall.

During these past days of confusion, respite, and happiness, no one had been keeping up with the house chores. Amila's thoughts had been elsewhere. An exam, an article to write for Friday, she said. She'd been coming by Bristie less frequently, but she did see Simon in Trieste. Norina understood, and, on this score, she had nothing to complain about. Quite the contrary. The kids had gone out together that evening too, and it was better that way. Norina needed time to herself. With the point of her thick, smooth walking stick, she rummaged through the leaves of the pellitory nettles. She wasn't searching for anything in particular, just keeping herself busy. More than anything else, she was searching through her own thoughts with a sense of vigilance.

With the boy's arrival, a canopy had lowered itself, covering up all their habits and everyday things. Now the canopy was slowly rising again, and everything had again become what it was, if not worse. Their plaster walls were faded, cracked, and crumbling. One tile on the stairs was still a little wobbly. The kids skipped over that step, stretching out their long, agile legs, whereas she had to hold tight to the railing whenever she placed her foot there. And then the purple-and-white pigeon droppings on the windowsill. Norina hated the invasive birds, but she'd given up standing guard at the window, shooting water at them with her ridiculous toy gun. She no longer bothered with them, even when she saw them pecking in the garden or roosting on a polished marble surface. Let them do what they want, she thought. It had been a relief. But now everything was again covered in muck.

And what's more, she had plenty of doubts. For example, was Simon enjoying his stay with them? Well, yes, the answer certainly seemed to be yes. How many long discussions had

FEDERICA MARZI

they had together? He was always ready to listen to her, even if afterward he talked and talked about himself. He told her so many things, about himself, about Melbourne, about Ann, about Nevia, but with particular sensitivity, never letting his own role seem too grand, and always stopping at the right moment. Possibly because he noticed when Norina stiffened, even if she forced herself to smile, feeling the corners of her mouth tighten.

Nonetheless, at times it seemed as if Simon was about to say or do something, but then he'd squelch the idea. As if he were thirsty and was too considerate to ask for a second glass of water. That's it. At her place, it was like Simon still needed a glass of water, despite all the Coca-Cola she'd bought for him.

Norina went over toward the oak tree and leaned on the low wall. She closed her eyes and let herself be soothed by the light rustle of the leaves. A sound up in the branches distracted her, and she opened her eyes and raised her head. A squirrel or mouse must have passed by. As swift as lightning. Then it occurred to her that she could be the problem. Because she was always fantasizing about how everything must be down there, with Nevia. Everything bigger, everything brightly colored, always something better. The ones in Trieste were always worse in comparison. She could feel it; she knew that Simon had wanted to save her the shame of having stayed back, on the wrong slice of the globe.

Norina inhaled deeply, letting the air fill her lungs. From the humid soil wafted the fragrance of mint, which grew in large clumps in the flower beds.

What would be left for her when the house was empty again?

Simon would be leaving soon; he had to continue his trip.

From the moment he arrived, Norina had put a cross on the calendar each day, so that she wouldn't get mixed up and lose count. There were only two marks missing along the horizontal line she'd drawn with her pen. Simon would be taking a train and then a plane, going to Greece for windsurfing.

"A friend from Melbourne is waiting for me," he'd explained at dinner, looking up from his plate.

And suddenly Norina had recognized those eyes. The shape, the color, the darting glance. There they were. But only for an instant. Simon got up from the table; he was in a hurry to go see Amila. Norina had found those eyes again precisely when she was about to lose them for a second time.

On the floor above, the light was on in Mariano's room. Their home had become a dispatch center for emails and photo attachments, phones beeping from morning to night. Australia had never invaded their home with a similar degree of force. Whenever she could, Norina would sneak off like a snake, getting out of the way, or she'd say, "Yes and no, first *one way, then the other*." In short, she rejected Nevia and all of her Australia, just as she'd always done.

Nevia had hoped Simon would be able to put things right between the two sisters, as she had written to Norina in her letter last June. But when the actual person appeared, Norina hadn't wanted to share him with anyone. Simon and Norina had gotten to know each other as they were in the present moment, and that had been lovely. True, what had happened in the past was in the past, but it had also happened, and she hadn't forgotten. And if there were things she couldn't have, there were also things she didn't want to surrender. That was why she'd broken

FEDERICA MARZI

ties with everyone: relatives and townspeople, both those who were still living, with houses on this side of the border or the other, or on this side of the world or the other, as well as those dead in their graves. Let them rest in peace.

Now, at least, she had gotten to know her nephew. And he hadn't disappointed her—quite the contrary. Norina felt, strongly and clearly, the force of blood ties and the potential of an experience in the present that could fill up a life, instead of emptying it. Something that was possible, not impossible, and as such wasn't simply the typical nostalgia of an old woman.

But then, just before going out, Simon had stopped by the kitchen and asked her a question.

"What ever happened to my grandfather? Do you know anything, Auntie?"

Norina's upper lip beaded with sweat. She clenched her teeth and swallowed; dropping the rag she was using to clean, she leaned against the pantry. She'd looked into the boy's calm, clear eyes.

"*I don't know anything. No one does,*" she said, hurriedly, as Simon's face, which during his stay had become nicely tanned, took on a new shade of disappointment. She'd quickly given him a glass of water, after letting the faucet run so it would be cool and free of chlorine.

What else could she have said? That Nevia had left, taking everything with her, including Franco, so that the beautiful things in life appeared in double measure, but only for her?

Nevia, however, hadn't succeeded in keeping Franco for herself. He'd gone away. Forever. Where, Norina didn't know. It could be all or nothing; he could be alive or dead. Of course, she had heard something over the years. That he had been in South America. Rumors, rumors. People love to talk, but for her the world was just too big. And so she had stopped thinking about all of those faraway places. It was only when her memories resurfaced, in the evenings when she couldn't manage to fall asleep, that she would start questioning. And imagining possibilities. She would see Franco, still the same, still taking life as it came, taking and leaving even Nevia without a second thought, as if everything belonged to him.

Nevia, on the other hand, she'd never managed to understand. What could have possibly driven her to him? Love? And was it true love? When it came to her sister's life, these were the only facts that interested Norina, but they had no explanations. And then there were other questions. One in particular tormented her. Would Simon come back to see her again, perhaps in a year or two?

Norina breathed deeply again, taking in the night air. She pressed her hand to her forehead. It was too early to think about such things now, even if there might be some possibility he would. Perhaps Amila would be the reason he returned to Trieste? If Simon was falling in love with her, he would certainly want to see her again.

Something was about to happen; Norina was sure of it. The two kids were certainly hatching some sort of plot, though she wasn't sure it was a love affair. After all, Simon had been ready to leave. He'd even said that he was going to Greece with a friend.

In sum, you don't just dump your true love by the wayside, even if times have changed, and everything today was different—mobile phones, earbuds, the internet. None of that was the main point, though. Because, according to Norina, there were rules for love. And they were valid for good. They never changed.

"Okay, you're coming back, I get it. And then?"

"I don't know. We'll do something."

"For an afternoon? Hmmm, I'm not sure if it'll be worth it for you. It's a long trip."

"Yeah, but I'm always traveling."

Amila and Simon were sitting on a low wall between the bar and a pavilion that, during the day, was used as a ceramics workshop for psychiatric patients and then became part of the bar. They were finishing their beers, and they were the only customers.

Amila brought Simon to unique places, not the usual tourist spots. That evening they'd wandered through dark, grim buildings, some of them abandoned. Cautiously they went inside another pavilion filled with debris. Amila had screamed at the sight of a large rat lying in wait behind a collapsed beam and made it scurry into a pile of junk. Simon had traced his finger around the cracks and stains on an ocher-colored wall. They checked out the graffiti and stopped in front of the famous Basaglia-era slogan TRUTH IS REVOLUTIONARY.

"What if I told you it was done out of love?" Simon continued, lightheartedly.

"I would respond by saying, oo la la!" Amila said, with a tone as carefree and joking as she could. "And I'd ask if you were planning on making me a character in your next novel."

"Hmmmm . . . I hadn't thought about that yet."

"About what?"

"About my next book."

"Well, you should. Especially because by now it's a sure thing that you'll be a writer."

Simon had given her some of his unpublished short stories to read. Amila had found some of the characters unforgettable, sketches done with just a few, sure strokes in moments when their small, ordinary lives were about to be upended by an event that would forever change them. She loved the heroic fragility of those characters, and to her it seemed that Simon's ability to describe life deserved to be called talent. And it was also very different reading him in English. She'd found a side of him that had escaped her until then. It seemed to come out of nowhere, and more than anything, that's what she found beautiful.

"Nevertheless, I do want to see you again." Simon crushed his beer can. He took off his glasses, set them on the wall, and leaned into to her.

Amila moved over. "Listen, I've figured out that you're nearsighted! If you keep this up, you're going to break those glasses."

"Oh, definitely," he said, amused, as he squinted.

It was a lovely night, and they were happy together. They were on vacation, but their vacation was about to end. Simon had to return home, to another continent, but he was acting as if he had an apartment next to the Western Union on the corner of Via Pascoli.

Simon pinched her lips with his own. Amila let him do it, but she was confused. What did any of this mean?

"I leave from Athens and arrive in Milan. And at Milan, I take a train for Trieste. We absolutely have to see each other," he continued, speaking quietly. He brushed her cheek with his nose, then with his lips, and he caressed her hair.

"Can you manage to get back to Milan in time for your plane?"

"Yes."

"All right, then."

"So then, we'll see each other in eight and a half days." Simon put his hands under her T-shirt. "So long as you like the idea, at least a little."

Amila backed away. "Yes, of course. I just want to understand a few things."

"Such as?"

"Such as what am I feeling, and what are you feeling, and what do we do, now that you're leaving?"

Simon didn't seem at all upset by this line of questioning. Amila was worried she seemed like a stock character, something out of a Harlequin romance. But the issues at hand, as Papà Željko always said, had to be faced.

"As far as I'm concerned, we'll figure out something," he answered, as if that were the most obvious thing in the world, not something immense.

Amila shook her head and looked at him, perplexed. Then she closed her eyes and sighed. "Okay." She opened them again. "We'll figure out something." She knew that storico began, and then they finished. But they could also continue.

"Besides, I still haven't cleared anything up, have I?"

"Meaning?"

"The novel, my grandfather's story."

In fact, they had tried again to look for Simon's grandfather, this time on the internet, using Mariano's computer. But there too, they'd failed to find a Franco Radonich, or even Radoni, someone who might still be alive or have some connection to the place where they'd been. "So that means I have to come back soon."

"But didn't you say you're done with that story?"

"Yes, but now it gives me an excuse to see you again."

"Then better not to make this grandfather of yours turn up too soon, or else you'll run out of excuses."

"Well, we'll have to find new ones. Otherwise, what good is it being a writer or journalist?"

"We're really good at spinning out a pack of lies."

"Unbelievably good. *Fifty-fifty?*" Simon said, in English, shaking her hand.

"*Fifty-fifty,*" she replied, pushing him down off the wall. "Listen, though, I won't be at Norina's by that point. I needed to have an excuse too, you know. To keep from going to Bosnia with my family. But now the summer is over, so I don't need it any more."

"Well, I won't always be staying with my aunt. Where will you be?"

"What do you mean, where will I be? At home."

"And where is that?"

"Do you really still not know?" Simon shook his head, amused, even if for Amila this was the most serious subject of all. "In Via Pascoli! In the center of the city!"

CHAPTER TWENTY-TWO

The Outlines of Happiness
SEPTEMBER 2004, TRIESTE/TRST (ITALY)

AMILA WAS COUNTING the days until Simon's return from Greece, and the days passed quickly, but only after they were over.

One morning, while walking through the crowded streets downtown, she saw a green dress in a store window. It was satin, with long sleeves and a multicolored, geometric motif over its green background. Beautiful, summery, and, above all, expensive.

She didn't have anything like it in her wardrobe; she didn't even have a single decent skirt, as Mamma Selma often complained. Her mother had only convinced her to wear skirts when Amila was small. They still had a couple of photos, their edges folded and worn out, that gave proof of an era of small, white dresses and frilly skirts. But, in fact, that had been another time, back in Yugoslavia, and memory there got lost down a whirlpool. And then, as Papà Željko would note, with regret, Amila went straightaway into her teenage years and jeans. And after that, college. And she'd had nothing more to do with skirts and dresses.

Amila would soon be meeting Simon for the last time, although they'd said that it wouldn't be the last, and so she imagined herself beside him in an outfit of a sort she'd never had. She didn't think twice and walked into the store. She tried on the dress at home, in front of the big mirror in the hallway. She didn't even take off her jeans. She checked the length of the sleeves, the cut of the shoulders, the way the skirt fell. Amila imagined how Majda would have laughed at this clumsy behavior. "Hey, what's going on there, are you frozen or something? It's only a mirror!"

Amila held the skirt by its sides and spread it out. She crossed one leg in front of the other and tried to spin around on her heels full circle. She let go of the skirt and relaxed.

It wasn't true that she didn't like dresses or that they didn't look good on her. The one she was wearing was perfect, and she felt wonderful. So good it worried her, almost.

She sat down at the desk to check if Simon had sent her any emails from the Surf Club in Limnos. Usually they came around lunchtime. The computer had been left on, and the screen returned to a page on Yahoo that she must've forgotten she'd left open. On the search engine there was the name Franco Radonić.

Amila had gotten the idea to try writing the name in the way most familiar to her, which was different from how Simon wrote it, ending in "-ch." Under the name, a series of blue headings appeared. Some of them were in purple, which meant that she'd clicked on them, but without finding much of anything, only dates for births and deaths, an address with no relevance to her research, or the first and last names in bold, but appearing separately, together with other names. Amila had continued to look for information about Simon's grandfather, in part for fun, in part out of boredom. And because of her own innate, stubborn curiosity. But especially because, if she did happen to find something, Simon would have to come back for more than just half a day.

She sat there, scrolling through the headings she'd seen already. And for the first time she noticed that the name Radonić appeared more often next to another name, not Franco, but Franjo, and that the two sounded a lot alike.

On impulse, she wrote Simon a text. Her hands were shaking.

Is it possible your grandfather's name could be Franjo?

Amila typed the new name into the search box. In front of her eyes unrolled a list of entries and links. The main news came from June, and it had appeared on a few Croatian sites and newspapers, as well as some in Italian. Most of it was about a bar that the man owned, a nightclub on the outskirts of Zara called Eldorado, where there had been a fire for reasons that weren't clear. The building was closed for an official investigation.

Simon responded:

> What sort of name is that?
> Croatian, or maybe Serbian, I'm not sure. Is it possible he changed his name?
> Not that I ever heard.

Amila insisted:

Ask your grandmother.

Why?

Because I might have found something.

I'm calling you now!

I can't talk now. Call your grandmother.

She'll be in bed.

I don't know what to tell you.

Amila went back to clicking and searching, stopping at the title of an article that she could download as a PDF: "Flames During the Night at the Eldorado Club Throw Light on a War Profiteer." There was even a photo of him: short hair, streaked with gray, and blue eyes, long and narrow, giving the expression of someone secretly amused. Franjo Radonić was the owner of a nightclub where a fire had occurred, and it was suspected to be arson. A club for adults, exclusive and chic. He owned another very popular bar, named For Fun, on the Istrian coast, in Salvore. It was near Umago, where Amila had been with Simon. That detail could be important.

Her phone beeped. She had a series of texts.

My grandmother was still awake. She says yes. His name is Franjo.

Franco was only a nickname.

I swear though I didn't know anything about it.

What did you find? Can I call you?

Amila left her phone on the table.

The article summarized the biography of a self-made man, a career that hadn't followed a linear path, but had taken him to Argentina before he ended up in Croatia. Franjo Radonić was the head of a trucking company, cofounded with someone named Danko Bukić, a businessman, politician, and then general in the Croatian Army, a major figure in the Croatian War of Independence. A year ago, the Hague Tribunal had issued an extradition order regarding him, but Bukić died of a sudden illness at his home in Spalato. So he was never brought to justice.

Her phone rang. Amila pushed it away.

She returned to her online search, this time typing in two names together: Radonić and Bukić. She opened one window after another and clicked feverishly on links sending her to articles that didn't tell her anything new. Then she chanced upon a headline that made her jump: "A General Who Can't Be Prosecuted and His Entrepreneur Accomplice." This article had been written for an independent weekly in Croatia. The author described an association that went far beyond a partnership in transport. Radonić had supplied an enormous number of semitrucks and four-wheel-drive vehicles of every kind. Bukić had redirected them to the war front between the Croats and Serbs, to besiege and ransack territory in the Dalmatian backcountry, while the defenseless population fled in terror on tractors, in private cars, or on foot, leaving their farm animals behind to roam around or die, on land that in short order was burned to the ground. The events had earned General Bukić an arrest mandate for crimes against humanity: homicide, persecution, forced deportation.

Amila felt as if she needed to breathe, as if she'd been underwater too long and needed to come up for air.

When it came to Franjo Radonić, there were no pending international criminal charges, but his role as second fiddle to Bukić was obvious, as was his well-known function as enthusiastic intermediary in rushed sales of abandoned homes to Croatia's nouveau riche.

These days Radonić had become the owner of two popular nightspots. His old corporation Za.dr.Transp was no longer active. It had possibly used legal maneuvers and a foreign company in order to move its capital abroad. After the Eldorado fire, Radonić's whereabouts had become untraceable.

The fact is that sieges, bombing, and forced deportations have once again created the ideal conditions for the formation of a band of traffickers, smugglers, and war criminals. Not simply war profiteers, they are figures with a decisive role in manipulating and facilitating the conflict, by exploiting the issues of ethnic and religious identity.

Amila felt herself drowning in the murky water that she'd immersed herself in, stubbornly and without interruption. This man who might be Simon's grandfather was implicated, complicit, or at least had some part in a really ugly story.

When Mamma Selma and Majda called her, she flinched like a criminal, caught in the act. She got up in an instant, slipped off her dress, and threw it on the bed, putting on the first T-shirt she managed to find. She was in front of her closet when Mamma Selma and Majda joined her.

Mamma Selma's face fell. "What's wrong? Oh God, you're sick!"

Amila murmured, "No, it's nothing."

Mamma Selma approached her, perplexed. "That's enough of all this studying! It's giving you rings under your eyes!"

"Okay, Mamma," Amila answered, mechanically.

Majda noticed the dress on the bed, picked it up, and held it in front of herself. She smoothed out the dress and looked at her sister with an air of complicity that received no response.

"What's this? Such a beautiful dress."

Majda set it back down carefully. She came closer, with a questioning look in her eyes.

"Where's Papà?" said Amila, cutting things short.

"Where he always is when it's time to eat. Late."

On the desk, Amila's phone rang. She pretended to ignore it.

"What's going on, girl?" Mamma Selma was upset. "Why aren't you answering your phone?"

Amila shook her head. "I'm fine. I just need to be alone for a minute."

"But you're alone all the time! Did something happen?"

"No."

"All right, then. But lunch is almost ready."

"What's for lunch?" Majda asked, without taking her eyes off of Amila.

"There won't be any lunch, if somebody doesn't help me put something together, and fast," Mamma Selma responded. "We went to the university to get registration forms," she continued, pretending everything was back to normal. For Majda, and the major she'd been deciding on. Either political science or history. At home, it was all they talked about. "Don't worry, it'll be fine." Mamma Selma took Amila's arm, stroking it.

No, it wouldn't be.

Amila went over to the desk. She looked at her phone.

Can you please tell me what's going on?

The truth was that she really didn't know either.

She moved the mouse and saw reappear on her screen the last of the countless articles she'd read so feverishly. She saved it. The information it contained spun vertiginously in her head. In a half-deadened part of her brain, an old family lexicon was active again. In an earlier time, she had worn it like a second skin, having grown up inside it. She had struggled to carve a space for herself between the historic events in northeastern Bosnia and those years where she and her family had lived, first in a center for refugees and then in a house, in Northeast Italy. They were glued day and night to the news arriving from what by now was ex-Yugoslavia. They were accustomed to speaking one minute about violence and death and then toss off something like: "We'll relocate to Trieste, we'll rent an apartment, and we'll enroll you in middle school. No, not Zvornik, no, we can't go back there. Which sport would you like to sign up for?"

Not even when Papà Željko and Mamma Selma had begun to focus more on the Italian regional and national news, broadcast in prime time on the state channel RAI, did they manage to get rid entirely of their basic vocabulary, even if, by that time, the whole family had started speaking in a different

FEDERICA MARZI

manner, and not only in a different language. By then, Amila was in high school.

She turned off the computer. She glanced at the new dress lying on her bed.

Where had Simon brought her? No, the question ought to be rephrased. Where would she now be bringing him?

All at once, she felt the perimeter of her happiness beginning to narrow; she'd adapted too easily to finding herself within it. Its outlines had moved while she'd been waiting for time to pass, while she was distracting herself, dreaming, and buying a new, too-expensive dress, while she was searching online for information and unlocking mysteries and truths which perhaps should never have been opened. And now it seemed those outlines had become borderlines.

Majda called, from behind her door—lunch was ready. Amila found herself moving one step forward, then another. She opened up.

"Hey, big sister, what's up? Is everything okay?"

"Sure, sure, everything's fine."

Amila followed her into the living room. A large ceramic bowl of steaming-hot pasta presided over the table.

Mamma Selma announced, "Pasta with butter, okay? It's that or nothing." Furtively, looking at Amila, she said, "C'mon, hand me your plate."

"When will Papà get here?"

"Oh, bless me, girl! Who ever knows that?"

"Just a spoonful for me, please."

"But you need to eat! Food is therapeutic," Mamma Selma said, in her usual dramatic tone.

True. A moment like this did call for one of Mamma Selma's maxims.

Amila sat down at the table and took her plate, piled high with spaghetti, after Mamma Selma had grated some parmigiano over it. So that the pasta would be nourishing. So that they would start chatting about this and that. And so that the history she had just discovered, about a man who might be Simon's long-lost grandfather, would sink back into the depths again, like a stream carving up karst. But the river it fed would later gush out of the earth. That's how those rivers run. You couldn't pretend they would simply disappear into nothing. Somewhere or another, some way or another, they had to come out.

CHAPTER TWENTY-THREE

Opposite Shores
SEPTEMBER 2004, TRIESTE/TRST (ITALY)

AMILA ARRIVED AT the half-empty café in Piazza Cavana for her rendezvous with Simon. He was already there, waiting at a table outside. He was tanned, his hair was longer, and there was a light-colored layer of fuzz over his cheeks. He began to get up, but Amila sat down across from him and put her helmet on a chair between them, like a partition that left the two of them on opposite shores. She took it away, setting it down on the ground.

First curious, then confused, they looked each other over as if they'd known each other in the distant past, and now each needed to examine the other carefully, considering almost every detail, in order to get back in sync.

Amila had decided against the new dress. Simon glanced down at her jeans, ripped at the knee, over which she wore an oversized white shirt. She took off her jacket.

"It's hot again."

Simon leaned back in his chair. Under his wrinkled blue jacket was a T-shirt. He took out a pouch of tobacco, different from the usual color, and rolled a cigarette. "Would you like one?"

Amila nodded. On his thumb, Simon had a wide new metal ring.

A brief moment of silence passed. Amila put out her half-smoked cigarette and gestured to a waitress, so they could order. "A *capo*," she told her. "Would you like a coffee too?" Simon shook his head. So she asked him about his trip.

"Oh well, it was fine."

Amila took off her sunglasses and set them on the table. She hadn't slept well, but it seemed as if Simon hadn't slept at all. He puffed off big clouds of smoke from his second cigarette.

"And how about you?" he asked her.

"Oh, nothing special. I had a lot to do."

The waitress arrived with her order. Simon took out his wallet; Amila told him not to, that she'd do it.

Simon crushed his cigarette in the ashtray, then pushed it away. They stared at each other.

"Look..." Amila began, faltering.

The day that she'd found news about the man she thought was Simon's grandfather, she'd let the phone ring time after time without picking up. Then she'd turned it off. After hours, she decided to call him. Simon had bombarded her with questions, but Amila hadn't wanted to divulge anything to him over the phone. From that moment on, they'd stopped talking, as if, on both sides, there'd been a tacit agreement to interrupt their communications. For that reason, perhaps, the time had seemed longer than it was, which made things more difficult now.

FEDERICA MARZI

Simon set his elbows down on the armrests.

"I'm just going to say it."

Simon wrinkled his brow, hanging on her every word.

"The man who might be your grandfather made a lot of money for himself... during the war. And how he did it wasn't pretty."

Simon leaned forward.

Amila took the pages she'd printed out of her bag. "Take a look."

"What is it?"

"Read it."

Simon slowly leafed through the pages, pausing here and there, as if he could understand the language he was trying to read. Amila had written out translations of some of the headlines, and she'd underlined certain sentences and summarized them for him in Italian. When he got to the photo, he froze. His lips tightened. Amila nodded. Simon continued to stare at the image in black and white. His leg bounced nervously.

"Who is this?"

"It's him. The only photo I could find. His name is Franjo Radonić. He comes from some town, but it doesn't say which, near Umago, just like your grandfather. He spent many years in Argentina."

"Are you joking?"

"Absolutely not." Amila shuffled through the pages until she found the one she needed. Simon rolled another cigarette. "He got married to the daughter of a rich industrialist, which is where his fortune began, it seems. At some point, however, he came back to Croatia. Strange, isn't it? Just before the war began. Which is exactly what Livio and Orietta told us." Simon pursed his lips. "Here they say it was because of violent quarrels with his wife's family."

"And then?"

"It's complicated. The overall impression is that of a shady character tied to a general. You see this guy, Danko Bukić? He was a big deal. He died a year ago."

With trembling hands, Simon began to leaf through the pages again. "And what did this general do?"

"He was accused of crimes against humanity. He directed assaults on towns and villages in a strip of land between Dalmatia and Bosnia. Franjo seemed to have had a role in this story. There weren't any accusations brought against him, or at least no formal charges. But some journalists have pointed at him, suspecting him of being involved in activities that are much more serious than simply selling trucks to the army or snatching up houses abandoned by refugees. That's here, on this page. Some were smuggling, and some were doing the killing... They seem to be separate things, but they always go hand in hand. And in this case, they seem very closely linked. Too closely, in fact."

Simon swallowed. "And who is making these claims?"

Amila stared at him for a moment, confused. "The authors of the articles you have in your hand. There's one source in particular that I think is very reliable..."

"But is there any reference to Australia?"

"No, but..."

"When did these articles come out?"

"Almost all in June."

"So why now?"

"They burned down a bar."

"Where was that?"

"In Zara."

"How old is this guy supposed to be?"

"I don't know." She looked for the page and held it up. "It might be an archival photo, perhaps from a few years ago."

"Do they know where he lives?"

"Probably in Zara, but he's vanished once again." Simon looked at her, questioning. "Don't you see, it's always the same story," Amila added. "He shows up, does something, then disappears without a trace."

"But couldn't it be a man with the same name as my grandfather?"

"The same name?" Amila thought about it for a minute. "Sure, it's possible. After all, his first and last names are fairly common…"

"The last name is written differently."

"Because it's in Croatian. But maybe that was always his real name." Simon didn't seem convinced. "Listen," Amila said. "The photo is the only proof you have. Show it to your grandmother. I don't think there's any other way to figure it out. And then, if it isn't him, so much the better."

Simon took off his glasses and leaned back in his chair. "I can't." He paused for a moment. "She's old now, she's not well, and she might recognize him or not. You don't know how many questions she's already asked me by phone. In other words, with this I'd be creating a real mess, and there'd be no end to it. And then what? And then my mother. Another mess."

"True. And nobody ever wants to create a mess," Amila countered, bitterly. "But they happen. And in this case, it looks to me like there are plenty. I'm sorry, but to my mind there are just too many coincidences. His given name, his family name, his place of birth, his return to the homeland at just the right moment. Fine, there's no reference to Australia, but... they might simply have left it out. He wouldn't necessarily get recognition simply for having emigrated, just like any other poor devil."

"I don't know..." Simon leafed through the material, biting his lip a bit, and then he stopped and looked at a single page, the article about the Eldorado. Then he put everything away. "I'm about to go back to Melbourne..." Amila lowered her eyes.

"Hey, just listen." She looked at him. "I can't go home with a story like this... and, anyway, I really don't understand what we're fighting about."

"We're not fighting. It's just that, if I were in your place, I'd want to know if it was him, that's all."

"Why?"

"For the same reasons that you had. Until a week ago, anyway. I'd want to know what he did in that bloody war. After all ..." She started up again, with even more passion. "You've made it this far. Are you backing down now? Or did everything simply become a bit inconvenient?"

Simon crossed his knees and stared at her. "Could you please tell me why you're so upset about this?"

Amila shook her head vigorously. "I'm not upset."

"It certainly seems that way to me."

Simon wasn't entirely wrong. But the obvious reason her emotions were getting hotter was right in front of her, and it was him, even if she didn't want to say that to him directly. And then, yes, maybe she was upset, but for something that Simon hadn't understood or that she hadn't been able to tell him. In order to tell him all that, she would have had to follow a long and tortuous road into the past. The moment she attempted to start down it, she felt resistance and couldn't bring herself to go farther.

"In any case, I never planned to tell my grandmother anything," added Simon. "Not to mention my mother. So I'm not backing down. But at the moment, I can't keep my thoughts straight, and I'm all out of good ideas."

"I get it. But how do you plan to solve all this in the novel?"

Simon shrugged. "A bit of make-believe."

Amila stared at him. "That's a bad move. I think this is a story that needs some truth."

Simon leaned with his cheek on his hand, and during a long silence, he seemed to reflect on many things, and on everything together. Then he took his tobacco, his lighter, and his rolling papers, put them in his bag along with the bundle of papers, and stood up. "Look, why don't we get out of here? Let's do something. I don't think we want to say goodbye like this." He slung his bag over his shoulder and put on his baseball cap.

Amila stayed seated. She looked at her watch. "Maybe you're right. You can't just force things to happen."

"C'mon," he urged her. "The two of us can tough it out, can't we?"

We're a hard bunch... Amila had already told him that once. How great it would have been to be able to pause for a while, and just relax, not have to tough it out.

Amila stood up and picked up her helmet. "Will it bother you if later on I don't go with you to the train station?"

"Why?" It was obvious this stung.

Amila made a great effort to free herself of her dark, heavy thoughts. "That way, it'll seem like we're going to see each other even sooner, right?"

Part Four

CHAPTER TWENTY-FOUR

Climbing to Cùcolo
MARCH 2005, BRISTIE/BRIŠČE (ITALY)

WINTER DRAGGED ON so long that it seemed interminable, having followed a beautiful and dazzling autumn, a real Indian summer, as Amila liked to call it. And it didn't bring good news.

The first day of the year, Mariano went into the bathroom without using his walker. He became dizzy, the muscles in the leg under his wasted hip contracted, and he lost his balance. Norina found him lying on his stomach, bewildered, and uttering hoarse, incomprehensible complaints. In the days that followed, the hip got worse. The pain was acute and unbearable. And all of this weight bore down on the old, hunched-over back of Norina.

Mariano spent his days in bed, taking pain medication and sleeping pills so he could rest at night. It was lucky that his mind was as lucid as always, but his thought processes changed, along with his moods. The doctor said straight-out that Mariano was depressed, that dealing with the *"ssyche* was tricky business. Norina understood what he was telling her. Mariano had been feeling down, ever since the youngsters they'd had around that summer had gone away. She'd always thought she would be the one who gave up, but instead it was him. Such are the lovely surprises that old age has in store for everyone.

By the time February arrived, Norina couldn't take any more. The sleepless nights had sapped her strength, and the countless responsibilities made it impossible to breathe. Getting Mariano's pills and capsules, remembering each at the required hour. Something boiling on the stove, but forgetting it until the water evaporates and the pan burns. Twenty-five drops of bromazepam in a glass of water. Take it upstairs. In a hurry, legs dragging; the stairs up and down are long, with junk packed into every corner. Sorting through another pile, but all that does is serve as a reminder of how many others are waiting for their turn. No, Norina couldn't take any more. So one night, she got up the nerve and called Amila.

She wanted to assure her immediately; she wasn't asking for the same number of hours as during the summer. The nurses from the local hospital came daily, Anika stopped by often, and she was taking care of the housework. They'd been looking for some permanent help, but so far they hadn't found anyone.

Amila interrupted her and bluntly said no.

Norina didn't surrender. She specified that she was only looking for company, one morning a week, just to raise Mariano's spirits, and also so that she could take an occasional walk in the woods.

Amila listened and then repeated for the second and last time no.

Norina tried to make her point again with Mariano.

"*If she told you no, it's no.*" He ended the discussion, wagging his finger in front of her face.

Norina, sitting on the edge of the bed, shrank backward, like a young girl trying to hold back tears after a scolding.

The next day, she typed in the number again, from behind the bedroom door. She and Mariano had no time to lose. She walked into the room, handing the phone to Mariano, who was sitting on the bed, a copy of the newspaper on his knees.

"Amila."

Mariano glared at Norina, staring over the top of his glasses, as he did whenever he said she'd gone gaga, *insenpiada*. Then he gestured: she should leave the room.

Norina didn't know what they said to each other, except that it went well. Amila agreed to come back, but just on Saturday mornings and only for a few weeks.

As soon as she arrived, Amila asked Norina if she'd looked for or found someone permanent to help out, do housework, take care of the garden, and get groceries. She also asked, with a face like a harsh schoolteacher, whether Norina really understood the gravity of this situation. Or maybe she looked more like a niece or a daughter, as Norina liked to imagine her, someone who was laying down the law—as if she'd been a relative who risked having to assume full responsibility for aging family members. But Norina wasn't fooling herself. Amila would only be staying for a short while. She wasn't a daughter or a niece, and she didn't owe them anything.

In February, however, something else happened: Norina discovered the internet. She and Mariano had changed places at the desk. It was now Norina's territory, and she asked Amila to teach her to use the computer.

"You turn it on by pushing the button," Amila explained, without batting an eye. Amila was sitting next to her, just as she used to do with Mariano, but without the patience she once had. "Don't wear it out. Wait for it to finish loading."

Norina nodded obediently.

"Do you see the blue 'e'? Good, I'll introduce you to the internet." Amila pushed her chair backward on its rollers. "You need to double-click on that icon."

"*Like this?*" Norina pressed two times on the key of the mouse, as she'd seen Mariano, Simon, and Amila do a thousand times, but it didn't work for her. How could that be? Amila was already standing up. She placed her hand over Norina's, so that she'd see how to move her index finger. Norina nodded, even if she felt she hadn't understood a damned thing.

"You can write whatever you want in the search box. When you hit the return key, that sends it, then the whole world appears." Amila started off toward the door, then turned around again. "Double-click, okay?"

"*Wait a sec*." But Amila was gone already. Blessed girl. Norina liked it better back when Amila was laughing and making fun of everything.

Norina made an effort and started researching Mariano's medicine, its dosage and side effects, and she even found recommended treatments for insomnia. Incredible—everything was written there. She tried a search for "Moonee Ponds," the neighborhood where Nevia lived, which from her photos looked very pretty and modern. Her sister had spent the winter at the

FEDERICA MARZI

public hospital being treated for asthma. By now, she ought to be there, at home.

Then she noticed the icon for Mariano's email, and it was a real temptation. Amila had said double-click, right? The list of messages from Nevia appeared, interrupted by a pair from Simon. They were from back in August, and she had already read all of them. Nevia and Mariano, though, had also exchanged messages in October and November, and then again in December, up until just before his fall. Her eyebrows tightened until they were deeply furrowed, and she felt a spasm of sharp pain shooting from the center of her forehead.

Probably you needed to do the same in order to open the first email message on the list. It worked, but it scared Norina, as if she'd just seen the devil, even though these were only her own sister's words. She glanced at them, distracted by the feeling that she shouldn't be looking at a message that wasn't written to her. Giving in to her sense of panic, she moved the mouse rapidly, clicking wildly, and found herself back at the desktop screen. She bit down on her lip. At least she'd understood. She looked around furtively. On the bed was a pile of laundry for her sick husband, washed but not ironed—pajamas, underwear, sheets. She cupped her ear, but beyond the door she heard only the usual silence. Good. She was alone.

She clicked on the email icon again and found her way back to her sister's chitchat, which mostly talked about Simon. Norina widened her eyes, and her heart began to beat wildly. Nevia was recounting how Simon was working for a famous lawyer in Melbourne, and how much the lawyer liked him, and how he was teaching Simon his trade. He wore a jacket and tie now and came back home late every night.

Norina was really proud of this nephew lawyer who was dressing so nicely. The realization of a dream that was practically her own.

Her eyes began to notice the list of commands. She clicked, and suddenly a blank square appeared. The cursor where she was supposed to type in something pulsated intermittently, echoing her heartbeat. She tried to type with her index finger, without worrying about capitalization. Just gimmicks. And she wrote: "ciao its me, norina."

She clicked on the only button that said "send." She didn't have any idea whether what she was doing was sending or receiving or what might happen. She then found herself back looking at the same list as before, but with one additional address in boldface, waltermobili.

Norina shook her head, convinced that her words had been cannibalized, either by the computer or by that waltermobili. Offended, she pulled the plug out from the wall, as if she were condemning that number-crunching machine to death.

A few days later, she obediently sat down again in front of the screen. The computer slowly loaded its programs, spitting out incomprehensible formulae in white across the black screen, until she began to worry. But eventually everything was working again. When she opened the email program, an address appeared: nevia.benci.

It was Nevia, really her, and thank heavens that she'd stopped with the "my dearest sister." She'd written simply: "Norina, is that you?"

She answered spontaneously. Yes, it was her. Sent it, then turned off the computer.

And that was how Norina and Nevia began to speak with each other again, after so many years, within a virtual world they'd discovered almost at the same time. Initially, they exchanged only a few sentences, simply to verify their identities to each other. Norina was the first to tell the story of Mariano's accident. Then she decided to ask for news about Simon. He never called her, and it seemed, in Melbourne, that he didn't even have time to go to see Nevia.

Norina couldn't even have explained it to herself, but now that she didn't need to write actual letters, and there wasn't any more mail on blue onionskin paper, it had become easier to accept news from this new world. The computer gave both sisters a different voice, and this one didn't sound so bad. And from one thing came another. Norina thought of little else. Go see if there's email, she'd tell herself. It was definitely more interesting than watching television.

For days they continued to tell each other aunt and grandmother stories, bit by bit with Nevia more in charge of the situation, even though Norina behaved as if she knew a lot about it.

Simon was working long hours; he even had to go to the office on Sundays. But Nevia was worried about him; something seemed off. She wrote that he appeared distracted, distant, perhaps because Ann was always after him about something, and that annoyed him. That daughter of hers was too restless and apprehensive.

Each morning the flurry of emails intensified, though it was only morning for Norina and evening for Nevia. At times they would be writing at the same moment, which to Norina felt like a perfectly executed magic trick, since it saved her from the anxiety of waiting for a response.

Nevia also began to ask questions, and Norina began to answer. For example, she asked about that girl in the photos that Mariano and Simon had sent last summer, photos that she was keeping in an old cookie tin. Norina could finally contribute something of her own, in her own voice, since Amila and Simon had met in Trieste, and in that period they both belonged to her.

Oh, Amila is beautiful, really beautiful, Norina bragged to her sister.

Nevia asked about the girl's name.

I think it's Bosnian, Norina replied, even if she wasn't so sure, since it sounded very Italian. And that's when Nevia wrote something she shouldn't have. "For Simon—I'm sure of this—Amila is our homeland, recalling him. He loves her, I can feel that, but the two of them are far apart. We have to help these youngsters. No one ever helped us. That's why so many things didn't come out the way they should've."

With that Norina understood. She wasn't safe, not even with a computer. She pulled the plug on it again. Nevia had pushed too far; she'd gone and hit against something she never should've touched. What did she know about homelands? What right did she have to call this land hers, after she'd abandoned it? And Norina would also like to know what she meant by "recall," since people don't say that, they say "call." And love? Nevia had no right to even say the word.

No, Nevia should never have said those things, even if it was inevitable that, sooner or later, this all had to end with some sort of allusion to the one fact above all in life that had separated them. The fact of loving the same man—and that Nevia had gone where she wanted, whereas Norina, who hadn't wanted to, stayed where she was. When the discussion happened to land there, Norina felt like running and slamming shut every peephole into that world, like a contemptuous, merciless jailer.

This time, however, in the middle of it all they had Simon in common—the same blood as theirs, the only Australian who was also Istrian. Norina always felt herself in second place, and it wasn't fair, according to her, since she had been the first. But that's how it was.

She was too old, that was the truth, and now it was time to give in. She wasn't saying she would forgive and forget, not yet, but she would at least keep talking.

Amila startled her at the door to the kitchen, carrying a steaming teapot by the handle. Norina was trying to pull herself together. Amila looked her over, sternly, as if Norina were a small child with a runny nose. Amila seemed to be in a bad mood, so she definitely wouldn't stay and hear her out.

"*I'm going*," Norina said, as a way to excuse herself. She clapped, and Luli came running.

Amila answered with her usual, "Yes, of course," making it clear she wasn't planning on wasting time with Norina's bad moods and complaints. That girl had a big heart, but you could tell she was fed up.

Soon after, Norina was back in the woods. Winter was gone. Only the wintery climate of her home had not.

"You're free!" Luli raced off. "Go on, run!"

Where the path forked, her dog turned and sniffed. Norina called to her, "To Cùcolo!" Luli leaped forward, with her ears lowered and alert.

Norina's footsteps were muted by the soft ground covered in pine needles and layers of dried, rotting leaves, packed down by winter hikers. The ancient pines with their umbrellalike crowns seemed to touch the sky, leaving rays of light filtering through to warm her shoulders. The evergreen holm oaks created patches of dark cover; below it was still damp, and the cold tickled Norina's nose.

Before taking the path that climbed up, Norina followed Luli along a side trail. They wound up on a ridge of gray rock, a cliff overlooking the evergreen woods below. The sun was blinding. The sea was vast, a carpet of rippling silver, a beehive made of tiny, iridescent cells. Only the gray spirals and lines sketched across its surface reminded one that it was still March and the water must still be freezing.

This was Norina's favorite part of the hike: the chance to plant her boots in the slick stones, feeling that she still knew how to keep her balance. Between sea and sky.

Luli had clambered up to the highest holm oaks—trees holding tightly to the rocks, leaning over the void, with strands of their roots exposed. That was Mount Cùcolo. You couldn't find that name on the internet, but Norina had heard it from one of the town's old cranks. He'd talked to her about the time, during World War I, when the Austrians had invaded those woods.

Ever since then, she'd called that place Cùcolo. And she was *cùcola* too: a perpendicular form with a steep drop, slanted slightly, leaning on her staff.

The clouds had scattered and thickened behind her, behind the rounded peak of the mountain. It was raining in Friuli. Along the border of the Grado lagoon, you could see the coves and canals clearly, even the trees and houses. Extending in the other direction was Istria, with its tapered cliffs, hemmed in by reflected light from the horizon. Norina straightened her back and breathed deeply, filling her lungs.

She continued on to the lookout. From there she took a path down over gray rocks that echoed under the heels of her old leather boots. From time to time, in the brush, you could glimpse a trench, part of a bunker built from dry stone. In other spots, there were long, narrow limestone sinkholes. The forest had reclaimed the relics of war, softening them, wearing them away entirely and covering them in moss and foliage. Nature always conquers where humanity creates catastrophes. We should learn from her.

Norina noted wild asparagus that had grown as high as her hips. They'd pushed up out of the earth to show off their crisp, dark growth. The oaks were a tangle of knotty and still-bare branches; they were covered in small buds, nuclei ready to thicken and explode. Signs of life left in earthly things.

Norina used her stick to inspect some of the bushes. It was still too early to harvest the asparagus. She took up a handful of crumbly brown soil and closed her fist around it tightly, as she had done once before, as a youngster, before crossing the border between Yugoslavia and Italy. This time, though, she wouldn't leave it behind.

Land. "Our homeland," Nevia had typed. Norina was still angered by the expression. And now Norina could feel the soil of that land inside her hand, on her side, with whatever call it might still be able to release. It certainly wasn't much, but for her it could be everything, and to her it seemed that it might, for the first time, make a big difference in her life.

So if it were true that, for Simon, Amila was the land calling him back, and he loved her, as Nevia had written, then she needed to understand once and for all what had happened between the two of them. Norina would have to go back home and find some way to talk to the girl face-to-face. And then she would have to plug in the computer again and email Nevia immediately.

CHAPTER TWENTY-FIVE

An Answer for Every Question
MARCH 2005, BRISTIE/BRIŠČE (ITALY)

AMILA DIDN'T FEEL too good that day. Not that she wanted to be curt or impatient with Norina; she was just overcome by an incredible sense of confusion. She'd been wrong to go back to that house, even if Papà Željko had told her it was the right thing to do. She'd bowed to her father's principles, steamrolled by his sense of social justice and responsibility. Being there, though, in that house in Bristie, forced her to remember.

Everything at Norina's reminded Amila of Simon. And when they were in touch, all he did was complain: his job was a meat grinder, his boss was a prison warden, and holidays were crumbs that weren't enough for a trip to Trieste, even at Christmas. She kept telling him to write and focus on the novel. And he, too, kept repeating "write," meaning for the paper.

In the meantime, they got by on phone calls, emails, and texts at a set hour, because of the difference in time zones. Here it was morning and evening there, or vice versa, and that forced them to follow a rigid schedule, which occasionally broke down.

The appointment would be reduced to a short text message, arriving in the middle of the night. Trying to keep the relationship going like this was exhausting.

Amila had tried confiding in Olga, hoping for encouragement, expecting she would say, "Enjoy life. The world is full of boys." But this time, her cousin had thrown her a curveball. Over the phone, Olga told her, "Sweetheart, you're definitely in love!" She added, giggling, "We're going to have to send you to Australia. Finally, you'll get to live in a civilized country."

That prospect was seeming more and more unlikely, for her and for her family. Mamma Selma and Papà Željko had had to leave on an emergency trip to Zvornik. Miran, their former downstairs neighbor, had called to let them know that their old apartment in the Russian Building had flooded. After hearing him out, Papà Željko nodded, thanked him, and hung up their cordless phone.

He sat down at the head of the table. With an ashen face, he said, "We have to sort all this out."

Like a scalpel, his declaration had reopened an old wound and revealed a new question in their lives.

"We need to sell—just as it is now, like others are doing." Selling, or practically giving it away, if the decision had already been made—they wouldn't be going back. Selling and buying something to call their own. Selling and no longer living in a rental apartment in Trieste. Selling and settling down. Selling and getting rid of their summer apartment in Marijin Dvor too.

"What are you talking about? It's our house, we have to save it!" Mamma Selma insisted, trying to keep from sobbing.

They all began talking at the same time—no one could understand anything. Majda complained that having so many houses made her feel schizophrenic, that none of them should complain if she developed a personality disorder. Amila said the problem wasn't their three houses, and everyone should be free to live wherever they wanted. After all, they were all grownups. Papà Željko gave her a cutting glare, and Mamma Selma put her hand in front of her mouth, just as she did back during the dark times.

Up until now, the unshakable uncertainty about what to do with their Zvornik property had kept them quiet. But now the apartment was not only there, theirs again and empty, it was flooded. Given this additional problem, it now seemed inevitable that something would have to happen. And when the minimal supplies they needed for their emergency trip were packed and put by the door, Amila's anxiety began to build.

Having an apartment in Zvornik didn't make any sense, but that didn't make it any less of an obsession. It was back in the place where she was born, but also somewhere she felt like she'd never even been. She hadn't seen it since they'd gotten it back. She knew it was in an impressive block of apartments, and that it had a hive-like series of windows framed by brick-colored paint and unbroken rows of balconies on its light-colored facade. Or so her memories suggested—clear on some things, fuzzy on others. Their apartment was on the seventh floor. To get in, you needed to go around a corner, then past one entryway, and their door was the one after that.

To cross the street and get to the river, you had to take a raised walkway. Mamma Selma would say enigmatically that the Drina's left bank is in Bosnia and its right in Serbia, and it flows northward—as if that saying summed up the direction of their history and the destiny of their country. But Amila had never been able to imagine a river that flowed in what was—according to her mother—the opposite direction. She had grown up in a seaside city and knew nothing about the direction of rivers and the stories they had to tell.

"Mamma, get ready," Papà Željko had said in that apartment, years ago, after coming in and slamming the door. "We have to pack and leave by the end of the week."

This was Amila's clearest memory of her first home, perhaps because it was also the last. She could see again the brown leather couch, including the creases in its armrests and the crocheted doily across the back. Memory works in strange ways. Enormous black holes and then a few photographic images of insipid details.

Mamma Selma was stretched out on the couch, a bag of ice resting on her forehead. Majda was sitting on the floor, drawing. Amila should have been sitting on the carpet too, but she couldn't remember why. Maybe to do her homework; she'd bet on that. They were all performing rituals that they would repeat in many other homes or places that weren't home, in other living rooms, or in the common room of the refugee center, rituals that remained—when all was said and done—always the same.

"Do me a favor, Željko," replied Mamma Selma, without even bothering to look at him. "Spare me your jokes for once. I have a terrible migraine. I can tell you for sure, spring is coming."

"No, war is coming. Miran said that Serb families are getting ready to leave the city."

Mamma Selma sat up with a jolt. The bag of ice fell to the floor with a thud. "What? Who? Miran? The janitor at your school?"

"Why? How many Mirans do we know?"

"Just one."

"He says it's probably going to become dangerous for Muslims."

Mamma Selma went pale. "What are you saying? Which Muslims, which Serbs?"

"The ones the politicians have been talking about for months now."

Everyone had heard it, right? The October speech Radovan Karadžić had made in Parliament prior to the elections. If it separates from Yugoslavia, Bosnia-Herzegovina will be taking the "highway to hell."

"But what ideas have all of you been putting into your heads?" Mamma Selma said.

"Look what happened in Croatia. And it isn't over. They've been deployed for months now. It's about to happen here too. Just like Vukovar, like Dubrovnik. . ."

"What nonsense! And today while I went shopping, while I cooked all afternoon, so that you'd find dinner ready, and you, what do you do? You come home late!"

"We have to leave."

"Because Miran told you to?"

"He's a friend."

"What about school?"

"They'll be closing the schools soon."

"Where can we go?"

"We'll go across the bridge with Miran, and we'll stay with Darko and Ivana."

"Darko and Ivana from Belgrade? Friends of friends, and only acquaintances for us?"

"In this business, friends will be needed. I've already called them, and they've agreed. After that we'll need to get across the border and go to Hungary."

"I don't want to go to Hungary! I've never been there. The language is horrible, plus we don't have a single Hungarian friend."

"Listen, Mamma. I'm known all over Zvornik for my pacifist philosophy. But I swear that if you don't get moving and pack your bags, I'll tie your legs together and carry you away with me like a salami. This will not be the moment where you finally get free of old Željko. In Hungary, you'll be able to ask for a divorce, if you want."

"If that's the reason, Zvornik also has plenty of good lawyers. Because we're only going away for a little while, right?"

To this question, there was no answer.

Mamma Selma spent her last days making the house shine from top to bottom, along with blowing her nose every five minutes. "A spring cold," she complained. "An April headache." Amila wandered in circles around her, asking if she needed any help. But her mother would say no. No, no, go away.

Even Papà Željko, who always said crying didn't do any good, was crying in secret in the bathroom. Amila asked him why, and instead of giving her an answer, Željko took her downstairs straightaway, to Miran's, so she would leave her mother alone. Amila and Majda had always played with Miran's daughter, Nevena. The adults had conspired to get the girls to leave them in peace, so they could continue to cry and pack their bags, without feeling as if they needed to explain anything to anyone.

Whenever Amila told this story in Italy, explaining how Nevena's family had helped hers to leave five days before the tanks arrived and the National Army barricaded the bridge, she realized she was simply confusing even further minds accustomed to thinking only about clearly drawn lines and straightforwardly tragic stories. Once a film director had showed up at the refugee center in Jesolo; he'd wanted to make a documentary about them. Mamma Selma laughed and said, "Yes, of course, why not!" whereas Papà Željko explained how in Yugoslavia, at least up until the war, everyone could be friends with everybody, undisturbed. This gave their story a different meaning, plus it had also been shaped by a number of peculiar coincidences. But that young beanpole director with a vaguely hippie disposition never showed his face again. Perhaps for him there were only unhappy and incomprehensible aberrations in the story of how Yugoslavia ended.

The sudden flooding of the apartment near the Drina all at once blew up many of the levees that shape this story.

A story about Nevena, the last friend Amila had played with in Zvornik, the friend who had saved her life. Amila remembered two braids hanging down around a lively little face, a face that never really managed to pull its features together. For Amila, it brought to mind the Italian expression "argento vivo"—quicksilver. Nevena must've had it in her blood. She'd spent her early childhood in Serbia. She'd returned to Zvornik when the war in Bosnia was over and the bombing of Belgrade had begun.

As far as she knew, Nevena was the only one out of all the kids her age who stayed in the Russian Building. Amila had played with them all, celebrated their birthdays, even if the most fun they had was in running up and down the long staircase in order to provoke old man Stjepan, who lived on the top floor and who, everyone said, hated snot-nosed kids. Sanela, Lejla, Suada, Nenad, Emir, Siniša, Fehim, Otilija, Zoran, Aleksandar. Had she forgotten anyone?

The kids born in Bosnia in 1984 had disappeared, not only from the building, but also from the streets, from classes, and from the gyms of Zvornik—like so many black holes. "Missing" (one of the first English words the children learned), or else gone somewhere or other.

Some were without their papà or an older brother, others without their mamma. Some with shrapnel from a shell in their eye or stuck in their shoulder. Some went to friends or relatives in Croatia. Some went to Belgrade. Some with, and some now without, a passport. Some in Germany, with a mother or father who suffered from bouts of depression. Some were studying important things, like computer science or medicine, in some capital city in the West. Some came from a mixed family and got sent to whichever part of the country seemed better, which meant neither. Some had become champions in a sport they'd already started practicing in elementary school, fulfilling an old vow. Some never became anything, because they'd never made any vows. Some boarded a bus and were delivered to the International Red Cross. Some went to Hungary and stayed there. Some had relatives or distant family who went through Karakaj, and who didn't want, or didn't know how, to talk about it. Some were doing well, some not well, and both stayed well away from Bosnia. Some were beginning to come back for summer vacations. Some were returning, instead, to live on other streets with a new name and their signs in Cyrillic, that you might or might not understand. And some were coming back, but were moving to Sarajevo. And then some, like Olga, were staying in one of the hyperperfect cities in the north of Europe, where life was good, though happiness was something else entirely. No one, though, except Nevena, stayed in the Russian Building. Amila had no idea what had happened to those long braids of hers.

And Amila?

Amila had done the same as the others. The same as those friends with an abruptly interrupted childhood, who couldn't have become enemies, but who also could no longer be called friends. They had been too young during that time. They lived through everything from their own point of view, finishing elementary school, getting cured or operated on, playing in refugee centers, learning to live in another part of the world or learning to put up with a distressing postwar period with no real prospects. All of them continuing to see and hear things that kids their age shouldn't have to see and hear. But naturally no one had thought about children like them in that sense. About these kids, who might represent the future, or the lack of future, of postwar Bosnia, and who had left their old apartment near the Drina forever.

Now they were scattered around the world. Amila was one of them. They shared a common destiny, a seesaw that continued to tilt between decision and indecision.

The Ivo Andrić story "A Letter from 1920" came to mind; Amila had first read it in middle school and then again in high school. According to Papà Željko, that was too soon; she wouldn't yet be able to understand. But, in fact, she'd understood perfectly, because it was a dialogue about kids of different ages, about those who stayed behind and others who never went back: "No, no, you'll come back for sure. While, all my life long, I'll be struggling with the memory of Bosnia, as if with some Bosnian disease. What the cause of it is—the fact that I was born and grew up in Bosnia, or that I'll never be coming back again, I don't even know myself. Not that it matters."

That last sentence had shaken Amila, as if it were a seal placed onto her life. A question with no answer, other than that nothing mattered.

Papà Željko always said that every question had an answer. As a teacher, he wasn't able to accept when answers were unknown. And whenever he didn't know them, he would do the same as every other professor anywhere. He'd invent one then and there.

The same thing also happened with many of the important questions Amila put to grown-ups, when she was still a Bosnian kid and after she became an Italian girl. But one was more important than the others: How could this have happened? That question had never stopped echoing in her head, not even as a young *dijasporka*.

With time, since the grown-ups weren't talking, she tried to come up with an answer of her own. But she never managed to find one that satisfied her. Instead, she simply tried to forget everything that had happened to her country, just as the other ex-Bosnian kids must have done. And to forget as well some things that—given the date on her birth certificate—she couldn't possibly remember. Including the memory of Nevena playing with her—and with her dolls, perhaps—at a time when, smoking and crying, the grown-ups were bargaining with peace and war, safety and death.

In other moments, Amila turned the question around. But in that case, from that angle, everything became even more difficult. Who were the ones responsible for the war? What were they thinking, where were they living, and what were they telling their children at night? Did they also pretend not to know the answers? And, above all, what would they have to say to someone like her?

Amila ground out her cigarette on the top step of the stairs, which were flooded by sunlight. The oak tree was magnificent, an exultation of bare branches, towering and tangled at the limits with the sky. She picked up a handful of cigarette butts from the ground, so Norina wouldn't get mad. She still didn't know that Amila had started smoking. She brushed away the ashes with the bottom of her shoe. She went back inside and made to go up to the second floor. She opened the door to the bedroom, turning the doorknob quietly. Mariano was lying on his side. His uncombed thicket of white hair stuck out from under the covers. He was breathing deeply.

She went back to the kitchen and scribbled a note, making it as polite as possible. She didn't have a car—her folks had gone back to Bosnia to deal with an emergency. She needed to use the Panda for some urgent business. She apologized profusely for the inconvenience, and promised to return the car that evening.

She put on her parka and wrapped her scarf around the jacket without zipping it up. The keys for the Panda were hanging on a hook next to the door, where they always could be found. She grabbed them without a second thought.

She closed the front door quietly and squeezed into the Panda. Backing up two or three times, she managed to get out of the tight parking space. She went through the gate without wasting even a moment to stop and close it. First she would have to go back home and get her passport.

She tried to recall the road that led to the stone house where, some time ago, the man whom Simon continued to call Franco had been living. The main point. For Simon, but now a point in relation to her life as well. She was the one who'd bumped into him, who'd tracked him down—at first, almost as a game, even if it was anything but.

Amila wanted to go to the town where, according to Livio and Orietta, that man had gone back to live, at least for some time. She wanted to meet him, ask him some questions, and learn something from him that no theory could explain, but which, from now on, might be able to make sense of her life.

Probably what she was about to do was absurd, and yet she felt she couldn't do anything else. Perhaps this was what it meant to go and meet your destiny. But in her case, she thought, it was destiny coming to meet her.

CHAPTER TWENTY-SIX

Finis Terrae

MARCH 2005, BUROLI/BUROLI (CROATIA)

AT FIRST THE trip was a succession of white stripes painted on burning asphalt and, behind Amila, a truck driver flashing his lights to make her drive faster. After she crossed the first border, the road up the hill had patches of new grass on its edges, growing along with the dried stalks; in some spots, there were masses of these translucent threads blowing in the wind. At every roundabout, signs declared the names of towns no one would recognize, but only one of them led in the right direction. Once she'd passed the suburbs of Capodistria, there was a solid line of bare treetops and branches that showed wear and tear from tangling and untangling themselves. They were in sharp contrast with the dazzling sky, their outlines lacing it in black, immobile in their seasonal necrosis. A white, flowering tree suddenly interrupted the wall of scrub brush. Her heart skipped a beat.

The second border was an open stretch of asphalt, located downhill and surrounded by a row of enormous billboards. A red arrow pointed toward the last *menjalnica*, a currency exchange booth, as if that were the final sanctuary before setting off into no-man's-land. It was closed. There were no other cars. A police officer with pimply cheeks took his time looking over her passport, opening it and closing it again. He looked at her residency permit.

Then another stretch of road and a second glass-walled sentry booth to drive by, after the parade of flags with that red-and-white checkerboard shield. A flurry of messages arrived on her phone, welcoming her to Croatia.

The land was as it always had been, the soil brown and familiar, right up to Buie, which Amila reached after making the climb. The small city loomed above her, with its pair of steeples. After the intersection, she took the road down across the farmland. She knew she'd arrived when the soil became red as rust. It had been plowed into large, moist clumps. She passed by rolling, well-ordered rows of bare, twisted vines. Next were olive trees with iridescent foliage and piles of pruned branches at their feet. The light was different in this part of the world.

Amila turned into Buroli. She parked next to the signpost and continued up by foot, following a line of houses. There was the fresh scent of laundry in the air. Rows of savoy cabbage in the coarse earth marked the borders of the gardens. Late for this time of year. A dog barked.

The house where the man might be was at the edge of dense woods. Amila wasn't sure that she'd found the right place, in part because this time the door within the stone arch was open. A Mercedes was parked next to the house. Outside, a tall man, followed by a medium-sized brown dog, was crossing a fallow field, carrying a spade. He was wearing a gray coat that made him look like a priest, over a dirty pair of work jeans. His white hair came down to his shoulders. The dog growled as Amila came closer.

"Shussh!" the man shouted, making the dog run off. He looked Amila over.

"Buongiorno," she said to him. Her voice trembled. "I'm looking for Signor Franjo Radonić. I've been told he owns this home."

"Who is looking for him?"

"I need to speak to him about a family matter. Does he live here?"

The man stepped toward her. Amila backed up a bit. "I'm a friend of Simon. Simon Monforte, the grandson of Nevia Benci and Franjo Radonić. Long ago they all lived in Buie. Now they're in Australia."

The man scowled. "But who are you?"

"A friend of the family."

"And your name is?"

"Amila."

He watched her, squinting fiercely, as if he wanted to see her more clearly. "Amila what?"

Amila shook her head. "I'm just a friend. Not a member of the family."

"Amila, Amila," he repeated, irritated. "Where are you from?"

"From Trieste."

"Trieste?"

His eyes, which were a strange color of gray and became at times darker than blue, flashed a glint of mirth. His eyes were still young. They beamed haughtily down from his wrinkled face, with its high, marked cheekbones. Amila knew she had seen those eyes before, not just on the internet. She must have also seen them in Simon.

A woman wearing an apron and a scarf over her hair appeared in a courtyard across the way; it was full of rough-hewn tables, wheelbarrows, and farm equipment. "Dio, Franjo!" she called.

Amila flinched.

The man didn't respond to her salutation and didn't take his eyes off of Amila.

"Ha!" He lifted up a corner of his mouth in scorn. "A brazen case of beginner's luck! I'm Franjo Radonić."

It had seemed impossible, and yet was all too possible. It was him.

"What did you want to talk about?" Franjo's Italian sounded natural. A slight foreign accent, which might come from any language, occasionally slipped into his clear words and fluent phrases.

"About your grandson. He has gone back to Australia, but he had been looking for you."

"I don't have a grandson."

"I can explain. If you could wait a moment, I have a photo." Amila opened the zipper of her purse.

"I told you, I don't know him. I have work to do." He took back the shovel, which was leaning on a low wall, and continued on toward the brush.

Out of the corner of her eye, Amila looked for the elderly peasant woman. She was still there, pottering around in her storage area. So this wasn't a ghost town after all. It had its busybodies, and some low chatter in the background. She tried calling him back: "Excuse me! Excuse me, please!" But he didn't turn around. Amila didn't move.

Franjo reappeared, without his shovel, after walking around the house. He came forward slowly, then stopped, checking to see where the old woman was.

"I don't talk about anything with anyone in public," he declared. "Inside, if at all," he added, with a distrustful look.

"That's fine," Amila said. "As you like."

"Go ahead," he urged her, waving the dog over to the door. "Shussh!"

Amila hesitated for a few seconds. Then she followed him.

Given his stature, Franjo filled nearly the entire opening of the doorway. Before going inside, he wiped his hands on his pants. Amila found herself in a small dining room with a single window, its shutters open, but little light coming through. A curtain served to divide the space in two. There was a fire in the *sparcher*, with a sharp smell of something that had burned. Amila heard the door close behind her. The room darkened, and then Franjo turned on the lights.

"Please sit there." He indicated a rough-hewn table of unfinished wood. He quickly set out two bottles and a glass, pouring himself a golden-colored liquid. He drank a sip and clicked his tongue. His mutt was lying under the table, at his master's feet, his muzzle between his paws.

Amila did her best to look at him calmly, but she felt as if the sound of her heartbeat echoed through the entire room.

"So, you have a photo?"

She rummaged through her purse and held it out to him, the only photo she had, taken months earlier, by Livio in Buie. It caught Simon before he had a chance to pose. "That's Simon."

The man took the photo and looked it over. Then he set it back down nonchalantly on the table. "No. It doesn't tell me anything."

"Are you certain of that?"

Amila sat straight up in her seat, without touching the backrest. Her hands held tightly to the handle of her purse.

"Did they send you here?"

"No, I came on my own."

"But who are you? And why are you speaking to me in Italian?"

Once again those eyes began to squint, staring at her as if they wanted to drill through her.

"Italian is my language."

"What, are you joking? Where are you from? From your name, I'd say Bosnia."

"I was born in Zvornik."

The man was searching through his memories, circling around her like a hunter with prey. The silence was unbearable. "I've never been in that region. But I know it was a real shit show." Franjo wiped his mouth with the back of his hand and poured himself some grappa.

"Listen..."

Franjo raised his eyebrows sharply. "I think we've said enough."

"Simon has done some research. He wants to know something about the world his grandparents came from."

"The world has changed," he retorted, clearly annoyed. "Australia, Australia! What the hell do you all want from me now?"

"Simon wanted to know if you were alive."

"You see that with your own eyes."

Franjo turned toward the *sparcher*, opening its door and adjusting the flame. The plaster had blackened. Next to that old woodstove, there was a brand-new kitchen stove and, hanging on the wall, two copper pots. He filled his glass again.

"C'mon, out with it, why did you come here?"

"I told you. Your relatives are looking for you."

"They're not my relatives!"

"According to everyone in that family, Ann is your daughter."

Franjo sneered. "Born like every other child in this world." He began to get up.

"Wait. Simon is no longer in Europe. He's gone back. But your story...your story interests me." The man looked at her attentively. "I would like to ask you about the war. That war concerns me and my family. I need to know some things."

"I wasn't in the war." He downed the contents of his glass. "I just know that war only always brings you shit."

"For some people, though, it also brought money." This voice seemed to come out of some other, second self. "I read in the papers about the Eldorado."

Franjo slapped his hand down on the table. "You are a journalist!"

"I'm not a journalist."

"Fucking demons from hell! The hell you're not!"

"I've told you I'm not."

From one side of the curtain, a child popped up. The man turned toward her. Her black hair fell over her shoulders. Her large, almond-shaped eyes stared at him, amused. She wore a sky-blue dress with bell-shaped sleeves. She had no socks or shoes.

"Shussh!" Franjo held up his index finger, commandingly.

The little girl paid him no attention, as if he were the least important being on earth and not a boss or commander; she continued to watch the scene, giggling. Amila was especially interesting to her. She looked at her, her eyes wide open. Only after she was bored with this novelty, and after Franjo had begun to shout, "Antonia, Antonia!" did the girl disappear behind the curtain, like a pixie.

Franjo moistened his lips. "The Eldorado is gone. I don't think there's anything more to say."

"Except for some small details."

"Oh yes?" he egged her on.

"I read about Za.dr.Transp." The man seemed indifferent. "I would like to know what role you played in the business."

Franjo's features seemed to change from moment to moment. He was young, he was old, he didn't bat an eyelid, he growled, and above all he was enjoying himself. He turned up a corner of his mouth. "Why should I tell you anything?"

"If you don't have anything to hide . . ."

"No, nothing."

"You were Danko Bukić's business partner. He was wanted by the Hague Tribunal for political and ethnic violence, for homicide, looting. . ."

"The Hague Tribunal! Ha!" he spat out, livid. "A tribunal with no jurisdiction. Western judges that speak English and have never even set foot in the Balkans."

"Some people have argued that you and Bukić organized everything together and divided up the jobs."

"Completely false."

"But you did know where your trucks were going and what they would be used for?"

"Trucks roll over asphalt in peacetime and in war."

Amila swallowed. "In '95, those trucks were used to occupy villages and towns and loot them."

"Really? Where?"

"You must know already."

"Since you know everything, why don't you tell me?"

"In the Krajina. Along a triangle of roads between Drniš, Knin, and Kistanje."

"Krajina? I don't recognize any place called Krajina. You're referring to Lika, Kordun, and Banija."

"It makes no difference how many names are given to the region. Terrible things happened there."

"But also in '91, right?"

"Yes..."

"Very good. So now I'll give you another three seconds."

"Civilians were killed and forced to leave their homes, which were burned. The houses that were left were resold to the highest bidder in a ghoulish game of real estate speculation. Some people have claimed that you were in charge."

"Oh, really?"

A large and shiny green fly buzzed next to the two bottles. Franjo waved his arm to shoo it away. It occurred to Amila that for him, her hands, with her nails chewed to the nub, her words, and her ideas were worth as much as that fly—though it might have managed to escape.

He started staring at her again. It was unnerving.

"Tell me, why are you so interested in the Serbs?" he asked, with a snigger. "You're not one of them."

Amila felt trapped by her ethnicity like a butterfly on a pin. "Victims aren't Serbs, Croats, or Muslims. They're just victims."

"Many of your compatriots wouldn't agree with you. Are you aware of that?"

Amila lowered her eyes. "Yes, I know."

A heavy silence followed.

"So what, then? What should we say about it?"

Amila gripped the edge of the table, as if she wanted to dig her fingernails into it. "The war was organized extermination and a free market for criminal gangs. And you know that better than me."

"No." He shook his head, decisively. "It was something else."

"What then?"

"A war of independence. You had to choose. Either the Croats, the Serbs, or the Muslims."

"Those ethnicities lived together—they were mixed. Yugoslavia was born in the name of friendship between peoples."

"I was always against Yugoslavia. Ethnicities can't be mixed together."

"So, what ethnicity are you, then? Italian, Croat . . . what?" Amila became impassioned. "Or maybe you think your blood is pure?"

"This is my house, and now I've had just about enough of you!" Franjo thundered.

Amila closed her eyes for an instant. She waited for the echo of his shouting to subside. "You've never been in your own home. You're just another emigrant, like everyone else."

"That's none of your business!" he said, slamming down his fist. Amila sat back in her chair.

Franjo turned toward the curtain. "Antonia!"

Above the copper pots hanging on the wall was a series of cracks climbing up through the plaster toward a large, moldy stain. Around it the plaster seemed to shudder with each of his shouts.

"So then, why would you have moved to Argentina?" The man glared at her furiously. "And then why come back just as the war began? Odd coincidence, don't you think?"

"I said, enough!"

"You can't always claim you're not a part of anything and never answer for any of it."

"Yes, I can."

"Even so, even if you deny it, the opinions you have show you to be guilty."

"Of what? You're the one who came to my house! And opinions change. Air! Give me some air!" he said, waving a hand toward her.

"Opinions have weight and responsibility."

"If that's how you see it. . ." He stood up, knocking over his chair.

Some footsteps could be heard moving behind the curtain Franjo didn't move.

"I'd like my photo, please."

The man held it out to her, disdainfully, saying, "Simon, Simon . . . C'mon, move along!"

Amila left the house of stone. The light outside blinded her— because it was still day, even if the day was done on that other side of the world, over there where the land seemed to come to its ultimate end. *Finis terrae*. Soon the sun would set here as well. She looked across the street, toward the storage lot of the old woman wearing a scarf. She had gone. Not a soul to be seen over there. No one who might look at her, no one whom Amila might look at, just to shake it off. No one to know that her tennis shoes were still there, even here, on the other side, leaning on the earth of this world. One step, then another. She didn't turn back. She sped up. No longer seeing anything at all, she began to run.

FEDERICA MARZI

CHAPTER TWENTY-SEVEN

Exotegrity

MARCH 2005, IZOLA/ISOLA (SLOVENIA)

FRAMED BY THE window, the sky was leaden and heavy as it continued to drool its dark tongues onto the sea. The glass was splashed by raindrops that split and striped it as they moved slowly downward. The neon light had been turned on, revealing stains on the wall and making the room seem surreal. A droning sound could be heard from the hallway, voices exchanging instructions, some muffled giggling.

Amila touched her body, the part that was skin and not wrapped in heavy bandages.

She was still there, still whole.

That youthful, female body behind the wheel of the Panda had run into a truck, enormous and overpowering, along a seesawing roadway. What she had seen emerge in front of her was its metallic blue grille. The horn sounded like the howl of a wounded animal. Amila had lurched the steering wheel abruptly.

Her wheels locked. And then nothing—the Panda slid into the guardrail, demolishing it.

Crushed with the car, she had buckled, compacted—a nucleus of her self and her story, unfinished business that had been waiting for her, that she needed to deal with. Her roots came from that place, and it wasn't simply about a country, a land, or a language. Her nerves were exposed, and her encounter with that man, Franjo Radonić, had reactivated them. Something there cut to the quick.

The doctor from Osijek, who had treated her the first night, stopped by to see her. He read her medical chart and nodded a couple of times. Amila would need to begin therapy to treat her pain and become used to sleeping on her back. The doctor assured her that she would be released the following day. As he had the last time, he also asked some personal questions, about her studies, what sort of job she wanted, and if she wrote her articles in Italian or Bosnian. He said that his story was similar, although learning Slovenian must have been easier.

"So you're also a writer?"

"Well, after the papers for my classes, my honor's thesis, and dissertation, I've limited my writerly output to medical charts and prescriptions." Amila grinned. She felt as if she hadn't smiled for ages. "Why else would anyone study medicine? So you never have to write anything else in your life. Not that sort of writing, anyway."

"Do you do emergency care?"

"Yes. I hate being bored."

From seventh grade on, Amila had hated being bored too, and that's why she kept charging ahead. She'd been good, really good, at turning things around the right way, to get the most from her life, thinking that she had every right to choose where to live, what language to speak, what school to attend, what to study, where to spend her vacations, where to fall in love, and what apartment she should live in. And where she felt she ought to stay, despite all sorts of things—having her foreign passport always at hand, along with the impossible spelling of her family name—that told her that she was only fooling herself. Still, she dribbled around such obstacles, like when you dart past the defense and go straight to the basket.

Now she felt like, at some point in the game, she'd cheated, and things weren't adding up. Because it was no longer about affirming her right to choose, it was about making a choice. Not about wanting; now it was about knowing. Knowing what would always stay right in the middle. She felt they should call it something like exoticity. Or, better yet, exotegrity, which in her case could even be written with a capital "E." A mix of exoticism and integrity. That's who she was. Everything was in that word: her self, her family, her story. She'd wanted to understand her apprehensions about uncertainty—wanting but never succeeding in choosing a clear direction. And yet you certainly couldn't live going in two directions simultaneously, that was clear enough.

She fell asleep leaning on the raised backrest of the bed, her head propped up on thick, hard pillows and her arm with the IV extended along her side. She slipped into a sort of sleep that wasn't really sleeping, more dozing in and out. She heard the voices of her parents arriving while she was dreaming. When she reopened her eyes, she had them next to her: Mamma Selma as tight as the string of a violin, ready to intervene; Papà Željko disheveled and ready to talk.

Amila felt a flash of pure and simple happiness cut through the fog that enveloped her, and the throbbing in her cheek flowed down into a vortex that concentrated all the pain in a single point. Mamma Selma hugged her, careful not to squeeze her too tightly, though she did make the iv totter.

Her parents started talking at the same time—a flood of questions: How was she? What had the doctors said? Amila answered as if she'd become a child again; at times it seemed they were speaking about someone else. At last, the inevitable request for an explanation. Amila felt like Alice in Wonderland, growing inside of a space that crushed her, unable to accommodate her new dimensions. She had again become a twenty-one-year-old girl, with adult responsibilities.

She asked Papà Željko if she could be alone with him for a moment. Mamma Selma looked offended. Željko nodded, suggesting to Selma that she might get herself a cup of coffee. He walked with her to the door, whispered something in her ear, and gave her a kiss on the forehead. He sat down on the edge of the bed and drummed his fingers on his knees, waiting.

"Papà, I've made a huge mess," Amila said, her voice broken. She felt the tears she'd held back till now falling down her cheeks, and her body again felt wrecked, aching in so many places. Željko stayed still, his eyes saddened. "I'm sorry," she added, turning toward the window. The clouds were moving across the horizon, changing colors. "Papà…" She turned back toward him, but quickly stopped herself.

"Yes."

"There's a boy."

Using the point of his finger, Papà Željko adjusted his glasses, without taking his eyes from her.

"He's Norina's nephew."

"Ah," he said.

"That Australian boy who came to visit her last summer, remember?" Amila would have preferred if everything were lost in silence.

"Were you two together the day of the accident?"

"No, he's living in Melbourne."

"You're in love?"

"Yes... but that's not it."

"So what is it, then?"

Amila fell silent.

"Young lady," Željko urged her, gravely. "Would you please tell me where you went?"

"Not far, Papà. Just over the border in Croatia."

Željko waited for Amila to continue. He sighed again and said, in a serious tone, "I can't help you if you don't tell me what happened and what you were doing driving around in Norina's car."

Amila shook her head firmly. "Daughter," he continued, with tension in his voice, "at least tell me nothing has happened to you that I have to worry about."

"No, I swear, nothing. Don't worry."

Amila thought again of Franjo's mocking smile, and his merciless lucidity, despite all the alcohol he'd downed. How, for him, it all seemed normal. He'd managed to turn all the cards his way without ever showing his hand, or by showing only a glimpse, in order to corner her. Trucks roll over asphalt—his word against everyone else's.

He had evaded every demand for information, pushed back against every accusation, heightening her sense of foolish impotence and depression. So yet again, one more time, nothing had been explained. Other than the fact that destiny wasn't some incomprehensible, inevitable fate; it was instead bound up with everyday good and evil, as well as an infinity of other random outcomes.

"For heaven's sake, what happened? You can't end up in a hospital like this without even telling me where you've been!"

Amila said only, "In a place where that boy took me once, where his grandparents had been living." Papà Željko looked perplexed. "He wanted to write a novel and..."

"And?"

"And nothing... I'm sorry, but this isn't a story that can be told." Papà Željko's face was colored by a look of utter bewilderment. "I can't," she whispered. "I'm sorry."

Papà Željko looked toward the window, and an icy silence fell between them. Amila dried her tears with the back of her hand. "Could you hand me a Kleenex, please?" Željko took one out of the box on the bedside table. His lips tight, he held it out to her. "Papà, I'm really mixed up." He nodded, worried. Their conversation went forward in pauses, the words dragging along. Each time they had the clearest opportunity to say something, they would falter. "Could you tell me something?" He nodded again. "Where did we all go?"

"We all?" he stiffened.

"Neighbors, colleagues, friends from Zvornik. My friends from school, your students. Papà, we've forgotten them all."

"For some time, I thought about all of them during every endless day of my life. And then less often," he admitted. "But you can't always think about everything."

"The thing is, when I try to think back on those years, all that comes to mind are vague memories. I feel lost. I don't even know anymore where all the parts of myself have gone."

"Feeling yourself divided, and not even in equal shares, is the least that can happen to people like us."

Amila shook her head firmly. "But Papà, we're safe. We got away."

"You don't know how many times I've regretted not knocking on all the doors in our building."

That moment, Amila thought, with its broken line between after and before, may have been the first impossible watershed in her life. Perhaps, in that story, no one had really been saved.

"But I was only thinking about us." Her father's voice was faint.

"Papà, listen, I'm not accusing you of anything. You saved your family, and I'll always be grateful to you for that." Željko shook his head. "You did what you could. It's just me. I can't not make my own peace with it, you see?"

"Unfortunately, peace is much more difficult than war."

A very long silence followed, thick with things they'd never told each other. Željko's eyes had reddened.

"Papà?"

"Yes."

"What about Nevena?"

"Miran's Nevena?"

"Yes." In her mind's eye, Amila was able to see the features of her old friend, childlike but determined, the girl with quicksilver inside.

"She speaks English well and works as an interpreter for an NGO. As long as all this lasts, she has a ready job. But she, too, would like to leave."

"Why don't we help her to come to Italy?"

"What are you saying?"

"Maybe you and the union could do something?"

Papà Željko slipped off his glasses and rubbed his eyes. "My girl, it just doesn't work like that. With the new law ... you have to wait for the new immigration quotas to be announced. And then, at minimum, she would need to have a work contract."

"But they helped us, Papà."

"I know, but that's not the issue. Listen to me, dear. Miran ... well, a lot of things are not so clear to me ... I mean, during the war ..."

"What are you saying, Papà?"

"I'm not sure. I've heard people saying things."

Amila felt as if she were trying to stay afloat, swimming with her arms as hard as she could, while a whirlpool was pulling her down by the legs toward the bottom, where even the clearest things were spinning in murky waters. "And who said it?"

"Fehim."

"Who's that?"

"One of my colleagues for years. Just before the war, he was teaching the last year at our school. The father of Sanela and Emir. Do you remember them?"

Amila remembered those names, and maybe a vague outline of kids in red and blue turtlenecks, corduroys, and brown boots with heavy laces. Two ex-Bosnian children, like her and Majda. "He came back too, for his house. But he's selling everything, and they're staying in Germany."

Amila looked her father straight in the eyes. "What rumors did you hear?"

"It's not certain, but it seems as if... honestly, I don't know; there are so many rumors running around."

"But they're the ones in charge now, and Miran's working for the city, isn't he? He isn't still a janitor? He got promoted?"

Željko shook his head. "But that doesn't necessarily mean..." He couldn't manage to go on. Between them, another painful silence followed.

"Papà?"

"Yes?"

Amila felt herself kicking, getting her head back above the surface, and taking a breath of fresh air. "Even if what you're not saying is true, would Nevena have to be involved?"

"Of course not. We don't know anything."

Amila closed her eyes. Papà Željko had reached his limit. And she'd had to force him. For years now she had tried never to disappoint her father. Because her father had always pushed her to do her best. But now, she was the one to feel disappointed.

They remained there, each closed off inside their thoughts, until Željko decided to go and get Mamma Selma. He stood up slowly and seemed exhausted.

"Papà?" Amila stopped him at the doorway. "A lot of things with Norina will have to be worked out. She stopped by the hospital yesterday, and she was upset about having to report to the police. I think the car must be a wreck... I can't tell you how sorry I am."

All Amila wanted now was to fix everything and keep as far away as possible—from the house in Bristie, from all that story. And from that point, the end point where Simon had brought her.

Papà Željko nodded, solemn and reliable. He would know how to do what was right for Norina, how to repair the damage. Amila was grateful for that.

When her parents returned to the room, rays of sunlight were angling through the clouds, covering them in shades of red. Pretending to be calm, Mamma Selma forced herself to hold back her anxiety and emotion, but that only made it more difficult for Amila. Luckily, the dinner cart arrived, and her mother let herself be distracted with things to do and organize.

Amila asked about the apartment. Mamma Selma uttered a mysterious "oooh"—which could mean anything, or nothing—while she was energetically tearing the cover off of a yogurt container. Papà Željko explained they'd hired a contractor, and he described to her the work of painting, flooring, retiling, and replacing the water heater.

When her parents put on their coats, the sun was hidden behind the clouds lined in purple.

"Mamma, once and for all, could you please tell me what you've decided to do with the apartment?"

Selma wrinkled her forehead and glanced over, worriedly, at Željko. He opened his lips slightly, without responding.

So there they were—her parents. Stuck with her inside a tight bubble of old pain, something that they'd never really been able to talk about, even after all these years. The pain of having been betrayed by their country, and of also being the ones who had betrayed it. Of having escaped from the slaughter without a scratch. Pain that they were ashamed they even had, compared to those who'd lived through something much worse. And then the pain of having rebuilt a life for themselves in some other place, while still remaining different, suspended within this sense of difference.

Mamma Selma broke the silence. "We need to have the work done, whether we sell it or keep it; otherwise it's worthless. We can't start before summer ... but you don't need to worry about this too. Not now."

"How could we ever go back there to live?" Amila asked.

"Exactly," Papà Željko stated. "We can't. But if we give it away, we'll always feel something is missing."

And so, in the end, there was also the pain of having gotten back what had been theirs in Zvornik, but knowing that they no longer wanted it.

"Mamma, when you're there, what sort of memories come back to you?"

"Memories?" Mamma Selma stuttered. "I'm not sure." She put a hand over her mouth to help her think. "Here's one—the smell of cabbage in the stairwell at dinnertime," she said, with new light in her eyes. "That I remember well."

"Is it still there?"

Mamma Selma's lips widened into a forced smile, and then she shook her head. "No, I don't think so... Or at least, not that I noticed."

"Why did you like it?"

"I didn't like it at all! I was always irritated by it, and that's why I remember it."

Amila laughed. Even Mamma Selma let herself really smile a bit. They were laughing at something sad, but it helped just the same.

When her parents were leaving, Mamma Selma said again that they'd be back the day after to pick her up; Papà Željko gave her a kiss on her head, as if she'd become a little girl again. The sky was dark, and the clouds had thickened.

Amila was left alone with a rough, confused idea, not knowing where it came from—an idea that cleared a way for itself, groping around in her head. She hadn't yet figured out how to put it into practice, but she did think she knew why she wanted to. Because she felt that she always came up short, and all the patches she put over her various flaws had started to fray. Because she wasn't happy, and it wasn't easy to feel this way, as if you were someone who always wanted something else. A malcontent.

The nurse with the long red ponytail came in. She changed the IV and told Amila to get some rest. Then she turned off the light.

Amila picked up her phone and looked up a number with two prefixes. She dialed it quickly.

At that hour, in the other hemisphere, it was the dead of night, and so, after a notice saying the phone was off, the voicemail message played.

"Ciao, it's me," she said, mechanically. "Sorry for not having answered you until now. Don't worry, I'm fine. I hope you've managed to speak with Norina. The Panda is out of commission, but my father will set everything right. And also..." Also, again, there were those words that were difficult to say. "I wanted to tell you that I went to Buroli. I met Franjo Radonić. He was in that house. He's your grandfather. I don't know why he was there, or how long he'll stay there. Seems absurd, doesn't it? As for everything else ... Well, I don't know any more than what we already knew. He denied everything. I'll tell you everything when we see each other. Even if I don't know when.

"And on that point ... tomorrow I go back to Trieste, and, honestly, I've got a real mess in my head. There are many months and a lot of distance between us ... It's always been like this, too much distance in my life. I can't do it anymore.

"We were wrong to dream about impossible things. Or maybe we did the right thing, but now I wish we could have met at some other time. I don't know, maybe ten years from now. When you'll have a well-paid job and normal holidays, and I won't still be an immigrant; when I'll be a citizen of some country, free to travel wherever and whenever I choose. I'm sorry, but for now I have to sort out my own life. I need to write my thesis and then maybe ... maybe I won't stay here. I'd also like to travel, like you do. And so, even if it's sad, I think it's better if I disappear from view, at least for a while.

"Do me a favor—please tell Norina what has happened. Somebody has to explain to her the mess we've made. It's none of my business. You're her nephew. You do it."

CHAPTER TWENTY-EIGHT

Things That Have to Happen

OCTOBER 2005, BRISTIE/BRIŠČE (ITALY)

NORINA GOT HER Panda back earlier than expected. Amila's father brought it to her in Bristie, repaired, washed, and good as new. Amila wasn't with him—she couldn't drive, but she didn't even stop by either. Of course, she had told Norina, both on the phone and at the hospital, how sorry she was. She apologized a thousand times during those days of confusion, when everyone was calling. But, according to Norina, her strict obligation would have included coming in person to explain how everything had happened, instead of making things even more complicated. Norina didn't hear anything else from her.

So when Amila's father, whom she'd never seen before, showed up, it was really difficult. At minimum, Mariano ought to have gotten out of bed and talked to him, man-to-man. But no. As usual, she was the one who had to do it, intimidated by such a courteous, refined man. Tall, and wearing glasses, he was brought up properly, so he didn't seem to notice his surroundings, though he surely saw the squalid state her house was in once again. He offered her a check, for the inconvenience—that's how he explained it, with that particular accent of his. Although Norina read something else in his words: so you don't make trouble.

But she'd been honest. Amila shouldn't have any problems with her residency permit. At the Slovenian police station, Norina officially declared that she had loaned Amila the Panda, just as anyone would with a member of the family. She knew plenty of stories about passports and residency permits—given out or taken back each time the wind changed. Everyone should have their own piece of paper, that was only fair, without having to go through such business. And to affirm this right, she was prepared to lie, so that's what she'd done. But a check? That she couldn't accept.

For many weeks, Norina didn't touch the car, as if she didn't trust it, as if it had been dirtied, roughed up. Another fall arrived. Mariano's condition was unchanged. Norina had to go down to the city, do the shopping, buy medicine. The usual things, so she'd have to reconcile herself, at least with the Panda. She started using it again.

One morning, Bristie was covered in thick fog, and from the valleys all you could see emerging were dark branches, stiffened and covered with dried leaves. Norina found an email in her inbox. It was her sister.

They didn't write each other much anymore, just once in a while, and only to tell each other really silly stuff. This time, though, the message was long and dense, the sort that Norina had only ever read in letters. Norina's vision blurred. She squinted, forcing herself to bring the text into focus. Nevia didn't start off with "my dearest sister," a salutation that had disappeared from their exchanges. But she also didn't begin with the usual "ciao," "ciao, it's me," "ciao, Norina, are you there?"

The subject came out of nowhere, as if the words had been taken out of context. Nevia talked about how, when she was young, she had been sent to several camps to process refugees. Even though they were decent people, she wrote, she and her family ended up there. Their only fault had been wanting to remain Italian. In exchange, they got contemptuous looks from people in the city, as if they were impoverished, as if they'd had some infectious disease, or they'd arrived from who knows where. It was only the smell of garlic, their worn-out clothes, their exhausted faces, and their eyes full of fear that had made them seem different. They were Italian like everyone else, and it was unfair that they had been treated like that.

Norina stopped, leaning back in her chair. She couldn't understand if this message had been sent on purpose, or if it was a mistake. It seemed that Nevia was confessing something to someone who couldn't be Norina, since she already knew the story. Maybe the message had been left in her outbox; maybe Nevia had forgotten about it. With email, a moment of distraction and it was gone. Messages got sent who knows where, and they couldn't be erased, torn up, or destroyed.

Her sister explained how it had been awful to leave behind her father, mother, and sister, like a criminal. But that's how things were going. When there was nothing left to hope for, if another life was promised to you, you left.

On the freighter *Flaminia*, everyone suffered from seasickness, and, to get over it, a woman told Nevia that she should eat two days' worth of food and stare at the horizon, first with one eye and then the other. You needed to get used to the horizon. It had worked. Nevia had stayed with a few other passengers in the ship's dining room, which was set for people who weren't eating and had nothing left in their stomachs, nothing to keep down or to vomit.

Norina imagined her sister with a pallid face, her hair nicely combed and styled with the pearl barrette on one side, her long, slender hands leaning on the edge of a round table covered with fancy plates and extra silverware. The white tablecloth that hung down to her feet was her only dining companion. She was sitting straight in her seat, with her eyes wide open. She wasn't speaking, just waiting for food to be served. Nevia appeared inside a weak, yellow beam of light that cut through the dense penumbra surrounding her. Norina could see her as clearly as if she were there right in front of her. That had never happened before.

Italians were separated from the Greeks, Nevia wrote, but they didn't all sleep together, even if there were many, many women in the four-story bunk beds in steerage. The point was to find some space. Before it was refurnished for the transport of people, the *Flaminia* had been a merchant ship. Some passengers managed to get a cabin. That's how it went.

Franco was there too, on the same ship.

Norina closed her eyes. But it was too late: "I loved Franco, but only for a short time, and I never hated him for leaving. Things that have to happen, happen no matter what."

FEDERICA MARZI

It was too late to pull the cord out of the computer and turn it off. Norina had read it.

If Nevia admitted to having loved Franco for only a short time, perhaps it hadn't even been love at all. And when had this love for a short time happened? And where? Already in Padriciano, before leaving, or on the ship, or in Australia?

Norina wiped her eyes, but the tears were trapped inside. That form of relief, available to everyone else, was barred to her. Even after rubbing them, her eyes wouldn't moisten.

Those eyes would have to get used to knowing what, during their whole life, they'd always feared and expected they'd read one day.

Nevia had always known that Franco would leave her: "He wasn't who I thought he was, or maybe he was, but I was different too. We all were."

She had been nothing more than a very young woman, alone and foolish. But still, the child that she felt growing in her womb, who would become her first child, had given her so much happiness. For that reason, it hadn't been a mistake. It had happened, and it was a good thing, proving that happiness was possible everywhere. Because happiness comes whenever it wants; it doesn't require a new country, a beautiful house, a particular job, or money, or whatever. We're not on this planet to get everything for free, and we need to accept that.

Australia had been a dream, but it had also been reality. And dreams have their price. Nevia, too, had been sent to the Bonegilla migrant camp, like everyone else, and she wasn't ashamed of it. Because if something in your life is painful, that pain must first of all be removed from your own heart.

Nevia wrote about having landed at the port city of Fremantle, during a sandstorm, a phenomenon as strange as the heat was that day, even though they told her it was winter. The red sand stuck to your skin. The refugees were held aside at customs. Nevia remembered men wearing hats and women with bonnets on the side of their heads. The Australians were wearing clothes that were more old-fashioned than those of the immigrants from Istria and Trieste. Nevia threw up for the first time.

Might that have been caused by her condition, wondered Norina, apprehensively.

Luckily, her sister continued, that had just been the first stop on their journey. They were allowed to get back on the ship and continue to Melbourne. Unlike Trieste, it seemed to be a very old port. Before she was sent for a medical inspection and then to the passport office, she had a label stuck onto her clothing. They did that to all the immigrants, like they were a herd of cattle. Those strangers were putting their hands on her, speaking to her incomprehensibly, and giving out orders, full of contempt. You could see it in how they acted, how they moved their mouths and their hands, and from their eyes, which only pretended to be good and understanding, but were really cruel. After the examination, she, too was free to go. But she didn't know where, even though that city had been, as it was for everyone else, the chosen destination.

She walked. There wasn't anyone on the streets. The roads were dark and covered in mist. She remembered a clock tower appearing at night in the middle of nowhere. She couldn't get the vision of it out of her head, as if only in that moment

FEDERICA MARZI

she had finally realized she'd crossed for good the threshold of her new life.

When she got back to the ship, her luggage had been confiscated, with the promise that it would be returned upon arrival. They had her board a train that appeared to have been built centuries ago. Everything inside creaked, and a folding door opened and closed continuously.

The trip took twelve hours; from the window you could see fields of eucalyptus trees, thousands of sheep, and a house from time to time. At one stop, country people were serving tea with milk—a sort of tea that Nevia had never tried before. After twelve hours, she arrived in Albury, where she boarded a bus and traveled for another hour. She got out in front of a reception camp surrounded by a metal fence.

Norina stared at the screen, rooted to her seat. She had never realized, or imagined, that arriving in Australia would have meant going to a camp exactly like the one Nevia had fled. *"Mamma mia, what did I do!"* Nevia wrote. But they made a point of assuring everyone that they would be able to go in and out of the camp freely. Still, there wasn't the promised work, the food they ate was disgusting, and you could only buy cooking oil at pharmacies. She left when she found work in a textile factory. At that point, her pregnancy had almost come to term.

The story ended there, as if it were actually finished, leaving the rest in suspense—the birth of Ann, the hurried marriage with Carmine, the twins, all their moves, the dressmaker's shop. And not another word about Franco. Nothing to give some real meaning to the oppressive weight Norina had been carrying inside, ever since he and Nevia had left, leaving her behind.

Though now Norina did know that her sister had conquered the horizon only to end up—both of them, or perhaps only Nevia—in a camp for immigrants.

Norina wiped her mouth with the back of her hand. She stood up and turned off the computer. She took a paper towel from the roll and pressed it over her eyes; it moistened only slightly. She walked around a bit to stretch her legs. She went over to the window. The garden was barren. The foliage of the oak tree was blazing in yellow and red. Soon all the leaves would fall.

Norina no longer knew what to believe. She felt old, as dried-up as the branches of her oak would be soon. To an email like Nevia's, there was nothing you could say. She didn't know what else she could do.

She certainly never would have imagined that those would be her sister's final words, so that it mattered little whether they had been meant for her or for someone else. To words like these, she never would have been able to respond.

A few days later, unexpectedly, came the phone call from Simon.

"Nonna Nevia is dead," he said. His delicate voice—that had been the real surprise for Norina; she had been looking for his eyes and instead found his voice. Yet now, in that tone which she loved so much, he was giving her awful news.

Norina sat down on the couch. She pushed the cordless phone tight to her ear and put her hand in front of her mouth. With a crack in his voice, Simon explained not only what had happened, but even how it had happened. The neighbors had found her, face down, in her garden. After she was brought to the hospital by ambulance, the doctors confirmed that she had died of a heart attack.

No one knew if she had suffered, or what her final moments had been like. Her asthma had kept her from doing more than a brief daily walk, but otherwise her health had been good. Which only made her death all the more impossible to understand.

When he finished, Simon stayed silent, without even an "I'm sorry"—perhaps because they were related, and regrets were shared equally between them. Norina also didn't say a word. She would have liked to cry, but her eyes stayed dry. She would have liked to express her sense of dejection, but instead she remained frozen on the couch. Simon, of course, could neither see any of this nor understand it. Perhaps she should have regretted the inability to show her grief. Sooner or later, though, she would do and feel all of these things at once, and then she would go out into the woods.

No one could have understood what it meant to have remained separated from a sister for an entire life. And then, as an old woman, having gotten back into contact by using a computer. And now, to have lost her, with no chance of finding her again. The funeral services would be taking place down there.

Simon called again after the burial. Norina was no longer checking her email; she wasn't watching television, and she'd been going regularly out into the woods. Mariano was sending her out, telling her she needed to change her behavior. He didn't need any more nurses, or anyone at all; he just wanted to be left in peace. She should leave him in peace. His movements had become more and more limited, just the bedroom and the bathroom, and he kept looking even taller and thinner.

He read the local paper from front to back, to pass the time. He stared out the window, turned on his side, his head sunk into his pillows. He ate by himself, because he couldn't manage the stairs, and Norina was fed up with sitting on the edge of the bed with an empty stomach. They didn't talk much, only whatever was necessary. This was the only thing that had gotten worse since Nevia's death, perhaps because Mariano, too, hadn't been able to cry. Not speaking to each other was their one way of staying together.

Over the phone, Simon described the details of the burial. All the daughters and the grandchildren and the husbands and the boyfriends and girlfriends, and also a number of Italians from Melbourne with other wives, husbands, children, and grandchildren, had gathered together in the church. For Nevia. Some had also come from Sydney. And from Buie many people had called, though only Orietta from Sucolo had also thought to call Trieste. Norina had never felt more alone. It was lovely that Nevia had had so many people, even if she'd died so far from her home. It was also sad, but maybe even more sad for Norina, who, even if she died in her own land, wouldn't have anyone with her. Even death had managed to make the two sisters compete. Would that story ever end?

Maybe it would.

Simon broke the news that he wanted to come back to Europe. He was looking for a job in London, and he had already gotten plane tickets. He also wanted to spend a few days with her and Mariano. Norina felt tongue-tied. Simon began to stammer out things that made no sense—he didn't want to disturb them, staying in a hotel wouldn't be a problem, he wouldn't be staying long.

Norina didn't know how she could explain it to him. Had she heard right? Her nephew, who didn't call her, and never wrote, who only occasionally called at Christmas—no, not even that, the day after, on Santo Stefano, because the day before he was busy—and who, yes, had also called last spring, when Amila had gotten in the accident, the police had her Panda, and everything was upside-down, well, now her nephew was telling her that he wanted to move to Europe, which meant not so far from her. So were they, after all, a family?

The family Norina had always wanted was Nevia's. Norina no longer knew if her sister had taken it away from her, long ago, or whether she had instead always wanted to offer it to her. In any case, it was a fact that Norina had always refused that bond, but now she did want it. She needed it, and she felt it was hers.

At last, she managed to say, for the first time, through her tears, "My poor, poor sister."

Around the World and Back
NOVEMBER 2005, TRIESTE/TRST (ITALY)

AFTER ALL SAINTS' Day, Simon was back with Norina. They were sitting at the dinner table, even though it was past lunchtime. And Simon was already about to leave again. This time Trieste had been only a very brief stopover.

He had brought something for her. It was from Nevia, wrapped in simple, white paper. Along with a pair of earrings, his grandmother used to say, it was the only possession she had from the old world. They had buried Nevia with her earrings; Simon had found the pearl barrette in the box of photographs that Ann now kept on a shelf in the living room.

Norina recognized it immediately. For her too, it would be one of the few, precious objects from Buie, from her home, that place where she'd been born. The barrette was back, after going around the world. She held it in her hands.

Simon was waiting for a taxi. He fiddled with his passport and plane tickets. He had a job interview in London. Mariano was convinced this was an excellent opportunity for him, and the mere fact that he could imagine his nephew in Europe, established in a prestigious profession, put him in better spirits. His health was improving.

Simon took a piece of paper, folded twice, from the large backpack kept between his legs. He was a young man who'd always had all he needed, but that was all he'd packed for what could be a new life, free of old baggage. Maybe he'd just be getting rid of lots of useless things.

And that was how Norina found herself face-to-face with another truth—or perhaps it was only a lie—about her life. A truth that came out of the computer. She was expecting it; by now she was used to those inane, cheap sheets of paper that cranked out of printers.

Prepare yourself, she said, as she unfolded the paper. For what she would see, though, there would be no way to prepare herself.

Even though he was standing in front of her, Simon disappeared for a moment from her field of vision; the two of them stared at each other without managing to speak a single word. After an infinitely long instant, her nephew asked if the man in the photo was his grandfather. He spoke like someone who was in a hurry—or continuing a conversation he'd had a thousand times already.

Simon had gotten thinner, his hair was longer, and his face seemed rougher and more angular. He took off his glasses. His veiled, impenetrable eyes searched anxiously for an answer from Norina, though she would have preferred to keep it to herself.

She looked at the black-and-white photo. It was part of a newspaper article. She could manage to read only the title, in large, boldface type, but she didn't understand "Slavic"; she understood only the word "Eldorado."

At first it was difficult to recognize a boy in this old man's face. But even Franco wasn't immortal, that was clear. Time had left its marks: his heavier face and gray hair, his receding hairline, the wrinkles in his neck. But that man couldn't be as old as Norina, no, he must be younger.

"Auntie, my taxi will be here soon."

Still, his eyes with their sparkle were unmistakable, even if they were blurred by the dark ink. The folds around his lips gave that notorious devil-may-care attitude to this now worn-down face. And the more Norina became convinced, the more the layers of that face thinned out, allowing the youth of a former time to emerge. Norina felt the corners of her mouth turning upward. She felt her stomach jump. The dead can come back to life.

To her nephew, she nodded. Yes, she was sure of it. It was him.

"But is his name Franco or Franjo?"

"Huh?" Norina couldn't make herself stop looking at the page.

"Auntie, what is his name?" he insisted.

"*Franco. We only called him Franco.*"

Simon explained that the article had been published after a fire in a bar Franco owned.

That got Norina's attention quickly. What sort of bar?

"A nightclub."

"*What?*"

"A strip joint. Or something like that."

Norina blinked and moistened her lips with the tip of her tongue. Everything always happened with the speed of light, and it all began to seesaw around her, as usual.

She realized they'd have little time to say far too many things. Instinctively she asked the question that was most obvious, that everyone wanted to know, for which there had never seemed to be an answer.

Simon said something that was new and old at the same time. Franco was living in Buroli, that was certain. So, the trip around the world was over and done.

But how, Norina thought to herself. Her mouth opened wide, but no words came out. Simon repeated what he'd said; he even assured her it was true.

But where did it say that? Simon didn't tell her. Instead, his words began to take long, tortuous paths, intentionally turning in opposite directions—something that even she, at her age, noticed.

It was difficult for Norina to follow this young man, who mentioned Buie, Livio and Orietta, the people she'd brought money to pay the bill at the cemetery. She heard his words ringing like coins falling into a tin coffer. His voice had a piercing inflection. Those names came from his mouth for the first time, and the sound of them didn't suit him at all.

Norina forced herself to do her own thinking. She cleared her throat and looked at him squarely. "Did you meet him?"

Simon shook his head. Then she heard him mention Amila. She had translated the article for him. A millstone rolled over in her stomach. What did Amila have to do with all this, at this point—an outsider who didn't know anything about their family? Norina couldn't repress her irritation—and shame—that two kids had gone sticking their noses into a story as old and private as this.

She and Simon were moving forward, one behind the other, over dangerous ground. At every step, you could slip and take a nasty fall.

Norina thought again about the car wreck last March and how Amila never even gave her a word of explanation. Norina suddenly was overcome with alarm. Where had Simon been in that period? According to Amila, in Melbourne. And so?

And so, what about the car? Simon said he didn't know.

This was a very tangled thread, and Norina wasn't able to find the end, even if she felt she must have it in her hand. Simon wasn't telling her something. This was about more than two kids being in love—which meant both everything and nothing—but she couldn't get any farther than that.

"Nevia knew about all this?"

"Auntie, why are you speaking Italian now?"

"How would I know?" answered Norina, twitching with irritation. The taxi arrived.

"No, she didn't know. But she might have intuited something." Norina had become the last remaining witness.

So what was he planning to do now? Simon could at least tell her that, couldn't he?

All he said, in the calmest tone ever recorded, was: "Oh, nothing much. I'll just be getting ready for my job interview."

They said goodbye in a hurry—and in embarrassment and uncertainty as well—without even a hug, in the middle of their interrupted conversation. Simon pulled the straps on his backpack tight and checked to be sure he had everything. He gave Luli a distracted pat on the head. In the doorway, he paused, as if having second thoughts.

For once, Norina didn't ask if he was planning to visit them again soon. Because it was clear that, for one reason or another, Simon would be coming back. Kids always have needs; they always have something buzzing around their brains, and that's why they come back.

Just the night before, eavesdropping behind the door of the guest room, she'd heard him say on the phone, "Nonna Nevia is dead. I don't know, maybe that man should be told about it."

It was obvious. That story still hadn't ended.

CHAPTER THIRTY

The Moon, from the Other Side

NOVEMBER 2005, TRIESTE/TRST (ITALY)

BUJE/BUIE (CROATIA)

AFTER SIMON LEFT for London, Norina kept returning to the photo her nephew had left her. She slipped it into her small private drawer in the living room, full of things she'd rejected or things that had rejected her. Every now and then she'd open it up and peek inside. The wrinkles on his forehead, forming deep grooves over his eyebrows, gave the impression that Franco was scowling. From his eyes oozed his usual condescension. Ha! The black-and-white image made him look darker. Norina took a step back. And the word Eldorado, written in large type, gave her a vague sense of disgust. So then she would quickly slide the drawer shut, to cover up that face. Soon after, though, she stopped opening and closing it all the time. Mariano needed her, and that was a good thing.

Norina received a call from the hospital about an opening for his operation. The date would be here soon, too soon. She and Mariano did everything necessary: showing up after fasting for the pre-op visit, packing a bag for him, and leaving Luli with Anika (even for several days, if it became necessary); then she got in the Panda, and he got in the ambulance, to proceed to the private clinic downtown.

Norina stayed for hours in the waiting room. She rubbed her thumbs, watching the ticking of the big, white, round clock on the wall. She was given five minutes where she was allowed to go into a dark room, with three beds filled with people who had been operated on that morning by the same talented doctor. Mariano was awake, with an iv and a catheter attached. He had a pale, yellowish look and dry lips. But he was talking; in fact, he was the one to ask first how she was doing. Norina told him to take it easy. She was fine. She put her hand over his and held it tight. It was cold, and he squeezed too, though feebly.

That hand had changed. It felt large, bony, and wrinkled. Norina hardly recognized it. She took her hand back and held the paper cup to his lips, advising him to take just a sip. She told him they would move him, maybe tonight, into his own room, and so by tomorrow his life would be completely different. Mariano nodded. Norina asked if he was in pain, but he shook his head. He was still sedated, so maybe it was true that he wasn't feeling anything. Or maybe, as usual, he was denying it, as if none of it mattered to him, or he refused to feel it.

The other sort of pain, though—Norina couldn't really know what toll it had taken on him. If it had been muffled or intensified in those long years of chatting, quarreling, and prescriptions in the house in Bristie, the only solid ground they had. And yet they were still together, even if only in a hospital room, both telling each other that tomorrow would be a whole different life, at the end of the path, and from there, no one could see beyond.

FEDERICA MARZI

Mariano closed his eyes. Norina told him again to rest. But then she had to leave; they'd given her only five minutes. She planned to come back the next day.

She closed the door and started down the long hallway. When she was outside the clinic, Norina realized she had nothing else to do. She simply felt tired. Outside it was a nice day, though cold. She buttoned up her overcoat—the one that these days she only put on to visit hospitals. She started walking quickly toward the Panda, which was parked on a busy street.

Not having to worry about anything or anyone waiting for her, or about anyone who might need her, freed her mind, but it also made her realize how much her mind was usually cluttered. Maybe that was why it seemed to her that she could never put two and two together and find the total. Or respond appropriately, laughing or crying. Norina felt as if she needed to find the courage she'd never had, to take her life into her own hands, even if those hands of hers had few skills and were deformed by arthritis. There was something that she needed to do.

She got into her car, being careful not to crease the tails of her overcoat. She checked to see if she had her ID card in her wallet, and if it was still valid. Written on it was her place of birth: "Buie d'Istria," then the year, then "estero," foreign. She thought it was probably time to get that changed.

She only wanted to go for a few hours, not simply to remember what she had lost she'd been doing that her whole life—but to see and understand what had changed.

She turned the key and fastened her seat belt. She'd never driven all the way there by herself. Over the years, that trip had kept getting longer, with the new borders and the countries changing, until it became impossible. She warned herself to drive at a snail's pace and trust her instincts. She hit the turn signal and pulled out of her parking space. It wouldn't be hard—she knew the route by memory, even if the roads had all been redone. The first border: Rabuiese, and on the other side, Scoffie. That's where she had arrived with her parents and her sister, in a van crammed full of household furnishings. The crossbar barrier they'd had there was gone, replaced by anonymous, functional buildings, platform roofs, and kiosks. She'd heard on television that within a year, all of it would be torn down. That's how these stories would end. They would send bulldozers to flatten that ugly wound inflicted on the earth, so that it would seem like nothing had ever happened.

The bored eyes of customs officials glanced at her ID card. Old women got treated badly even at checkpoints, or maybe it didn't matter at all if you were young or old. Whoever might be coming or going, definitely nobody was there to welcome you in.

The second stage: Capodistria. You needed to follow the road signs—easier said than done; with all the yellow signs, and blue signs, and the cars speeding past you, and so many new houses dotting the side of the road, you could miss even the few landmarks that were left. There was much less cultivated land, and more brushwood, curves, and interchanges. When she didn't know where to go—which happened often—she pulled over on the side of the road. She asked for directions, and everyone answered in Italian. She'd start up again, aiming straight for the horizon. When she had to merge into the right lane at the traffic light, a few drops of perspiration slipped down her temple. She made a mistake, of course, and the car horns were deafening. Norina hit the button to turn on the emergency lights and drove very, very slowly into the right-turn lane. A rude kid gestured at her with his middle finger; not resorting to that level of drama, she, too, wished him an appropriate fate, without taking her hands off the steering wheel. She turned on the radio, lowering the volume, so she could concentrate. She continued on, carefully following the road signs.

The final border: Dragogna. No one would be tearing that one down. It would continue to keep watch over her house, located just across it, on the other side.

After two and a half hours total, the houses began to look more familiar, but she hadn't kept up and didn't know any longer who owned what in town, who had left and who had stayed. She didn't see any people around. She parked the Panda on the side of the street, as close as she could to the trees, next to a house that stood apart from the rest. The last stage: Buroli. She'd arrived.

She wiped the sweat from her lips. A few rays of sunlight slanted in through the window on the passenger side, giving her the impression that she might rest in its warmth. She waited for some time for something to happen, but nothing did. She looked around apprehensively.

At last, in the field opposite the house, a man appeared with a bucket in his hand. He was wearing jeans and a down jacket. He went across to the woods and disappeared. He came back, swinging the bucket, with a walking stick in his other hand. His white hair was down to his shoulders, a detail that wasn't in the photo that Simon had brought. Norina felt as if she recognized his height, and also something about the way he walked, though he did limp a bit now. There was a glimpse of his face, but only as part of the whole. It could be him.

A small girl came outside; her hair was long and black as charcoal. She went up to the man, and he listened to her, nodding. Like a grandfather, he tousled her hair and sent her back inside, pointing his finger toward the door. He set his bucket down, planted his stick in the ground, and looked over toward the Panda, for a time that seemed to be ages. Norina pressed her hand to her mouth, holding her breath. The other hand kept gripping the steering wheel. She prayed to God that Franco wouldn't come any closer. I beg you. I beg you.

The man picked up his bucket and went back into the house, same as before, to continue his life, which was made up of buckets and sticks carried this way and that, and of children who had nothing to do with Norina's family. Franco had become a man who was from that town, much like Mariano, though in better health—someone who had once been different, someone for whom she had waited, for so long, at least so long as she'd been able to imagine him vividly. Afterward, she didn't. Afterward there had been something else. Life had quickly taken its own course, and now it was done.

Norina had never really looked hard enough for happiness. She'd gotten stuck like a bump on a log—*come un pedocio de scòjo*—to the idea that she'd been born, and that she lived on the wrong side. Her land was still there, but she was somewhere else. And between these irreconcilable opposites, her land and her self, the arc of her life had been stretched, like a bent, twisted metal wire.

Yet even the new world, which had always eluded her, had gone the way it'd gone. No doubt that was what Nevia had wanted to say in her last, long message, which perhaps she had sent knowing already that death was near. Norina now knew that Nevia's words had been meant for her—to tell her there hadn't been any better world anywhere.

Franco had gone back inside his home. He had been just a few steps from her. He'd gone, like so many other things. Now it was time for her to go too.

She drove quickly through Buie. She opened the car window when she was at the traffic light at the bottom of Lama, the point where the old city and the house with the *rosèr* were stitched together with the new city, with its other houses. Between the cemetery of San Martino and that other, where her own dead were buried. At the intersection of a road that, behind her back, led out to fields of red soil, while, in front of her, it would go down in the opposite direction, sending her back to the border. She hoped that a bit of breeze, even for a moment, would bring the voices and fragrance of Istria inside the cold cabin of her car. But nothing came through—just the night, its blanket of silence, and the glare of a new store sign. It was too late to add another stop. She drove through the intersection and glimpsed, too quickly, the two bell towers poking up above the town.

After driving down the hills and through the rotary, she drove into the night. After she passed yet another curve, the moon appeared. Large and full, with its face bright and pulsating in its many shades of gray. From its edges emanated an orange halo, lighting up a corner of the sky. She would have liked to pull over to look at it more carefully, but on the side of the road, there was only brushwood interspersed with gravel lanes leading out into the fields. The occasional house or commercial building caused the moon to disappear, only to reappear after the following curve. Norina would soon change directions, and then who knew where the moon would be.

She looked into her rearview mirror; there was no one behind her.

Slow down, she told herself. Slower, slower, slower. She turned her head and looked.

And now it all was coming back to her. She remembered. In Istria, the moon shines differently. Norina would never see it again. The road would bring her back, for good or not, slowly or quickly, to Trieste. To the place that had become her home.

CHAPTER THIRTY-ONE

At My Place

"SO YOU'RE BACK." Amila forced herself to smile at him.

"Yes, to see my uncle. There's a direct flight from London."

"How's he doing?"

"The operation went well. He's in a rehab center, and he's walking. He's even walking in a swimming pool."

"Incredible! Give him a big, big hug from me."

Simon nodded. For Amila it was damned hard to be in front of him and feel anything—like how hard her heart was beating—and get it to stop. But she'd agreed to meet him, and she suggested they do it somewhere that, for once, would make things easy for them both.

"So, let's go." Simon put his hands in his pockets and started off first toward the beginning of the boulevard, where the crowd was headed.

The air was humid, with a thin, invisible rain that stuck to hair and jackets. The biting cold had begun, that very day.

"I wanted to tell you, I'm really sorry about your grandmother."

"Thank you."

"It must have been awful for Norina too."

Simon looked at her, squinting in that way of his. But he also seemed different. Thinner, older, more real—or maybe it was only Amila who saw him that way, because she, too, had changed.

"I'm sorry, you know," she said, "but I didn't have the nerve to call her."

"Her number hasn't changed, so you still can."

"You're right. I should," she said, hesitantly, knowing it was the right thing to do. Norina and Mariano had nothing to do with it, so she ought to at least call.

Amila and Simon moved slowly past the white tents that, each year, appeared again in the same place.

"How is your shoulder?"

"Oh, it's fine now. It was already better last summer."

"Were you in Sarajevo?"

"No. I stayed in Trieste. We stopped having that sort of summer routine. Plus, I had to swim, for my shoulder."

A salesman with a microphone headset was calling the crowd for a live demonstration of the Festival of San Nicolò's official vegetable grater. His hands shaped forms and ornaments out of produce, as if he were performing miracles.

"When you get it home, it never works." Amila made a sign that they should leave.

In the mist, triangles of yellow and white light opened up onto shelves where multicolored piles of food and clothing rose above the crowd. The fragrance of marinated olives, big as dates, mixed with the oversweet smell of cotton candy, marzipan, and roasted hazelnuts. Gloves gathered into petals were

·

hanging over the heads of salespeople chilled from the cold. Attached to the elevated structures were fur-lined wool caps, with pom-poms or animal faces.

At the next booth, Simon tasted a sliver of ginger, and it made him cough. Amila took a handful of black and pink peppercorns to sniff. Simon treated her to a candy apple on a long stick; fire-engine red, it looked like the apple of love and poison from fairy tales. Amila licked the caramel and was disappointed by its somewhat bitter taste. Then she bit into it and the crust crumbled. The apple was grainy and very sweet—a reassuring taste straight from her childhood.

They left the crowd and continued down a side street; both had their hands in their pockets, their shoulders hunched into their jackets. In the end, they hadn't bought anything other than the apple, and they still had everything to say to each other.

"How far along is that novel of yours?"

"Oh, it's nowhere. Just frozen."

"Are you joking?"

"No, but I have published the short stories."

"Really? That's fantastic news! And you didn't even bring me a copy?"

"Well, I wasn't all that sure I would see you again. But I'll bring it to you next time."

Amila smiled in embarrassment. To tell the truth, she hadn't reckoned with the possibility of a next time. "And how is it going?" she said, hurriedly, to change the subject. "The story collection, I mean."

"Not bad at all. But it's a really short book."

"So what's the title?"

"*At My Place.*"

"Wow, that's great!"

"Really?"

"Really."

They spent a moment in silence. Amila knew that the moment had come to spell out what had been left up in the air between them. She had to.

"So, look . . . What have you decided to do about your grandfather?" Amila took a cautious step toward the subject. "Are you thinking about going to see him?"

"At his house in Buroli? Definitely not."

"No? So what will you do about the rest of it?"

"The rest of what?"

"Didn't you always say there was only one part you still needed?"

Simon shrugged. "I've crossed him off my list. I'm keeping my roots short. And anyway, my grandfather was someone else. His name is Carmine."

"I get that. But then, why come to Europe?"

"To keep a certain distance."

"But you'll actually be closer!"

"That could be."

They were waiting at the traffic light. Cars were crawling by at a snail's pace. "You're not curious about what happened with him?" Amila asked, with a hint of resentment.

"Well, actually, yes, I am."

The traffic light turned green, but neither of them moved.

Amila took a deep breath and then said, "It was difficult. But I'm convinced that the information we found about him is true. Unfortunately, though, it will still take a lot of time—too much time before certain facts are generally known. Some things will never be known. In the meantime, people will simply have to be satisfied with what little is certain. It's painful, but that's the way it is. So, anyway, what I mean is... do whatever you feel is right. Write your novel." Simon almost began to speak, but Amila didn't give him time. "London will be great. And anyway, I'm finding my own path too... I'm going to Bosnia," she added, forcing herself to keep a neutral tone.

"To Bosnia?"

"Yes. I'm taking a trip I still haven't done."

"When?"

"After the New Year."

"Why?"

"It's tough to explain. Maybe it's not about going back, but about moving forward. I have enough money to get by for six months. Just think, I'll be realizing one of my father's oldest dreams. A sabbatical year. Well, I guess that means I have to do it for him too."

The traffic light again turned green, and this time Amila took the first step into the crosswalk. Simon followed her, and they crossed.

"What will you do there?"

"I'll write and try to sell my articles to major newspapers. I'm going for it."

"What will you write about?"

"Oh, about Bosnia. I imagine there will be plenty of news, and if I don't find any, I'll think of something."

They arrived at the end of the festival area. Next to the theater, the booths seemed more isolated and bare.

"Should we go back?"

"Okay, but first I'm going to roll myself a cigarette. Are you smoking?"

Amila also pulled out a pack. "I always smoked with you."

"Not seriously."

"I guess this means I've become serious." Amila laughed and got him to light her cigarette. The cloud of smoke mixed with their breath, white vapor tunneling through the humidity.

"So are you going back to your hometown?"

"To bolster my nerves, I signed up for an international peace parade."

"How did you find out about that?"

"Oh, back home you can always find that sort of thing."

"What will you do there?"

"My folks have had some remodeling work done on our apartment, but, so far, they haven't been able to sell it. It's a story that never ends, as my mom says. But I, well, I would like to go and see what it's like."

Simon shook his head. "I'm sorry, but I just don't get you." He puffed out the last cloud of smoke and threw the butt down.

"Some things just can't be understood."

Not even Mamma Selma understood. She said Amila's latest idea was just plain crazy. Majda kept repeating, angrily, that she wanted no part of it, and Amila should leave her in peace. And even Olga, on the phone, had been speechless. Amila had heard her light a cigarette and loudly puff out some smoke, as long seconds of silence ticked by. At last, she suggested that Amila come to Vienna if she really needed to get some distance. But that was the proof. Olga didn't get it. Because it wasn't about that. Only Papà Željko proclaimed that what she needed was completely normal and, in fact, indisputable. But he, too, was exaggerating.

Amila was sure she wanted to go to the place where that old apartment was, near the Drina, even if she didn't really know what she was looking for there. In the meantime, however, she had understood something about what she didn't want. The remnants of Bosnia that had been retraced in their summer vacation apartment in Marijin Dvor, for example. She'd never felt it was her own. And in any case, by now, even without discussing it, their family had agreed to give that up. They couldn't afford the luxury of keeping three apartments, so they'd let go of the one that was easiest to get rid of. For Amila, the three-year diploma she'd received in the fall also didn't seem enough anymore. She'd achieved the better life she wanted, but she also knew that another was possible too—it might be worse, but anyway, it was worth trying to do something more than simply imagining it.

"But there aren't any Muslims left in your city, so what will you do?" Simon stopped in the midst of the bustling crowd. His hands had become red from the cold.

"Someone is always returning. And, anyway, I'm used to being the only one."

For a long time, Amila and her family had thought they'd lost everything forever. And with their expulsion from Zvornik, they had also been subjected to a prohibition against returning. They'd been forced to scatter across Western Europe, they'd returned intermittently, and they'd left the future of their apartment unsettled. In some sense, they had repeated the same logic that had cast them out.

"Also, I'm going back as an Italian, with something more," she added. "Or as a Bosnian, with something less. It's either the most comfortable or the most uncomfortable position to be in. I'm not sure which."

Simon continued to look at her skeptically.

"Look, I have no idea what it will be like, or if I'll like it, but I know I can do it, and that makes an enormous difference. Plus, I want to go and find one of my friends. I haven't seen her since we left our home. She's still living in the same building."

From the moment she'd made her decision about changing directions, Amila felt herself freed from her exotegrity, and from the pain that had deposited, layer upon layer over the years, from the anxiety of wanting to understand, and from the frustration of not being able to remember, from all Mamma Selma's *sant'Iddio*s, and from the summer debates and maxims of Papà Željko. Freed to do something else too, if she wanted. Freed to sort something out, something that itself might not last forever.

"Didn't you always say that Trieste is your home?"

"I did indeed. I'm leaving my home."

"Won't you miss it?"

"Of course. But if it's your home, then you can also leave it."

"When did you make your decision?"

"I'm not exactly sure, but I think it was after the accident." They started walking again. "That was when I started dreaming in Bosnian."

"And before that, you never did?"

"No."

"How can you know what language you're dreaming in?"

"You just know, period. So, well, I thought to myself, hmmm, now that must mean something."

Simon breathed heavily, as if he had just finished a marathon. And he, too, seemed to have arrived at a conclusion of his own.

"So, can I come there to see you?"

"You're a freeborn citizen of this world, so far as I can tell."

"Here, I'm a noncitizen, like you."

"Noncitizens from English-speaking countries are allowed into Bosnia without problems, like everywhere else."

"So then, I'll come, the first vacation I get. If they give me the job."

"Do you think they'll give you the job?"

"I'm sure they won't take the first person they interview."

"So where was this interview?"

"Ohhh... at a really posh law firm."

"So then, I'm sure they'll give you the job," said Amila, laughing.

Simon laughed too. "In any case, I'm not leaving Europe. We'll see if London will be my place."

Until then, Amila hadn't understood that Simon was taking it seriously. Just like she was. "Europe is a big place," she said, goading him.

"Not for me. And you know what I think?"

"No, what?"

"Geography doesn't always work against our dreams."

"At least dreaming hasn't yet been prohibited. I think we've figured that much out."

They were almost back to the point where they'd begun, and Simon's hand brushed hers. He pulled it back quickly, as if he'd had second thoughts. But then he caressed her palm with the tips of his frozen fingers, and Amila responded, brushing his with hers, which were equally cold. They shouldn't be doing that, definitely not. Nonetheless, Simon's fingers searched for hers again, and her hand answered his.

In front of the Janus fountain with its double masks, under a cluster of balloons, stood a San Nicolò giving out chocolates with his image on them; he patted the heads of timid children and waved his staff, saluting all the cameras. Simon convinced Amila to get her picture taken.

"Oh, my grandmother would have been so happy to see me here."

"Then you should get your picture taken, not me!"

"But a photo of you will look better." He pushed her forward, so she'd go with a small group of kids.

San Nicolò swung his head and gave Amila a clap on the back, as if she were a big, mischievous child, or an adult that didn't want, or wasn't able, to let go of her childhood. The children laughed.

San Nicolò took out a small sack of chocolate coins for Amila too. She gave it in turn to a little boy with his cap pulled all the way down to his eyebrows. The boy looked at her, his mouth agape.

Acknowledgments

PART OF THIS book was written during a residence at the Casa degli scrittori/Kuća za pisce/Hiža od besid (Writers' House) in Pisino, in a place and space where I felt at home from the first day, surrounded by breathtaking landscapes and the intense, unique beauty of Istria. I thank sincerely the Program Council of the Casa degli scrittori, and, in particular, Neven Ušumović, the director of the Biblioteca civica Umago/Gradska knjižnica Umag (Umag City Library), and Iva Ciceran, the director of the Biblioteca civica Pisino/Gradska knjižnica Pazin (Pazin City Library), for having believed in this book and for having given me the opportunity to experience one of the best months of my life. A special thanks goes to Lorena Monica Kmet as well for her engaged reading and extensive advice.

An important stage in my long journey was at the Virginia Woolf Writing School-Librati, the Libreria delle donne (Women's Library) in Padova, together with the profound literary sensibility of such people as Barbara Buoso, Ilaria Durigon, and Laura Liberale, whom I thank for their reading, for their encouragement, and for so many precious suggestions.

I thank as well my other early readers for their extensive feedback, and especially for their support and affection: Elisa Billi and Stana Stanić. And a thank-you to Raffaele Oriani for having been, in his special way, in this story.

I'm grateful to those who accompanied me during my travels in Bosnia, to Irvin Mujčić, for the long hike on hidden paths along the Drina, and to Violeta Savić, who threw open her doors for me in Zvornik, welcoming me as a friend. My first trip to Zvornik, however, dates back to many years earlier. My guide then was Veronika Martelanc, to whom I am also in debt for her essential juridical clarifications.

I thank Erica Costantini for some explications of the effects of traumatic events, and Robert Stoppari for his testimony and for the documentation which he agreed to share with me. To him a special dedication is due.

A sincere thanks to Rosanna Bubola, for her help in reading the sections written in dialect.

I am also extremely appreciative of and grateful for the entire Bottega Errante Edizioni team, who always believed in this book and who followed it across forking paths and helped to push it across "its" borders. And thanks, as well, to my publishers at Sandorf and Sandorf Passage, who carried this novel beyond those borders, taking it to another somewhere else.

Last but not least, a giant thanks to Jim Hicks (and to Anna Botta, the first editor of all Jim's translations) for having done much more than translate: for having re-created this novel, in a second language, where it belongs.

FEDERICA MARZI

FEDERICA MARZI was born 1974 in Trieste, Italy, a town situated in the far northeastern corner of Italy, on the border with Slovenia. She grew up in a family of post-World War II Italian refugees who departed from Yugoslavia after the Free Territory of Trieste (divided into a Zone A, controlled by the British-American troops, and a Zone B, controlled by the Yugoslavian troops) was dissolved in 1954. Part of this family story has migrated into her novel, *My Home Somewhere Else*. After her studies in German and English literature and language and comparative literature, she has been employed as a high-school teacher. Her short stories, many of which have been translated into Croatian and Slovenian, are set in the borderland culture of her hometown, Trieste, where she lives. *My Home Somewhere Else* was published in 2021 and is her first novel.

About Sandorf Passage

SANDORF PASSAGE publishes work that creates a prismatic perspective on what it means to live in a globalized world. It is a home to writing inspired by both conflict zones and the dangers of complacency. All Sandorf Passage titles share in common how the biggest and most important ideas are best explored in the most personal and intimate of spaces.